Why on earth should an innkeeper's daughter from the Yorkshire Dales want to become a doctor in the 1920s? Even Rose Stanton herself did not quite know why. But her father had sacrificed everything to send her to medical school and now, as she faced an examining board of hostile and sceptical men, she knew that no matter how insulting they were, she must succeed in her ambition.

How could she know that walking out of that room with the job under her belt would just be the beginning of her troubles? The beginning of a long and weary fight with her crusty male partner in the practice for the right to open a family planning clinic, and with the husbands of desperate women for the power to advise on contraception. The beginning of a life-long love for a married man which she would fight with all her strength to resist.

Also by Elvi Rhodes

OPAL

and published by Corgi Books

Elvi Rhodes

Doctor Rose

CORGI BOOKS

DOCTOR ROSE

A CORGI BOOK 0 552 12607 1

Originally published in Great Britain
by Century Publishing Co. Ltd.

PRINTING HISTORY
Century edition published 1984
Corgi edition published 1984
Corgi edition reprinted 1987

This book is set in 10/11 pt Lectura

Corgi Books are published by Transworld Publishers
Ltd., 61–63 Uxbridge Road, Ealing, London W5 5SA, in
Australia by Transworld Publishers (Aust.) Pty. Ltd.,
15–23 Helles Avenue, Moorebank, NSW 2170, and in New
Zealand by Transworld Publishers (N.Z.) Ltd., Cnr. Moselle
and Waipareira Avenues, Henderson, Auckland.

Printed and bound in Great Britain by
Cox & Wyman Ltd., Reading, Berks.

TO HARRY, WITH MY LOVE

I acknowledge with gratitude the help of
Dr R. A. Leake, who checked all the medical
details in this book.

Chapter One

Rose sat upright in the high-backed, leather-covered chair. She was small, slightly built, and if she leaned back at all she thought it would engulf her. Clearly it was not a woman's chair. It was a chair built for the kind of men who faced her in a semi-circle across the polished table; solid-looking men with dark suits of best Yorkshire worsted; with high, stiff, gleaming white collars – and with gold alberts slung across ample stomachs; men whose shapes and appearances befitted them for their roles as Town Councillors of Akersfield.

It was not so much that they faced her as that she must face them. She was the sole object of attention of all seven members of the Health Committee. On these men depended whether she did, or did not, get the job. And she wanted the job. She wanted it badly.

'Have any of your family been doctors, then? Does it run in the family?'

The questioner, sitting on the Chairman's right, was different from his colleagues; younger looking, with no sign of grey in his dark hair, his face lively and alert. Up to now he had seemed to be the one most in her favour. But better not take anything for granted, Rose thought.

'No Sir. I'm the first of my family to qualify.'

'Speak up Doctor Stanton. You young people all mumble nowadays. There's no need to be nervous, you know. Just answer the questions in a nice clear voice.'

The speaker this time was an elderly man whom the Chairman had earlier addressed as Councillor Patterson. Rose had already diagnosed that he needed his ears syringing – that or a deaf aid, poor man. From the irritated looks his remarks drew from the others she guessed that he made this complaint at every meeting.

'I'm sorry,' she said, raising her voice. 'I said I'm the first of my family to train as a doctor.'

'What does your father do?'

'What made you want to do it?'

'Don't you reckon it's a rum job for a woman?'

The questions now came from all sides, as if they wanted to shoot her down with rapid fire. The last speaker seemed especially hostile. It wasn't his first antagonistic question. She manifestly found no favour with him and she wondered how much influence he had with the rest of the Committee.

'My parents keep an inn in the Dales,' she said. 'In Faverwell. It's been in my father's family for four generations. Just a small inn.'

Too small, she thought, to bear the expense of her training. And yet it had. Her parents had never made enough money to save much and it was only by mortgaging the inn to the bank that they'd been able to send her to Medical School. It was a measure of her father's love for her that he, who had never owed a penny in his life and couldn't bear the thought of debt, had steeled himself to go cap in hand to the bank and to put all he owned at risk for her career. That was one of the reasons she needed this job, so that she could begin to repay her parents.

'As for what made me want to do it,' she said. 'It's difficult to tell. I just know I've never wanted to do anything else ever since I can remember, ever since I was a child.'

That was true. She recalled her mother complaining to a neighbour 'Our Rose doesn't play with her dolls properly. Not like Emily does. She paints measles spots all over 'em and puts 'em to bed. Or puts their arm in slings and their legs in splints. It's not natural in a little girl.'

The tetchy-sounding man was repeating his question.

'I said don't you think it's a rum job for a woman?'

She met his disagreeable look with her own direct one, schooling herself to speak calmly, hoping her irritation didn't show in her face. It wasn't the first time she'd been asked that particular question and it was too much to hope that it would be the last.

'I agree that there still aren't many women doctors,' she said. 'Though there are more now than before the war. But in this case I think being a woman gives me a real advantage. Whoever works in your Welfare Centre will be dealing all the time with women and children, mothers and babies. I like to think I understand them.'

'I reckon Doctor Stanton has a point of view there,' the

man on the Chairman's right said. 'A very good point.' He had a pleasantly deep voice with slightly drawn-out north country vowels. It was a reassuring voice.

'But she knows nothing of the married state,' another man objected. 'Now some of our other applicants are family men, with wives and children.'

'Doctor Stanton - if she were to be appointed - wouldn't be without a man's guidance,' the Chairman said. 'She'd be working under a male doctor.' He looked towards Rose. 'The Medical Officer for our welfare services is a man, a Doctor John Stanton as it happens. Now *there's* something that could cause confusion, I'm afraid. Two doctors with the same name!' He shook his head as if he had suddenly found an insuperable problem.

'Which I'm sure could be sorted out,' the man on his right put in. 'She could be Doctor Rose, I daresay.' His eyes twinkled and he lengthened the sound of her name, rolling it off his tongue slowly as if he was reluctant to let it go.

I like the sound of that, Rose thought.

'Yes, well, there's a lot more to be settled than that,' the Chairman said hastily. 'Now I suppose you're not engaged to be married or anything like that, are you? You're not courting?'

'No, nothing like that.'

Just as well, she thought, that Gerald, busy in his veterinary practice up in the Dales, couldn't hear her decisive reply. It wouldn't please him.

'Good! As you know, we don't employ married women.'

And that's something I'm prepared to argue about, Rose thought, but not just now.

The Chairman shuffled through his papers, scanning them as if he sought fresh inspiration.

'Well then Doctor Stanton,' he said, not finding it, 'I think that's about all. There's nothing wrong with your training. Leeds is a highly-respected Medical School. It's turned out some good doctors. I see you won a scholarship. And then you've had a couple of years on the wards of our own Akersfield hospital and they speak well of you. I think also we've fully explained what the job is.' He glanced around the rest of the Committee. 'Have any of you gentlemen any more questions for the young lady?'

A man raised his hand.

'I'd just like to ask Doctor Stanton why she isn't considering going into private practice?'

Rose hesitated before replying.

'Naturally I have considered it. I suppose most doctors do. In the first place I have to admit that I couldn't afford to buy into a practice. But if I put up a plate on my own I might have to wait a long time for patients to come to me. I couldn't afford that either.'

'You mean people don't trust women doctors like they do men? Well I'm sure that's true enough!'

The speaker was the awkward man. I've played right into his hands, Rose thought angrily.

'But more important,' she continued firmly, ignoring his interruption, 'is that I know I'd like working in the Infant Welfare Centre. And it would be good experience for me too, especially here. I know how go-ahead you are in Akersfield in these matters.'

A wide, satisfied smile spread over the Chairman's face. I've hit the target, Rose thought.

'We pride ourselves on it,' he admitted. 'We pride ourselves on it. Oh, there are those in the West Riding who are bigger than us, have the advantage of having started out sooner. We can't expect to compete with Bradford, though we've learnt from them. But we do our best, and our best is pretty good, eh gentlemen?'

He looked around for approval, which came in the shape of nods and grunts and murmurs of 'hear, hear' from the other members of the Committee. But Rose knew he spoke the truth. Akersfield's reputation in health matters was way ahead of most other towns of its size.

'But . . .' The Chairman was well into his stride now. '. . . In common with the rest of this land of ours, four years of bitter war have diverted our resources into other channels, like that of defending our shores, defeating the enemy. But that's all over now, praise God. It's nineteen twenty, and from now on things are going to get better and better. Me and my fellow Councillors will be proud to march ahead, leading Akersfield into a new and more prosperous age . . .'

His rhetoric was interrupted by the awkward man.

'I still say it's a waste of time and money, training women to be doctors! All they do is get married and have children. Money down the drain!'

But my father's money, not yours, Rose wanted to say. And he believes in me.

The Chairman, coming down to earth, took a gold hunter from his waistcoat pocket and looked at the time.

'Well, Doctor Stanton,' he said. 'As I'm sure you know, we still have one more applicant to interview. So now we'd like you to wait outside and we'll call you in again – if need be, that is. If need be.'

As Rose stood up the man on the Chairman's right gave her an encouraging smile. Leaving the room she tried to take the thought of that with her rather than the bland, non-committal, or downright discouraging expressions on the faces of the other six members of the Committee.

The waiting room offered no comfort. It was a narrow room with a door at each end, and on one wall a high window which looked as if it had remained firmly closed since the town hall was erected. The window was glazed with opaque glass so that it was impossible to see the sky, even if that had not been obliterated by the November fog. Ugly yellow wooden chairs stood against two longer walls. Brown linoleum, scarred with cigarette burns, covered the floor. The room could have been specially designed, Rose thought, to subdue the spirits of whoever had to use it.

The other five candidates had ranged themselves around the room, leaving at least two chairs between themselves and the next person so that there would be no need to speak to each other. As Rose came in from the Committee room five pairs of eyes fixed themselves on her. She couldn't help but smile.

'No decision, gentlemen! I'm to wait until called for, like the rest of you.'

A young man of about her own age returned her smile. The rest, when the last one to be interviewed had gone into the Committee room, lowered their heads again. But they can't be worried about me, Rose told herself. I'm no threat. They're simply in competition with each other. The cards are stacked against me all right. How many of *them* have

13

been told it's a rum occupation for them to follow? And if they happen to be married it's in their favour. She took a seat two empty chairs away from the man who had smiled at her. He leaned towards her and spoke.

'Would you like to look at my newspaper while we're waiting?' he asked. 'I've read it.'

'I'd be grateful,' Rose said.

The Akersfield *Record*. She unfolded it and looked at the first page. Sugar rationing was to end next Monday. Butter was still in short supply and likely to continue expensive. She turned the pages. The weather would be unsettled and foggy and, of more immediate interest, they were advertising fur-trimmed velour cloth coats at four pounds ten shillings, which wasn't bad. If she got a job she would buy one. She had not had a new winter coat since the middle of the war.

But she couldn't think about that now. She couldn't concentrate. Her thoughts were all on the other side of that door. What would she do if she didn't get the job? Her hospital appointment finished at Christmas. All she had been offered so far was an assistant's job to a doctor in the better-class area of Akersfield, for three days a week. It was not residential and the money wouldn't be enough to keep her in food and lodgings, however meagre. Also, she didn't fancy it. Knowing the doctor – she had met him in the hospital – she was well aware that she'd be used as a dogsbody, as cheap labour, rolling pills, dispensing potions, kept well away from all the interesting cases which the doctor would claim as his own. In any case, she really wanted this job in the Welfare Centre. She was drawn to it. It was in the kind of neighbourhood – far from well-to-do – in which she wanted to work. She was sure she could make something of it.

She folded the newspaper and handed it back. 'Thank you,' she said. 'I'm afraid I can't take anything in just now. Too nervous, I expect!'

He grinned sympathetically. 'Aren't we all?'

She liked the look of him. If she didn't get the job herself then she hoped he would. She wondered about him. He looked too young, too untouched to have served in the war. The men who had been in France had the experience written in their faces, as if they saw life through different eyes. If she was not to work with women, then she would have liked to have used her skills as a doctor to help some of the men she saw around her all the time; in the streets, in the hospitals, everywhere. There were many who would need help for a long time to come. They had a sickness of the heart and mind which was often worse than the wounds they had brought back in their bodies. But it was an area of medicine which was closed to her. As a woman she could not be expected to understand men.

All heads were raised as the door to the Committee room opened and the last candidate emerged. His expression was non-committal. No-one spoke as he sat down. Twenty minutes passed, each one of them an eternity, before the door opened again and a man came out. He looked around at the candidates and consulted the piece of paper he held. Rose felt her heart thumping so strongly in her chest that she was sure the others must hear it. She gripped her handbag tightly. Please God! Please God!

The man approached the candidates in turn, speaking quietly to each one. As she sat farthest away from him she would obviously be the last to know. She watched the others as, one after the other when the man had spoken to them, they rose to their feet and left. He was with the young man next to her now and she heard his words.

'Would you please go back into the Committee room, Doctor Cartwright.'

Disappointment engulfed Rose like a wave seeking to drown her. And as they said happened to a drowning person, all the hopes, fears, trials, difficulties she had gone through to reach this point came together before her. But she managed to smile at her neighbour as he set off for the Committee room.

'Congratulations!'

'Thanks,' he said.

She started to rise to her feet but the man with the list stood in front of her.

'No, you're not to go, Doctor Stanton. Will you wait for a moment or two and then go into the Committee room when Doctor Cartwright comes out?'

Oh well, it was something to have come second, she

supposed. Not that it was any use to her. She wondered, in fact, whether she should bother to wait to receive the Committee's condolences. But she'd better do so in case she ever had to come before them again. There was the future to think about, however bleak it looked at the moment.

She didn't have to wait long. Doctor Cartwright soon emerged, still smiling, but not stopping to speak on his way out. A minute later she was back in the Committee room, sitting on the edge of the same large chair, waiting for the members to stop whispering to each other. Come on, she thought impatiently, get it over with!

'Thank you, gentlemen,' the Chairman said, bringing them to order. Then he looked at Rose.

'Well then, Doctor Stanton, we've all discussed your application very thoroughly, very carefully. It hasn't been easy. It's an important matter for us and, if I may say so, for Akersfield itself. The health of our Mothers and Children . . .'

Oh no, Rose thought! Spare me the speech! She couldn't bear it. Not now. She looked towards the man on the Chairman's right and as she did so he carefully lowered one eyelid in what amounted to a wink.

'. . . and the citizens of the future upon whom our town, nay, our country, will depend in the future as they have in the past . . .'

She stopped listening – and when the words came, the words which changed the world for her, it was as if she heard them from a great distance.

'. . . And so, Doctor Stanton – Doctor Rose Stanton as I suppose we shall have to learn to call you – we are pleased to offer you the post of Assistant Medical Officer in our Welfare Centre at a salary of three-hundred-and-seventy-five pounds per annum.'

She must pull herself together, quickly! She was going to faint, or burst into tears – and she mustn't because that was exactly what the beast of a man who didn't approve of woman doctors was waiting for her to do! She looked at him and saw it in his face.

She took a deep breath. 'Thank you, gentlemen. Thank you very much. I'm grateful. I shall try to serve you well.'

16

'Not only us,' the Chairman said sententiously, 'Not only us, but Akersfield.'

This time she would have been prepared to listen to him, to let him have his fling, but it seemed he had almost finished.

'See the clerk before you go,' he said. 'There are one or two things for you to sign. And your appointment starts on the first of January 1921.'

'Thank you,' Rose said again. 'Thank you very much.'

As the Councillors gathered their papers together, preparing to leave, the clerk came towards her. While she was still answering his questions the nice man on the Chairman's right passed on his way out.

'Congratulations, Doctor Rose,' he said, and was gone. She hoped that wasn't the last she would see of him. She felt he'd been especially kind to her, that all along he'd been on her side.

The man standing by the far door of the waiting room watched Rose as she left the Committee room. He saw a small, slender woman, whom he supposed must be in her mid-twenties though she looked younger. She had a country complexion: clear, flawless skin tinged with pink, and a deeper flush of pink on her cheeks. The severity of her straight-brimmed felt hat fought – and lost – against the deep auburn hair which escaped in tendrils from under it: against the short, tilted nose, the gently-curving mouth which looked as though it had just finished smiling and might start again any minute. The tailored lines of her coat and skirt, which ended decorously a few inches above neat ankles, were softened by the red scarf she wore at her neck. The fact that its colour shrieked against the auburn of her hair only added to the vibrancy which was exuded by her whole being.

She had not seen him as she crossed the room, her head held high, her face alight with happiness, but when he stepped in front of her, barring her way, she raised wide-set, slightly-puzzled green eyes to his. But the puzzlement could not hide the joy in her eyes.

Rose saw a man so tall that she had to tilt her head back

17

to look at him. He must be more than six feet. He raised a fawn trilby, revealing crisp, fair hair. He had a thin, pale face and blue eyes which, meeting hers, were at one and the same time, humorous and serious. There was also, if she was not mistaken, a hint of admiration in them.

'I'm sorry,' she apologized. 'I wasn't looking where I was going.'

She had a pleasant voice too, he thought; clear and soft; a north country voice with its short vowels, but not from the West Riding.

'Don't apologize,' he said. 'I can see you have other things on your mind. Pleasant things, too, if I'm not mistaken.'

'Does it show so much? But you're quite right as it happens. It's turned out to be a special day for me.'

'I know,' he said. 'That's what I want to talk to you about.'

'You know? How can you? You weren't on the Committee were you?' He couldn't have been. She had studied the face of every single member. She would not have forgotten him.

'Were you one of the candidates?' she asked. 'If so . . .'

He took a card from his pocket and handed it to her. 'As it says there, Alex Bairstow, Akersfield *Record*. I'd be grateful for a few minutes of your time, Doctor Stanton.'

She looked genuinely puzzled now.

'How do you know?'

'I knew the interviews were taking place,' he said. 'I also knew there was a woman on the short list. It's my job to know things like that. Then I met Councillor Worthing, the Deputy Chairman, as he was leaving, and he gave me the news. He seemed very pleased about it. Allow me to congratulate you, Doctor Stanton.'

Councillor Worthing? So he must be the man on the Chairman's right, the one she had known all along was on her side.

'I see,' she said. 'So you've come to cover me – like Births, Marriages and Deaths?'

He smiled. He had a particularly nice smile. It widened his already generous mouth and brightened his eyes.

'Not quite! I used to do that when I was a cub reporter, before the war. At this time of the year I attended funerals most days of the week. Since I returned I've been promoted. No more Hatches, Matches and Despatches, not even chapel bunfights. I go after stories. You know the kind of thing? Local boy makes good, or preferably, for our readers, goes to the bad! The human element, especially if it's controversial.'

There was a sharp edge to his voice, as if he didn't quite take himself seriously. And yet he does, Rose thought. I'm sure he does.

'And I'm controversial?' she queried.

'I'm sure you know you are. But you were at the interview, I wasn't. I'd be delighted to hear that it was one hundred per cent in your favour but I'm not sure that I'd believe you.'

The clerk came and interrupted them.

'I'm sorry, Doctor Stanton, Mr Bairstow. I have to lock up these rooms now.'

'Right, Tom, we're moving,' Alex Bairstow said.

Rose walked with him down the wide staircase into the lobby of the town hall.

'We can't break off the conversation at this point,' Alex Bairstow said. 'And I'm sure you don't want to continue it in the town hall entrance. Will you let me buy you a cup of tea? To celebrate. There's a cafe quite close by.'

'Honestly,' Rose said, laughing, 'There's not much to know about me. I'd be taking your tea under false pretences.'

'I'll be the judge of that,' he said. 'Let's go.'

Outside the town hall's impressively pillared entrance he tucked his hand under her elbow and guided her across Market Street and through a labyrinth of narrow back streets to a small basement cafe, halfway up a steep hill. He walked with long, easy strides and Rose had difficulty in keeping up with him.

'I always have toasted currant teacake with my cup of tea,' he said when they were seated. 'Would you like one?'

'I'm really not sure what I'm doing here,' Rose said. 'But since I *am* here - yes please. I miss my mother's teacakes.'

'But these are very good,' she admitted a few moments later.

'You were trying to tell me you weren't controversial,' Alex Bairstow said. 'Well maybe *you* aren't - I haven't decided about that – but you must know your appointment is. Five men short-listed and they pick a woman! The first woman doctor we've had in the town, let alone working for the Council. So tell me, how did the interview go?'

'I don't propose to tell you that,' Rose said sharply. 'The interview was confidential, as you must very well know.'

'All right I'll tell you,' he said. 'I've sat in on enough Council meetings to know. Councillor Worthing would be for you. He's a fair-minded, enlightened sort of chap, and what's more he likes women, especially pretty ones. Councillor Thwaites – he's the Chairman – would sound off about the glories of Akersfield and his part in its making. Councillor Patterson wouldn't hear half that went on and Councillor Rogers would be against you. I daresay he told you that a woman's place is in the home?'

'More or less,' Rose admitted. 'It's what most men say. I'm used to it. I daresay it's what you tell your wife.'

'I haven't got a wife,' he said. 'I suppose I haven't really got a home. I live in digs. And I know you're not married or you'd never have got as far as the interview.'

'The Chairman said, "Are you courting?"' Rose giggled at the memory.

'And are you?'

'Not really.'

'Ah! Then there's someone?'

'Yes and no,' she said thoughtfully. 'And please don't write that down and use it.'

'I won't,' he assured her. 'It isn't part of my plan to make things more difficult for you. Besides, you don't sound very sure, and I like to get my facts right. When do you start the job?'

'In the New Year.'

'And what are you going to do between now and then?'

'Well,' Rose said, 'I shall be working in hospital up to Christmas. Also I'll have to look for lodgings. You can put that in your paragraph if you like. Someone might make me an offer. I'll probably go home for Christmas. Home is Faverwell. My parents keep a pub there and they can always do with extra help at Christmas. Anyway, you've no idea how beautiful the Dales can be at Christmas.'

'Oh yes I have,' he contradicted. 'Before we went to

France my Company was stationed in Swaledale. I'd have been glad to have stayed there.'

'Did you have a bad war?'

'Are there any good ones, then? But mine was better than some. As you see, I'm here, and all in one piece. And I've got a job, which is more than can be said for some. Was your friend about whom you're not sure in the Army?'

'No,' Rose answered. 'He's a vet. The only one for miles around so he was needed on the farms. But he looked after army horses sometimes, when they were stationed nearby.'

'I see. Well, Doctor Stanton - by the way, has anyone told you that your boss's name is Stanton?'

'Yes,' she said. 'I've settled for Doctor Rose.'

'Doctor Rose. Nice. Can I quote that? The human touch that endears itself to our readers.' His voice was mocking. 'Now if I could also say that you're fond of animals that would go down really well.'

Rose flushed.

'It's your idea to write something about me, not mine. It makes no difference to me.'

'Ah but it could, you know. Never underestimate the power of the press, Doctor Rose, either for you or against. But don't worry, the editor won't give this item undue importance. It's not front page stuff.'

'I'm sorry,' Rose said. 'But if I decide to rob a bank or murder Councillor Rogers, I'll be sure to let you know.'

She had thought at first that she quite liked Mr Bairstow. Now she was not so sure. He was too cocky by half, too full of his own importance. But what did he matter anyway? She'd got the job. That was all that mattered. Everything would be good from now on.

Alex Bairstow was grinning at her.

'Thanks,' he said. 'I'd appreciate that.'

Chapter Two

When the train drew into Grassington station Rose's brother-in-law, Christopher, was there to meet her. As she stepped down from the carriage he took her case from her.

'Whatever have you got in it?' he asked. 'It feels heavy enough for gold brick. How long are you here for?'

'Would it were gold bricks,' Rose replied. 'Warm clothes and Christmas presents mostly. And I'm here until almost the end of December. How are you?'

To her eyes Christopher always looked the same. No different now, at thirty, from ten years ago when he had married her sister. But since they had all known each other since they were children he had never changed in her eyes and she supposed he never would. He was tall, broad-shouldered, with the ruddy complexion of someone who had spent most of his life out of doors. His features were well put together but unremarkable.

'Can't complain,' he replied. 'And you? We were pleased to hear about the job.'

'Isn't it wonderful,' Rose said. 'I was so lucky.'

She followed him out of the station to where his Morris car stood by the kerb.

'It's good of you to meet me,' she said. 'I wasn't at all sure there'd be a bus and I didn't fancy walking all those miles. I've done it often enough, goodness knows; but Christmas Eve isn't the time.'

It was raining as they left the station; a thin, mean sleetish rain. Outside the village Christopher turned the car down the hill towards the river, then north on to the narrow road which led to Faverwell, seven miles up the dale. In an hour or so it would be dark, but as yet there was still some light in the cold, grey sky. It was a sky which promised snow to come. And true to its promise, after two miles or so of the twisting road, which followed closely the bends and curves of the river, the rain turned to snow, falling in soft, thick flakes.

Rose, not speaking – one of the nice things about

22

Christopher was that you could enjoy a comfortable silence with him – watched it settle on the high green fells which rose on each side of them. It began to mark out the tops of the grey limestone walls, walls which climbed to the summits, now going straight, now diverting to form fields of strange geometrical shapes. When, in Leeds or Akersfield, Rose thought of home, it was the whitish-grey walls running up the hillsides which she pictured.

'I'd hoped it was going to be a white Christmas,' she said. 'It seems so right.'

'Shows you're not a farmer,' Christopher said.

'I know. Still I *am* a daleswoman, so I should know better. But it does look so very beautiful.'

'Well we've got all the sheep down from the tops, so I'm not too worried,' Christopher said. 'At least there's no wind to speak of, so it won't drift.'

'How's the farm been this year?' Rose enquired.

'Not too good. Sheep are fetching a poor price. I wish I knew some other way of making a living but farming's in my blood. The Bishops have been at Fellside as long as the Stantons have kept the Ewe Lamb. It takes someone like you to break away.'

'But I'm not breaking away,' Rose protested. 'It's simply that I can't do my job here. But however far away I go I shall always come back. I'm sure of that.'

'Anyway it's good to have you back for Christmas,' Christopher said. 'Emily will enjoy it, not to mention your Ma and Pa. She gets a bit down, Emily does. And when she's down she gets to thinking about Robert. Not that I don't think about him as well, you understand; but having the farm to think about helps me.'

Robert was their only son. He had died two years ago, aged five, from diphtheria; by coincidence at a time when Rose was doing her stint in the fever hospital, so that every small diphtheria patient she saw there reminded her sharply of her nephew. Christopher and Emily had two other children, Helen, who was nine years old and four-year-old Kitty; but Rose suspected that Robert had always been the most deeply loved.

'I understand,' Rose said. 'Or at least I try to. But some members of the Health Committee, when I had my interview, seemed to think it was impossible to understand something if you hadn't experienced it.'

'I daresay someone like you can understand a lot,' Christopher said thoughtfully. 'And you can sympathize. But you can't know what it feels like unless you've gone through it.'

'Do you think that applies to something like marriage, or giving birth?' Rose asked.

'I think so,' Christopher said.

They could see Faverwell now. The winter afternoon was closing in and the lights were showing in the cottages and on the farms.

'I'll drop you at the Ewe Lamb,' Christopher said. 'I'll not come in. I've got jobs to do, and being Christmas Eve Emily'll want to get the children off to bed in good time.'

'When shall we see you?' Rose asked.

'Tomorrow for dinner. After the Ewe's closed. Your Ma and Pa aren't opening up in the evening.'

'I know,' Rose said. 'It's about the only evening they have off together in the year. Well I'll see what help Mother needs, and if there's time tell Emily I'll walk over in the morning.'

When Christopher drove away, it being not yet opening time and the front door of the Ewe Lamb being locked, Rose went around to the back. Before she could raise a hand to the door knob her father was there, his eyes bright with welcome, his thin face creased in a smile.

'My word, lass, it's good to see thee! Tha's a sight for sore eyes, an' no mistake!'

It was a measure of his excitement that he spoke in the dialect. It was not his usual way, though he could speak it with the best of them, and did so when the occasion called for it, and always when he was moved or excited.

'It's good to see you, Father,' Rose said.

They embraced warmly. He was alight with happiness, Rose thought, and marvelled that once again her homecoming could do this to him.

'Where's Mother?' she asked.

'She's around at the church, giving a hand with the decorations. You'd think she had enough to do without that, wouldn't you? She's been up since five this morning.

She'd have been here, only we didn't expect you quite so soon.'

'It was kind of Christopher to meet me,' Rose said.

The kitchen door opened and her mother, bringing a flurry of snow with her, entered.

'Coming down fast now,' she said. 'Somebody'll have to clear that path up to the church or it'll be real slippy for early service.'

It was her mother's way, Rose knew, not to show outward emotion. She was quite unlike her husband in that. She took off her gloves, scarf, coat and hat, placed the gloves in the dresser drawer, put the pins from her hat in a small vase on the mantelpiece, hung her coat behind the door and put her hat on the dresser before she turned to speak directly to Rose.

'Well then, Our Rose?'

'Well then, Mother. How are you?' Rose leaned forward to kiss her mother but Clara Stanton, as if by accident, turned away, so that the kiss landed only lightly on the edge of her cheek. She seemed unable to show affection, though Rose knew that it was in her. As a child she had longed to have a mother who would kiss and cuddle her, like the mothers of her friends. She had determined at an early age that when she grew up and had children she would hug and kiss them a lot. They would never have to wonder about her love for them.

'Have you put the kettle on, then, George?' Mrs Stanton asked. 'I daresay we could all do with a cup of tea.'

'Meanwhile,' Rose said. 'I'll take my case upstairs and unpack. After that I'm ready to give a hand with anything you want me to do.'

'No call for you to start working. You haven't come back to work,' Mrs Stanton said. She was getting out cups and saucers. The best china, Rose noted; delicately thin, gilt-handled, decorated with pink roses. She should have felt complimented but she was not. The sight of the flowery china on the embroidered linen cloth saddened her.

'I've come because it's my home. I wanted to come. I wanted to be with you and Father and the rest of the family.'

She put out a hand and touched the back of her mother's hand as she arranged the cups. 'I'm not a visitor, Mother. Please don't treat me like one. The kitchen cups are good enough for me.'

'Well . . .' Mrs Stanton hesitated. 'Well you *are* a doctor!'

'I'm your daughter, same as I always was. But all right, just this once to celebrate we're together. After that don't you dare!'

She went upstairs to unpack. She had slept in this room, with its small window overlooking the beck which ran down to join the river, ever since she could remember, sharing it with Emily until her sister left home to marry. Every night of her childhood she had fallen asleep to the sound of rushing water, for even in the hottest summer the beck never ran dry. When she had first gone to Medical School she had returned home every weekend that she could find the return fare from Leeds, but a few months later she had become so involved in this and that Society in the university, in weekends spent walking or cycling with new friends, or in rather pleasurable and not too strenuous efforts to raise comforts for the troops, that she had come back less and less often. If she was now regarded as a visitor she supposed it was partly her own fault.

When she went downstairs again her mother was pouring the tea and there was buttered currant teacake on the table.

'I had a fair currant teacake in Akersfield,' she said. 'Not as good as yours, though.'

She had seen Alex Bairstow a couple of times since that first occasion. Once, meeting him in the street by chance, he had taken her to the same cafe; once he had taken her to the cinema to see 'Beyond the dreams of Avarice'.

'You said in your letter you were pleased with your new lodgings,' her father said.

'I think I'm going to be. Anyway, they're cheap, which is important.'

'And clean too, I hope?' her mother said sharply.

'They looked fine to me. Of course I don't start living there until after Christmas.'

'How did you come by them?' her father wanted to know.

'Through a friend. Well, an acquaintance, really. His name is Alex Bairstow. He's a reporter on the Akersfield *Record*. He has digs in the same house.'

In the act of refilling her husband's cup Clara Stanton paused, her body tensing.

'You'll be living *in the same house*?'

Rose laughed. 'Really, Mother, don't look so shocked! It's all right. Wherever I'd gone into digs there might have been young men. Alex is quite respectable, I assure you. If it's any comfort to you we're not on the same floor.'

Mrs Stanton finished pouring her husband's tea, spooned in more sugar, added water to the teapot, fetched hot mince pies from the oven.

'Gerald's coming over in the morning, barring emergencies.'

She was trying to sound casual, but Rose was not deceived. Her mother never lost hope that her daughter would make a go of it with Gerald. To be a vet's wife would be a good position and, more important, it would keep Rose within the world Clara Stanton knew and understood; the country world of farms and animals, of villages and small market towns. Just once, when Rose had qualified, Clara had visited Leeds. She hadn't liked it at all, had been glad to get home to Faverwell and didn't care if she never saw a city again.

'On Christmas Day?' Rose queried.

'He reckoned it might be his quietest time, though you never can tell with a veterinary.'

'Well it won't be *our* quietest time in the Ewe Lamb,' Rose said. 'And before you say another word, you're not doing me out of helping in the bar for a bit. You know I enjoy that. I also told Christopher I might go over there for an hour. And then there's the Christmas dinner. What about that?'

'I can manage,' her mother said firmly. 'Gerald will want to have a bit of time with you, coming over from Wensleydale. It's only natural.'

George Stanton looked at his watch and stood up. It was time to open the bar and it would be a busy night in spite of the snow. Passing his wife, he pressed his hand on her shoulder.

'Leave it be, Clara! Leave it be!'

'I'll be with you in a minute or two,' Rose called after him. 'Give you a hand.'

She turned to her mother.

'It's no use, Mother. I'm not going to marry Gerald. I've made up my mind.'

'But he's always been that fond of you,' her mother protested.

'I know. And I'm fond of him. But I don't have plans for marrying anyone. I've got a job to do and I'm looking forward to it. Can't you understand that?'

'If you *had* to be a doctor,' Mrs Stanton said, 'then I don't see why it couldn't be in the dales. There's sick folk here as well as in the towns.'

'But not so many. Anyway there's no place here for a doctor. Doctor Harper is good for a long time yet.'

'He might take you as an assistant,' her mother said. Rose sighed. 'Mother, of course he wouldn't. He couldn't afford to pay me enough. Anyway, no-one in the dales would take me seriously as a doctor. I'd always be Clara Stanton's little lass. And what I'm interested in right now is working with mothers and babies.'

'Plenty to do if you had your own babies,' Mrs Stanton said sharply. 'You ask our Emily!'

It was clear to Rose that her mother wouldn't mind her throwing up her entire training, for which she and her husband had made so many sacrifices, if only her daughter would marry Gerald – or someone like him – and settle down near to hand and raise a family. She left the kitchen and joined her father in the bar.

'Don't you worry about your mother,' George Stanton said. 'Deep down she's as pleased as Punch, as proud as Lucifer of you. It's just that it's a new pattern and she can't get used to it. You see, lass, you're the first woman in the family ever to work away from home.'

'What about Great-grandmother, Mother's own ancestor?' Rose reminded him. 'She went off to America. Perhaps I've got it from her, though I've never thought of going so far.'

Her great-grandmother had lived further up the dale, leaving as a poor emigrant in the middle of the last century. Many years later her daughter, Aurora, had returned, married an Englishman, and given birth to Clara.

'That was a long time ago,' George Stanton said. 'Anyway it's time to open up.'

On Christmas Day the fells were magnificently clothed in pristine white and on the road through the dale there were three inches of crisp, hard snow underfoot. But it had stopped snowing and the sky was clear and blue.

Gerald arrived at half-past ten. George Stanton, tidying up in the bar, saw his Rover draw up in front of the inn and unlocked the door to him.

'Merry Christmas, Mr Stanton,' Gerald said.

'Merry Christmas. What was the road like coming over?'

'Not too bad.'

'The womenfolk are in the kitchen. Go through. I have to finish in here.'

Mrs Stanton gave him the welcoming smile she reserved for a few, favoured people.

'Our Rose will give you a cup of tea,' she said. 'And perhaps something in it – a drop of rum – against the cold. If you'll excuse me I have a few things in the bar to attend to.'

Rose grinned at Gerald as her mother left them. If she and Gerald had not been such good friends her mother's heavy-handed tact would have been embarrassing. As it was they were amused by it.

'All the same,' Gerald said, taking off his overcoat, sitting beside Rose on the horsehair-covered sofa, 'all the same I'm glad of a minute or two alone with you. If this Christmas follows the usual pattern there won't be many of them.'

Rose's first thought when Gerald had entered the kitchen was how attractive he looked, more so, even, than she had remembered. His face was tanned, his hazel eyes bright and kind. Now, guessing what he was going to say as he sat down beside her, she thought what a pity it was

29

that she didn't love him – or didn't love him enough, for she had always been fond of him. If things had been different she could have done worse than to marry Gerald. But things were not different.

'Gerald,' she said quietly, 'Please don't say what I think you're going to say.'

'Is it so obvious?'

'I'm right, aren't I?'

He nodded.

'It's no use, Gerald,' Rose said. 'It's not just that I won't marry *you*. I don't want to marry anyone.'

'No-one? Ever?'

Rose hesitated. 'Ever is a long time. I can't say that. But it isn't part of my plans. Do you realize, for instance, that if I were to marry I'd lose my job? Have you heard about my new job?'

'I have. Congratulations. And I realize you'd lose that particular job. But that needn't be the end of your career. You could put up your plate in Wensleydale. Married to me, you wouldn't starved while you waited for patients.'

'Oh Gerald, you know you have a perfectly good doctor there already. Who would come to me? But even if they would, it's not what I want. When I was in Medical School we talked a lot about conditions in towns, about people who didn't have much, lived in terrible houses, were often sick. It's places like that where I want to practise. Places where I'm really needed. Does that make me sound self-righteous?'

'No,' he said. 'I know you too well for that. So I suppose until you get this out of your system . . .'

She felt her anger flare, clenched her fists to control her temper.

'It's not something I intend to get out of my system. Why can't any of you understand that? I'm sick of being treated as if I were simply playing at being a doctor, as if it's all a childish game!'

He had risen now and was standing in front of her. Before she could say more he had taken her in his arms. She struggled to free herself but he was too strong for her. He was kissing her, his lips hard, sweet and strong on hers. She could not escape, and for a few seconds she did not want to. He had never kissed her like this before. This was not the kind, patient Gerald she was used to.

He let her go.

'Perhaps that'll convince you I'm not playing either,' he said sharply. 'You don't give either of us a chance. If you let yourself go you might find you could love me. I wouldn't keep you from the job you've taken,' he said more quietly. 'I understand about that and I'm willing to wait a year or two - but not forever, Rose.'

'I'm sorry,' Rose said. 'I don't love you like that. Not enough to give up what I'm doing, even in a year or two's time. Selfish of me, I daresay. And I'm sorry. But there it is, and you must believe me.'

'You've made it quite plain,' Gerald said. 'If you'll excuse me, I won't stay. Anyway, I've got some visits to make. Animals don't stop being sick because it's Christmas Day. You'll find it's the same with people.'

'I already have,' Rose said. 'I spent last Christmas Day delivering awkward twins. I was on midwifery duty and I'd been out on a case all night. I know what it's about.'

'I'll let myself out the back way,' Gerald said. 'Make my excuses to your parents.' Then he smiled. He never showed himself out of humour for long. 'Your mother's going to be awfully disappointed, you realize?'

'In me, not in you,' Rose said.

How quickly men recover, or seem to, she thought. She was still shaking inside, still surprised by his kiss. He had aroused feelings in her, not for himself but for his sex, which she had thought she had well under control, feelings which she must learn to deal with. The world, certainly the world of Akersfield, would have to change a great deal before she could order her life as she wanted it; before she could marry, have children, and keep her job. It was an impossible combination.

She did not, in the end, walk over to Emily's house. There was no time. They were extra busy in the bar and she was kept hard at it, serving drinks, washing glasses, and in between chatting to old friends and acquaintances. It was four o-clock before her father could lock the door on the last customer and they could make final preparations for the

Christmas dinner. Emily, who had arrived an hour earlier with Christopher and the two little girls, helped Rose to lay the big walnut table in the dining room, a room only used for meals on ceremonial occasions.

'You look tired, Emily,' Rose said. 'Are you all right? It must be hard going with the work on the farm and two lively children to look after.'

'I can assure you it is,' Emily retorted. 'There never seems to be a minute to spare. You'll find that out for yourself if ever you marry and have a family!'

Rose was surprised by the edge in her sister's voice. Emily, always the more gentle, always - in her fair-haired, rosy-cheeked way, the prettier - had been the placid one, taking life as it came, making none of the demands on it her younger sister made. All she had ever wanted was to be married to Christopher, to have his children. But now, Rose thought, looking at her more closely, she had a drawn, discontented look. Of course she had never been quite the same since her small son's death. Who could expect it? But why is she so sharp with me? Rose wondered.

'But you're such a good wife and mother,' Rose said. 'Everyone admires you for it. You wouldn't have wanted anything else, would you?'

'As well I didn't,' Emily cried. 'There wouldn't have been enough for two in the family to be doctors. It took Father all his time for you.'

Rose felt suddenly sick to the stomach, not only at her sister's words but at the venom with which she expressed them. She was shocked by the jealousy she saw in the blue eyes which met hers. How long had Emily been nursing this grudge against her? She had never before suspected such a thing.

'You were the first,' she said quietly. 'You're the elder. If you'd said you wanted to be a doctor, Father would have found the money for you instead of for me. You never said anything that I remember.'

'Even if I didn't want to be a doctor, I might have wanted to go to university,' Emily said stubbornly. 'I don't remember that I was asked. And if I didn't say anything it was because I knew how hard it would be for Father. You never thought of that did you? All that mattered to you, all that has ever mattered to you, was your ambition! Anyway, I never came first with Father.'.

'But Emily that's not true!' Rose protested. 'He treated us equally well. And I was well aware what he was doing for me, the sacrifices he was making. I told him I'd pay him back when I could. And I shall – every penny. You'll see.'

She was angry, but underneath her anger a cold little thought clawed at her mind. Was what Emily said true? Had her ambition made her selfish, blind to anyone else's needs, taking everything she could get?

Emily sighed. 'I'm sorry Rose. I didn't mean it. I seem to flare up for nothing these days.'

But you did mean it, Rose thought. Every word. How long have you felt like this about me?

'The farm isn't doing too well,' Emily went on. 'Christopher works hard, far too hard, but in spite of that things don't get any better. We need more capital investment. I worry about him – about all of us. I worry all the time about the children's health. I never used to, but since Robert . . . well, things happen so quickly, don't they?'

Rose put out a hand and touched her sister.

'I do understand,' she said gently. 'And I'm sorry. Perhaps the farm will pick up this year.'

'I hope so,' Emily said.

'As for the children,' Rose said. 'I assure you I never saw two healthier looking girls. They're lovely!'

Emily's face brightened.

'They are, aren't they? And would you believe it, Helen, at nine years old, wants to be a doctor like her Aunt Rose!'

'Well I must have a word with her,' Rose said. 'And Kitty? What about Kitty?'

'Kitty? Oh she's like I was. Content to play with her dolls.'

'I think this table looks quite pretty now, don't you?' Rose said, changing the subject. 'Shall we see if we can give Ma a hand with the goose?'

Matters seemed all right again between them, but in Rose's heart there was a small, persistent doubt. She had seen feelings in her sister which she had not realized existed there. She was by no means sure that they had been laid to rest or that things would ever be quite the same again. She hoped she was wrong, and in the happy meal which followed, the exchanging of presents, the carol singing, the childish games they all played until the children were exhausted and had to be put to bed in the spare room, she managed to persuade herself that she was.

On the twenty-seventh of December, a day earlier than she had intended, she left Faverwell. Her mother bade her a brusque farewell while pressing into her hands a parcel of home-made teacakes, spice cake, and a Wensleydale cheese. Her father went with her on the bus to Grassington station - Christopher had an emergency on the farm and could not take her in the car. He embraced her before she climbed into the carriage and as the train moved out of the station she watched him standing there, a slight, thin figure, his coat collar turned up, his rounded shoulders hunched against the wind. She loved him so much. One day she would make up to him for all he had done for her.

Apart from her father, she thought, it had not been the happiest of Christmases. She had not fitted in as she once did. As the train drew away, steaming towards Akersfield, she realized that she was not entirely sorry to be leaving. She hoped that Akersfield would be more welcoming.

Chapter Three

On the doorstep of number fifteen Victoria Street Rose put down her suitcase and reached up to the bell, but before she could press it the door opened and Mrs Crabtree stood there, smiling a welcome.

'No need to ring, love! Number fifteen is Open House – except of course after ten-thirty in the evening when I like to lock the door because you never know who's about do you? Not since the war. Have you had a nice Christmas then? I think it's turning colder.'

Mrs Crabtree did not pause for breath. It was as if her speaking and breathing arrangements worked on separate circuits.

'Very nice, thank you,' Rose said. 'And yes, it is turning colder.'

The entrance hall of number fifteen was like many others Rose had seen. A door on the right of the narrow passage led to a small, bay-windowed sitting room where Mrs Crabtree liked to think (though she was wrong) that her boarders gathered for civilized conversation after meals. A door further along the same side led to the dining room where breakfast was served between eight and nine and a sort of high tea – which Mrs Crabtree referred to as supper because it sounded better class – at six-thirty every evening except Sunday, when there was a cooked dinner in the middle of the day. At the far end of the passage a door, kept closed, led to Mrs Crabtree's own quarters.

The stairs rose steeply on the left, the red-and-blue Axminster carpet – the pride of Mrs Crabtree's heart – held in place by stair rods of highly-polished brass. Rose's only desire was to mount those stairs to her own room on the second floor, but Mrs Crabtree stood in her way.

'Mr Bairstow's gone to Manchester to visit a friend,' Mrs Crabtree informed her. 'He left a note for you. I'll bring it up presently. Would you like a nice cup of cocoa? I'm afraid you've missed supper.'

'Don't bother, Mrs Crabtree,' Rose said. 'I'll take the

note now if you'll give it to me. Save you climbing the stairs.'

'No trouble, love. I'm used to stairs. I'll fetch the note and I'll bring you a cup of something at the same time. You look perished.'

That means she's going to stand in my room chatting, Rose thought. It had taken no more than the first meeting with Mrs Crabtree, when she'd called to inspect the room, to discover that her landlady liked to talk. Rose didn't feel like it now. She was tired, and a bit depressed. She wanted to make herself a cup of tea – there were gas rings in the bedrooms and the boarders were allowed to boil a kettle, even to make toast in front of the gas fire, though that was the extent of permissible cooking and woe betide any from whose room the smell of soup wafted down the stairs.

Her room looked smaller than she remembered it, more crowded but still pleasant. The chintz curtains at the window matched the cover of the one armchair. A well-polished chest of drawers, with a mirror on top, was reflected in the shining dark-green linoleum which covered the floor and was itself obscured in the middle of the room by a floral-patterned carpet square. Against the far wall the narrow bed was spread with a honeycomb quilt of dazzling whiteness and the small table by the window boasted a hand-crocheted cloth. Yes, her mother would have found it clean all right.

Rose crossed to the window, but before drawing the curtains she stood there for a moment, watching the lights of Akersfield. Starting from a denser patch of light in what must be the centre of the town, they were strung out like pale jewels – not bright enough for diamonds, more like milky opals – until somewhere on the outskirts they faded into the darkness. There was a street lamp right outside her window, its gas light flickering, yet managing to pierce the thin December mist which hovered and swirled around it. She hoped its light would not keep her awake. The winter nights were long and it would be morning before the lamplighter came to put it out.

She looked down the length of Victoria Street; a long, respectable road of houses built in the eighteen-seventies. It was about a hilly mile from the centre of the town, near enough for her to walk to the Clinic every day, just far enough out to miss the once-decent, now near-decrepit and multi-occupied houses closer to the town. There were no mills on the east side of the town, but the rest of Akersfield had mills in plenty. Here and there, where there was enough light from the gas-lit streets, she could see the outlines of the tall chimneys against the sky, not emitting smoke now, for the boiler fires were damped down for the night.

When she had closed the curtains she took two pennies from her purse, put them in the meter, and lit both panels of the gas fire. The room needed warming up. Then she hurried to the door as Mrs Crabtree's knock came, but the landlady had a foot in the door before Rose could stop her.

'I brought you tea, not cocoa. There was some in the pot and it's still quite hot.' She advanced and placed the cup and saucer on the table.

'A cosy little room I always think this is,' she remarked, looking around. 'I see you've got your own bits and pieces out.' She nodded in the direction of the photographs on the top of the chest and the small Corot print which Rose had hung by the side of the fireplace. 'Makes it feel more like home, I daresay. I like my ladies and gentlemen to feel at home.'

Anything less like the Ewe Lamb, with its spacious living kitchen, her bedroom overlooking the beck, Rose could hardly imagine. But Mrs Crabtree meant well. Anyway since she had not felt wholly comfortable at the Ewe Lamb on this last visit, it would be sensible to get used to this.

'I'm sure I'll be very comfortable, Mrs Crabtree,' she said politely.

'That is my aim,' Mrs Crabtree said. 'Home comforts. I made that my motto when I started this business. Of course I'd never kept a boarding house before and I wouldn't now if Mr Crabtree hadn't been taken so sudden. Appendicitis, they said - which is not what they called it before the late King Edward had it. Stoppage of the bowels it was then, and a fancy name didn't cure my husband . . .'

'Thank you for the tea,' Rose interrupted. 'Did you say there was a note for me?'

'Yes. Of course Mr Crabtree was well insured. Insurance

and sanitation were the two things he was most careful about. Ah yes, the note!'

She handed it to Rose and waited for her to open it. When Rose put it on the table without any sign of doing so she said, 'Well I'd best leave you in peace. It's been nice having a little chat, getting to know you. Everybody else is out, by the way.'

At eight o-clock on a Wednesday evening they would be. It was half-day closing in Akersfield; an evening for visiting friends, or going to the pictures or the pub. Rose felt suddenly lonely. At Medical School she had had lots of friends and in the hospital there had always been someone to talk to.

When Mrs Crabtree had left she opened the note. 'Taking you to a New Year's Eve party on Friday. Will give you a knock 9 pm. Be ready. A.B.' Nothing else. No polite 'would you like to go' or 'if you're not already engaged'. It would serve him right if she refused. But she wouldn't. Invitations for New Year's Eve weren't likely to come pouring in. Beside, she liked parties and she quite liked Alex Bairstow.

She cut herself a slice of spice cake and a wedge of cheese, unpacked a book, and settled down in front of the gently-hissing fire.

At nine o-clock on New Year's Eve Rose was ready, waiting to be called for. She had not seen Alex in the meantime. Mrs Crabtree said he had not yet returned from Manchester.

'Well, I'm sure he will,' Rose said. 'He's taking me to a party.'

Mrs Crabtree beamed. 'Just what you need, if you don't mind me saying so. You've been looking a bit peaked. You need to get out more.'

Rose had gone out the morning after her arrival back, to buy material to make herself something new to wear to the party. She had nothing in her wardrobe which would do. After much deliberation she had chosen a deep green crepe material, and a paper pattern of a dress with a low round neck, short sleeves, 'falls' from the waist down each side of the skirt, and the Turkish hemline, very much in favour at the moment. It had all cost more than she could afford and she would have to pull in her horns until she received her first month's salary. Thursday afternoon and all day Friday had been spent in a frenzy of cutting and stitching. It had taken hours to stitch on the sequins around the neckline and at the hem of the dress.

Now, surveying her upper parts in the inadequate mirror – she had to stand on a chair to see, separately, her lower half – it seemed worth it. The deep green colour, more subtle than emerald, suited her. She had pulled her hair back from her face into a soft chignon at the back of her neck. Tomorrow, for work, she would plait it and twist it into two businesslike 'earphones'. But what she really desired was the short, swinging 'bob' which was now so fashionable. As soon as ever she could afford it she intended to have her hair cut off. Long hair had really gone out with the war.

By the small clock on her mantelpiece it was already ten past nine and there was neither sight nor sound of Alex. It was too bad of him. She had been promised a party and had gone to a lot of expense and trouble. She picked up a newspaper to scan while she waited.

'Good riddance to 1920,' she read. 'It has reduced our money, stolen our trade, given us unemployment. We were promised a new world, homes fit for heroes. But where are they?'

Perhaps she should knock on Alex's door, if she could do so without Mrs Crabtree hearing her. Then while she was making up her mind she heard him running up the stairs. He beat a sharp tattoo on her door.

'Sorry to be late,' he said breezily. 'Blame the train. We had to stop to take on water. Anyway, a quick wash and brush up and I'm yours. Say in about fifteen minutes.'

He was gone before she could reply but in fifteen minutes he was back again, standing in the doorway of her room. He wore a dark suit with a stiff white collar and shirt. His hair was sleeked back with a liberal application of brilliantine. She had never seen him look so respectable.

His gaze swept her from the top of her red head to the Louis heels and pointed toes of her black kid shoes.

'Doctor Rose, you look lovely,' he said. 'I've never seen

39

you dressed for a party before. You come up a treat. I doubt if your patients would know you!'

'Thank you for the double-edged compliment,' Rose said. 'And speaking of patients, I start work tomorrow. I mustn't stay out too late or I'll be good for nothing.'

'I'll bear it in mind,' he promised. 'But we can't leave until we've seen the New Year in.'

'How do we get back into the house?' Rose asked. 'I gather the drawbridge is raised at ten-thirty every night.'

'So it is. But Yours Truly has wheedled a key out of our landlady.'

'Good,' Rose said. 'All the same, I wouldn't put it past her to be waiting up for us when we get back, no matter what the time.'

'Mrs C leads a vicarious life,' Alex said. 'Our parties are her parties, our friendships are her concern and, you'll find out if you ever need to, our troubles are her troubles. Don't underestimate Mrs C.'

The party venue, a double-fronted house in Picton Square, was within walking distance of Victoria Street, in a road which seemed to have retained its exclusivity in spite of its proximity to the town. It seemed, as they approached the house, that the party must be taking place in every room, since from every window light showed behind the drawn curtains.

'Who do you know who lives here?' Rose asked.

'A solicitor. Name of Peter Benford. You'll like him.'

She did, too, from the first moment of introduction. He was smallish, fiftyish, with blue eyes behind gold-rimmed spectacles and a handshake so strong that it made her wince.

'Glad you could come,' he said. 'Alex has told me a lot about you. What will you have to drink? There's sherry – or one of those new-fangled cocktails if you like.'

'Sherry please,' she said. She had never drunk a cocktail, wasn't sure what its effect would be.

He supplied her with a drink and then, after a few polite sentences, left her with Alex. She watched him as he moved among his guests in the large, crowded room and was impressed by his skill as a host.

'Here, let me fetch you another drink,' Alex said.

'I've hardly started this one,' Rose protested.

'Then I'll fetch one for myself. Stay right where you are. I'll be back in a jiffy.'

She had noted before that he drank swiftly, usually whisky, downing three to everyone else's one. But he seemed to hold his drink and, as far as she could tell, it had little effect on him.

Standing waiting – there was nowhere left to sit – she appraised the gowns of the other women. They were unexpectedly smart; well made, in beautiful materials and expertly cut. But she did not feel too out of place in hers. It was smart, yet inconspicuous enough to pass muster. And she had been right to choose the Turkish skirt. There was not a gown here which did not curve in towards the hemline. She would have expected the women of Akersfield to have lagged behind fashion, to be provincial in their taste, but it was not so. These ladies of Akersfield, she thought, could have held their own anywhere.

She was observing the scene with interest when her host approached her, accompanied by another man.

'Here is someone who insists on meeting you – and I can't say I blame him,' he said. 'How Alex can risk leaving you, even for a minute, I really don't know! But let me introduce Councillor John Worthing.'

'We've met, after a fashion,' Rose said. 'Good-evening Councillor.'

'Good-evening Doctor Rose.'

He had the same teasing look in his eyes, an air of not taking her quite seriously, of mocking in a kindly way. Standing close to her he was more attractive than he had been with a large table between them. He exuded an air of intimacy which was at once fascinating and slightly alarming. She wished Alex would return – and then almost immediately hoped he would not.

Councillor Worthing noticed her quick glance around.

'Let's move from here before young Bairstow comes back to reclaim you,' he said. 'The party's going on in the room across the hall also, and it's a bit less crowded there.' He took her elbow and began to lead her across the room.

'But I promised Alex I'd stay put,' she protested. 'When he comes back . . .'

'He'll see how foolish he was to leave you. Anyway, he knows his way around. He'll find you again. But not too soon, I hope.'

The room across the hall was identical in size and shape but, as he had promised, less crowded than the first. In the wide hall which separated the rooms a gramophone was playing and some couples were dancing.

'Do you do this stuff?' Councillor Worthing asked, weaving a way through the dancers.

'Given the chance,' Rose replied. 'We danced a lot when I was in Medical School. Sometimes in the hospital also.'

'I'm no dancer,' he said. 'Perhaps you should teach me? Anyway, I don't think you'll find much dancing in Akersfield's Infant Welfare Centre.'

'I don't expect to,' Rose said. 'But I shan't be living there, you know! I do expect to have a life apart from work.'

He would make a good dancer, she thought. He moved well, with good coordination. But dancing was more than doing the right steps and moving well; it required something in the soul. She was in no position to know whether Councillor Worthing possessed that.

'So you start tomorrow,' he said. 'Silly day to start, Saturday. You're not nervous are you?'

'As a matter of fact, I am,' Rose admitted.

'No need to be. You'll be all right. I knew that as soon as I set eyes on you in the Committee room.'

'Well, not everyone agreed with you!'

He shrugged. 'More fools they. Though the majority *did*, or you wouldn't have got the job. You don't need to bother about the others. And don't be too worried about John Stanton.'

Rose looked up sharply. 'Why should I be? Is he alarming? I haven't met him yet.'

'Which is part of the trouble,' Councillor Worthing said. 'He feels – perhaps he's right – that he should have had some say in the choice of his assistant.'

'And if he had, he wouldn't have chosen me?'

'Who knows? But he wasn't consulted. And then . . .'

He left the sentence in mid-air. Rose finished it for him.

'And then he doesn't want a woman?'

'Well, don't let him worry you,' Worthing said. 'You'll get used to each other. And I don't think you'd really find any man alarming, would you?' The look he gave her was bold, direct. She felt as though he was touching her, though he was not.

'You're wrong, Councillor Worthing. In fact I think I find you a little alarming!'

It was a silly thing to say and she was immediately annoyed with herself, but he threw back his head and laughed. He had a splendid, deep-throated laugh. It seemed, without being the least bit raucous, to involve his whole body. It made him seem years younger, not a day older than herself, though Rose judged him to be forty.

'That I don't believe,' he said. 'And by the way, you can keep the Councillor Worthing stuff for official meetings and the like. Otherwise I'm John and you're Rose.'

She liked this man. There was a directness in him which reached out to her, moved her. There was an intimacy which she had sensed even at the interview. Now it stirred her feelings so that she felt that they had known each other from a long way back, while at the same time promising more, much more, for both of them to discover. It was with a sense of disappointment that she saw Alex come into the room. He was in the company of a pretty young girl of about eighteen.

'Good-evening, John,' he said, joining them. 'So it was you who pinched my girl? I might have known!'

'You shouldn't leave valuable property around,' John Worthing said. 'It's too tempting.'

'I'm not anyone's property,' Rose said sharply.

'In the meantime, John, your daughter's been searching for you.' Alex turned to the girl. 'I told you we'd find him with some attractive lady.'

The girl smiled affectionately at her father, coolly at Rose.

'I came to remind you that we promised Mummy we'd be home early, to see the New Year in with her.'

Rose felt suddenly foolish, ashamed of the thoughts which had been in her mind only a few minutes ago. How could she be so naïve? He was like a dozen others she had met. And yet, meeting his eye as he stood behind his daughter, seeing the way he looked at her, she found herself hoping he wasn't. Somehow, it mattered.

'Come and dance, Rose. It's a one-step,' Alex said.

With a cool nod to John Worthing she took Alex's hand and followed him.

They left not long after midnight, staying just long enough for the 'first footing', when the darkest young man at the party went outside into the street, and was re-admitted as midnight struck, carrying a piece of coal to bring good luck to the household.

'It's too soon to go!' Alex protested. 'We're just beginning to enjoy ourselves.'

'I'm sorry,' Rose said. 'I really am tired – and I have to be up early.'

There was no sign of John Worthing. She supposed he had done his daughter's bidding and gone home to his wife.

When they left the house the night was fine and cold with a clear, starlit sky. Rose shivered a little and Alex drew her arm through his own, entwining his fingers in hers. When she tentatively tried to draw away he looked at her in surprise, so she let her hand lie in his as they walked through the quiet streets.

'Why wasn't Councillor Worthing's wife with him?' She asked the question carelessly, as if the answer was unimportant.

'She's an invalid,' Alex said. 'She's seldom well enough to attend parties.'

'Have you met her?'

'Briefly. They give a garden party each year for some charity. If she's well enough she puts in an appearance. She's a pretty woman – beautiful, I should think, before she was ill.'

'What's wrong with her?' Rose asked.

'I honestly don't know. I've heard that when John married her – they were both very young – she was the life and soul of any party. Linda was born a year after they were married and it appears Mrs Worthing has never been the same since.'

'Poor woman!' Rose said. Then 'poor man', she added softly.

'I'm sorry for both of them,' Alex said. 'Though John doesn't let it cramp his style too much.'

At the gate of fifteen Victoria Street he paused, then turned Rose around to face him, drew her into his arms and bent his head to kiss her. She had known, even before the evening started, that this would happen. A few hours ago the prospect had been pleasurable, her body already alive to the prospect. Now, her heart and mind full of that brief encounter with John Worthing, though she knew nothing could come of it, she could not respond to Alex. She wanted to, she tried to, offering her lips to his in submission. He kissed her once, then released her. She was sure he had sensed the submission.

'Happy New Year to you, Alex,' Rose said before he could speak. 'How do we know Mrs Crabtree isn't watching through a chink in the curtains?'

'We don't. Does it matter?' He sounded surprised.

'I wouldn't want to give her any wrong ideas,' Rose said. 'They *would* be wrong, you know.'

The Baby Clinic – that being the name by which everyone referred to the Maternity and Child Welfare Clinic – was in Beech Grove, occupying the first floor of a narrow-fronted, eighteenth-century house in a short street of similar houses. All were in a state of genteel decay, like so many elderly ladies, once beautiful but now gone to seed. None of them was in private occupation, most of them being divided up and taken over by lesser-known insurance companies, moneylenders (grandiosely named financial consultants) and the like.

Rose pushed open the front door and went in. The hall was untidy, with cartons, full and empty, sharing the space with a row of dark wooden cupboards and a wheelchair. A printed notice at the foot of the elegantly-curving staircase said, 'Maternity & Child Welfare Clinic First Floor, Dental Clinic Second Floor'. In a small room off the first floor landing, marked 'Enquiries', she found a young woman.

'Good-morning,' Rose said. 'I'm Doctor Rose Stanton. I start work here today. You are . . ?'

'Miss Mabel Pearlman. I'm the clerk. Pleased to meet you, I'm sure.' Her voice was hoarse and nasal. She was clearly in the grip of a nasty cold and Rose hoped she wouldn't pass it on to too many babies. But the girl's smile was welcoming.

'We've been looking forward to seeing you, Doctor Stanton. Doctor Stanton should be here any minute . . Oh dear!'

'Doctor Rose! To avoid confusion.'

'Doctor Rose. That's nice. Well I'll show you to your room. I've put out a white coat. I'm afraid it'll be miles too big for you,' she said, appraising Rose's figure. 'Oh, here's Nurse Butterworth!'

Nurse Butterworth filled the doorway with her comfortable shape. She held out a hand.

'You must be our new doctor!'

'Doctor Rose, we're to call her,' Miss Pearlman said.

'You're very welcome here,' Nurse Butterworth said. 'We can certainly do with an extra pair of hands.'

'I was just going to show Doctor Rose her room.'

'You do that, love. Then how about a cup of tea all round. Doctor Stanton should be here in about a quarter of an hour. I'll see you later, Doctor Rose.'

Rose's room was small, partitioned off from a bigger room, but the sash window, uncurtained, was a fair size, so the room was light. She put on the white coat which, as promised, was a mile too big for her and, sitting on the chair behind the heavy oak desk, looked around. This was where most of her waking life was to be spent for goodness knew how long.

There was not much to look at: two chairs, an examination couch, a hatstand, a wooden filing cabinet. The floor was covered in brown linoleum, the walls were dark brown at the bottom, fawn above, the ceiling had once been white. Then she saw the calendar. Someone had hung it on the wall facing her: a country scene with a village, as it might be Faverwell itself, and a tear-off pad with today's date showing in large red letters. January first, nineteen-twenty-one.

'I put it there,' Miss Pearlman said, entering with a cup

of tea. 'Doctor Stanton's arrived. He'd like to see you in ten minutes. Just give you time to drink your tea. His room's across the landing.'

He was sitting, white-coated, behind his desk when Rose entered. He had greying hair, and *pince-nez* set on top of a sharp nose, under which he had a dark moustache. He looked at her from cold grey eyes set in a pale face. Everyone in Akersfield looks pale, Rose thought.

'Good-morning,' he said. 'I understand we're to call you Doctor Rose. I find it a little frivolous, but in the circumstances . . .' His voice trailed off.

He doesn't like me, Rose thought swiftly. He doesn't like me and he doesn't want me here. Councillor Worthing was right.

'Nurse Butterworth will inform you about the routine,' he said. 'After that I suppose you had better sit in on my surgery. Naturally, I have no idea of your capabilities.'

'But my references, my application . . .' Rose ventured. 'My experience is written down there. I'm properly qualified and I've spent more than a year since qualification on the women's ward of Akersfield hospital.'

'While I, my dear lady, have been a doctor for twenty-five years, and my father and grandfather before me. I'm afraid I can't possibly turn you loose on my patients just yet.'

His voice was cold, his face stony. Was this his usual manner or was it reserved especially for her? Well whatever the case, he wasn't going to beat her. She wouldn't let him. She braced herself to speak as pleasantly as possible.

'I quite understand. Of course I'll be happy to sit in on your surgery. I'm sure it will be valuable to me. And then I hope it won't be too long before I can be of real help to you, Doctor Stanton. I understand there's enough work in the clinic for at least two doctors. I'd like to take my share.'

His head was bent over a sheaf of notes he had started to read. She might never have spoken. She wanted to take him by his narrow shoulders and shake him until his silly, prissy spectacles fell off.

'See Nurse Butterworth,' he said curtly, not looking up.

47

Chapter Four

Eva never liked to admit it, and she never would out loud, but she had quite enjoyed the war. Well, not enjoyed it exactly. That was a word which made her feel guilty. And you couldn't help but be sad even now, when it had been over going on three years, about all those men killed or wounded; on the Somme, in Gallipoli, at Passchendaele. Some of them were boys she'd gone to school with, boys who'd joined up under age, so eager were they to be up and at 'em. All the same, there were bits of the war, things she'd done, which gave her satisfaction. Her present life did not offer that.

'You'd be better off on munitions,' her mother had said from the minute Eva left school. 'Nice clean work and well paid.' But she hadn't wanted to go on munitions. She preferred her work in the hospital, even if she didn't earn much. She had liked the idea of looking after the wounded, helping them to get on their feet again.

Not that she'd actually looked after them. Not as if she was a nurse, which was what she really wanted to be, what she dreamed about. As a domestic she had washed up, cleaned the sluices, polished the ward floors until you could see yourself in them. Sometimes she shook up a patient's pillow if no nurse was around to restrain her. And on the side, unofficially, she'd run messages for the men; posted letters, placed sixpenny bets with Bert Sugden, the bookie. Once or twice she'd been persuaded into smuggling in a packet of Woodbines, which was how she'd got to know Jim.

'You know I shouldn't,' she told him. 'If there's a no smoking rule it's for your own good.' But he was so handsome, so persuasive - and with a bullet in his leg from Amiens what could a strong young man like Jim Denby do but smoke? He always seemed to have money and he was generous with it. 'Keep the change,' he'd say. 'Buy yourself some chocolate.' He didn't seem to know you couldn't get it.

When Jim was discharged from hospital and came out of the army at the beginning of 1919 it had taken him less than a month of courtship to get Eva pregnant.

'He'll have to marry you,' her mother said. 'We're having no bastards in this family. I'm saying nowt about you getting caught; that's easy done, as we all know. But since you are, it's marriage – and preferably in church!'

By this time Eva had not wanted to marry Jim, couldn't imagine what she had seen in him in the first place, but she knew she'd have to. So her dreams of being a nurse vanished. Not that they could ever have come true. For someone of her class it was impossible. She knew of no-one who had stayed at school after the age of fourteen and when she'd been there some of the children were still half-timers: half-time in school, half-time in the mill.

But dreams cost nothing and they kept you going. As she pushed the pram along Babcock Street, the new baby tucked in under the hood and eighteen-month-old Dorothy propped up at the other end, she was at it again. Then, right in the middle of saving the life of a desperately sick man by her devoted nursing, she heard this voice. It could only belong to Mrs Harris. No-one else had a voice so loud.

'What are you calling the new bairn then? Have you picked a name?'

There being no gardens to the back-to-back houses in Babcock Street, Mrs Harris, plump, slatternly, was sitting on the step outside her door, enjoying the afternoon sunshine while keeping an eye on everything that went on in the street and supposedly guarding her several small children who were playing in the gutter. How *could* she sit out on the street like that? Eva wondered. It was so common. Though her own family had never been anything other than hopelessly poor, she had been brought up to dread anything common.

'We haven't quite decided, Mrs Harris,' she replied. 'I thought perhaps Meg, short for Margaret – or Mary is always nice, don't you think?'

Mrs Harris's fruity sniff showed what she thought. 'I like something a bit different myself. Something special. Gloria or Pearl or Angela. Give a child a nice name and you set it up for life.'

Three less suitable names for Mrs Harris's runny-nosed female offspring Eva couldn't imagine, unless it was the ones she knew they already bore; Hyacinth, Miranda and Selina.

'I get them out of novels,' Mrs Harris confided. 'Whenever I see a name I fancy I jot it down, just in case it might come in handy.' She chuckled. 'It usually does!'

She got up from the step and peered into the pram, touching the sleeping baby with a grubby fat finger.

'Well you'll have to think of something soon, love. You'll have to get her registered. Going on six weeks, isn't she?'

'That's right.'

'I thought so. What does Jim say?'

'He doesn't mind. He leaves it to me,' Eva said.

As he left most things. He didn't go much on babies anyway, regarding them as inevitable and inconvenient results of what a man must have as his right. He probably wouldn't care if she gave them numbers instead of names.

'Quite a posh pram you've got there,' Mrs Harris said. 'That didn't come off a Christmas tree!'

'Mam had it given by a lady she does for,' Eva informed her. 'She told Mam she kept it in the attic for years, waiting till she was past having any more. She reckoned the minute you gave the pram away you fell for another.'

Mrs Harris nodded wisely. 'She's right at that. And it happens to the rich as well as the poor.'

But not as often, Eva thought. Families of nine, ten, even twelve children were not at all uncommon here in the Ridgetron area of Akersfield, but you didn't see anything like that in the Park Moor district where the better-off lived. In Ridgetron when a woman couldn't stand the thought of another birth tearing at her, or despaired of feeding another mouth, she might pay a visit to old Ma Radlett who did mysterious things with a mucky darning needle. You didn't see many Park Moor women knocking on Ma Radlett's door and Eva doubted if they had her equivalent on Park Moor. So how? And why, and what? Perhaps the men were different there?

'I must push on,' she said. 'Mam's expecting me.'

When she reached her mother's house she manoeuvred the pram into the already overcrowded living room. 'I'm not leaving the baby outside,' she said. 'Too many cats and kids. And I don't want to pick her up. She's only just gone off.'

'Been keeping you awake, has she?' Mrs Foster asked sympathetically.

'Half the night. She doesn't seem to need sleep. And I don't think my milk's satisfying her. I don't think she gets enough.'

Mrs Foster snorted. 'How can she when *you* don't get enough? Now you sit down at that table and you're going to get a good plateful of sheep's head broth inside you. A nursing mother needs good food.'

'It's not that easy,' Eva said.

She sat to the table and started avidly on the food her mother put before her. The broth was steaming hot and thick with vegetables, the dumplings floating, light as feathers, on the surface. It was a strange dish for a summer's day but to Eva it was perfection. Her mother watched her with satisfaction.

'I know it's not easy, but I daresay Jim doesn't go short. He fathers these kids on you - bless their little hearts - and it's you has to bear the burden! Well next time I see him he's going to get a piece of my mind!'

Eva had heard it all before. And it was true. But Jim wouldn't get a piece of her mother's mind because he never came here and her mother didn't visit them. She had been once to the room where they lived, ate, slept - and decided that it was better for Eva to visit her. At least it got her out of that dump and she could see to it that she got a decent meal, and sometimes give her a copper or two that Jim needn't know about.

Eva scraped her plate clean, then wiped it round with a piece of bread. She felt better now, not so weak.

'Why did you push me into marrying him, Ma?' she asked. 'We'd have been better on our own, me and Dorothy.'

Her mother poked the fire, which had to be lit, though it was hot in the small room, or how else could she cook or heat the water?

'That's dirty talk, Our Eva,' she said. 'I'm surprised at you. A baby needs to be born in wedlock.'

'What about *my* needs?' Eva said. 'Don't I have any? Don't my needs count?'

'You should have thought of that sooner. You made your bed and you must lie on it,' Mrs Foster said sharply.

It had not been a time for thinking. Nor had there been a bed. Jim had been waiting for her at the hospital gate when she came off duty. Less than quarter-of-an-hour later he had taken her, on an uncomfortable bit of spare ground behind the hospital, both of them shedding the minimum of clothing because of the cold March wind. It was almost unbelievable that that single, swift, urgent – and for her painful – action could so have changed her life.

'I'm sorry for you right enough,' Mrs Foster said more gently. 'You know I'll do anything I can to help. And after all, you wouldn't have wanted to be without little Dorothy, would you?'

The baby started to cry, a thin little wailing sound, as though it was too tired to make the effort but knew it must. Eva took it out of the pram and held it close, unbuttoning her blouse to give it the breast. The child turned its head from side to side, reluctant to take the nipple which Eva tried to push into its mouth.

'She's always like this,' she said despairingly. 'She won't feed and I'm sure she's not gaining weight.'

The two women looked with concern at the baby, noting the pallor of its complexion, its pursed-up mouth, its delicate, bluish eyelids, the way the skin stretched tightly over the skull.

'Why don't you take her to the Baby Clinic, Our Eva?' Mrs Foster said in a worried voice. 'See what they think.'

'Jim doesn't go much on baby clinics,' Eva said. 'He reckons women should know what to do with their own babies.'

'Damn Jim!' Mrs Foster said.

Eva stared at her mother. She was seldom so vehement and she never swore.

'Perhaps I will take her,' she said. 'They say there's a new lady doctor at the clinic. I've heard tell she's ever so good.'

Mrs Foster looked doubtful. 'I'm not so sure about a *lady* doctor. After all, she won't be married, won't have bairns of her own.'

'Well I might go tomorrow,' Eva said.

The baby in her arms relaxed, stopped fighting and began to suck greedily. Eva leaned back and gave herself up to the moment. She was so tired. Perhaps the doctor would sort everything out. Perhaps she could tell the doctor her other worry. It had been present with her now for several days and it was something she dare not tell her mother.

Miss Pearlman watched Rose climb the stairs, and stopped her on the landing.

'You look hot, Doctor Rose.'

'I am, Mabel. It's stifling outside. Worse than in here.'

She had been down into the town in her lunch hour to buy some stockings. Whenever she could afford it she bought silk ones, rather than the more servicable lisle, but there was no doubt that they snagged and laddered very easily. But – she admitted it – she was vain about her shapely legs and slender ankles. In any case, Alex was taking her out this evening so she had to wear decent stockings.

There had been no air in the town with its narrow cobbled streets, stone-flagged pavements and high buildings – and every chimney belching out smoke. Not for the first time in the last six months she asked herself why she had chosen to work in Akersfield. It was the kind of day to be walking the fell tops, or discarding her shoes to dip her feet into Faverwell's fast-flowing river.

'Don't forget there's the Committee inspection this afternoon,' Mabel said. 'I was worried in case you were going to be late back. They could arrive any minute.'

It would have been another black mark against me, Rose thought, going into her room, donning her white coat. Goodness knows I can do without that.

Doctor Stanton had ceased being openly rude to her, and sheer pressure of work meant that he had to allow her to deal with cases, both in the baby clinic and in the ante-natal clinic: but he gave her no encouragement, showed no confidence in her. He would not allow her to see any new cases until he himself had dealt with them, decided all the treatments, given Rose her orders. He passed on the routine cases, keeping the more interesting and unusual ones to himself. There were no discussions between them about how to help particular patients. Rose could go to him with a question if she wished, though he would never mention any of his cases to her. But he was a good doctor, Rose allowed him that.

'He's one of the best,' Nurse Butterworth frequently said. 'We're lucky to have him.' Which was true. Nurse Butterworth was Doctor Stanton's strong ally, but she was never less than fair to Rose, never made her feel, as he did, that she was not part of the team.

She had been at her desk a few minutes, reading the case sheets which Mabel Pearlman had put out for the afternoon clinic, when Nurse Butterworth entered.

'Doctor Stanton would like you to see one or two of his cases this afternoon,' she said. 'He'll be busy with the Committee. There's nothing you can't handle. He's put off all the tricky ones until tomorrow or Friday.'

Trust him, Rose thought - but said nothing out loud. Where the others were concerned she refused to give any sign that all was not sweetness and light between herself and the Medical Officer. But unless they were fools, which they were not, they must know.

'This Committee is a damned nuisance,' Nurse Butterworth said. 'What do they know, anyway?'

'Which members of the Committee are coming?' Rose asked. 'Do you know?' It was the first Committee visit since she had joined the clinic. All she knew was that three or four members came, talked to Doctor Stanton, to Nurse Butterworth and - as a token courtesy - for about two minutes to Mabel Pearlman. So Rose presumed they would also want to see her.

'Councillor Thwaites - he's the Chairman - Councillor Rogers and Councillor Worthing,' Nurse Butterworth said.

At the mention of John Worthing's name Rose felt a tensing of her body, a sharpening of her breath. She bent her head over a file, afraid of what she might show in her face. She had fought against her feelings for this man, reminded herself that he was married, that most likely he was only amusing himself with her; also that she hardly knew him. She had had neither sight nor sound of him since the party on New Year's Eve.

'The other two are all right but Councillor Rogers is a bit of a tartar, doesn't approve of much,' Nurse Butterworth said.

'I know. I've met him. He certainly didn't approve of me! Well, if there are any new cases this afternoon I'll see them,' Rose said. 'If one doesn't see new people the first time they come, then they tend not to return.'

Nurse Butterworth looked doubtful.

'I suppose you're right,' she said reluctantly. 'I suppose you can take down the particulars and then arrange for them to come back to see Dctor Stanton.'

I shall do nothing of the kind, Rose decided.

It was very much a routine clinic that afternoon. Miss Pearlman admitted the mothers and babies; Nurse Butterworth weighed the babies and gave them a quick inspection before their mothers took them in to see the doctor, in this case Rose. The babies were too often underweight, their limbs less than straight; they had muddy skins and nappy rashes. The similarity of so many cases was depressing to Rose.

But the mothers were often in a worse state than their babies: undernourished, badly dressed, dull-eyed and tired-looking, though most of them were younger than she was. She had the feeling that life was one long struggle for most of these mothers. As well as the newest baby they were often accompanied by a toddler, even two, whom they struggled to discipline at the same time as trying to keep the baby quiet. Rose kept a small supply of jelly babies in her drawer to quieten awkward toddlers, though she knew the dentist on the floor above would be furious with her if he knew.

She would have liked to have taken all these tired-looking mothers, separated them from their children for a whole day, given them a *charabanc* outing to some beautiful place, with a great big meal at the end of it.

It was almost the end of the afternoon when Eva Denby

came in. Whatever the Committee members were up to they had not troubled Rose. Mabel Pearlman, bringing in the card for the new patient, said they were all in Doctor Stanton's room.

'There's a Mrs Denby here. She hasn't been before though she's got a little girl of eighteen months as well as the baby. Would you like a cup of tea, Doctor Rose?'

'Yes please. Tell Mrs Denby to come in.'

A timid knock on the door announced Mrs Denby's arrival.

'Come in,' Rose called. 'Come and sit down,' she said when Eva Denby hesitantly entered.

Just like all the rest, Rose thought. Tired. Anaemic without a doubt. Yet somehow she felt that there was a spark here. Mrs Denby was pretty – even allowing for the fact that she was too pale, wore a dress totally unsuited to the heat of the day, and that her dark hair hung lankly around her face. She had a Pre-Raphaelite appearance, with large eyes and sensuously-curved lips in an oval face.

'It's the baby,' she said. 'She doesn't seem to be thriving. And now the nurse says she's underweight.'

'Are you feeding her yourself?' Rose asked.

'As well as I can. She doesn't seem to take to it. Yet I had no trouble with this one.' She indicated Dorothy, who stood quietly beside her.

'Give the baby to me, let me have a look at her,' Rose said.

She laid the baby gently on the examination couch, talking meanwhile to the mother. The child lacked the plumpness, the creases in the flesh, the pink-tinged skin and vigorous movement of a thriving baby. It lay still, not kicking. It was clearly undernourished and weak.

'Well,' Rose said. 'There's nothing here that can't be put right, Mrs Denby. We shall just have to work on it. I'm sure she needs some supplementary feeding, which we can arrange. You see you can't feed your baby well if *you* are undernourished, and I think perhaps you are. Is your husband in work?'

'No,' Eva said. 'Not for the last six months. He has this war wound, you see. It plays him up in the winter and he gets laid off. Then he can't get back again.'

So she's probably been underfed right through pregnancy, Rose thought, handing back the baby. It was common enough.

'I wish you had come to see us when you were expecting,' she said. 'We could have helped. There's a free milk scheme for which you would have qualified, and free dinners at one of our centres. Still, it's not too late. As a nursing mother you can still have those. Your name would have to go before the Committee but I'm sure they would agree.'

It was one of the bugbears of the system; it annoyed Rose intensely, that in a case such as this not even Doctor Stanton could order free milk and dinners. Everything had to go to the Committee for a decision, even when it was a clear-cut case and certain to be agreed.

'I see you live in Paradine Street,' she said. 'Once it's agreed, we can arrange to have the milk delivered daily. Could you come to the centre in Slater Road for dinners?'

'I don't know,' Eva said doubtfully. 'I don't know that my husband would like it.'

'But it's for the sake of the baby,' Rose protested. 'Once you're eating properly you'll get your milk back and then the baby will thrive. It will be better for all of you.'

There was a hesitation, a fear in the woman's attitude which puzzled Rose. Surely no man . . . ?

'There's something else,' Eva blurted out. 'There's something else! I think I've been caught again! I think I'm expecting.' Her tone was a mixture of fear and despair.

Rose sat back, squared her shoulders, looked into the worried face of the mother. Not another one, she thought. Not another one. What could she do?

Mabel Pearlman came in with a cup of tea.

'Will you bring Mrs Denby a cup, please?' Rose asked.

'Rightho!' Mabel looked surprised. It was not the usual practice but Doctor Rose had her own little ways. 'As soon as you're through with Mrs Denby you're wanted in Doctor Stanton's room,' she said.

'You could be wrong, Mrs Denby,' Rose said gently when Mabel had closed the door behind her. 'The body takes time to settle down after a birth. It's sometimes difficult to know just what *is* happening. And your baby is only six weeks old.'

'I'm not wrong,' Eva said stubbornly. 'A woman knows these things. You feel it in your insides.'

'I suppose neither you nor your husband took any precautions?' Rose asked.

'Precautions?' There was scorn in Eva's voice. 'You don't know my husband when he's had a pint or two. Anyway, he reckons that's a woman's job, though how and why I really don't know. But I thought you couldn't get caught when you were breastfeeding.'

'That's not true,' Rose said. She had lost count of how many women had said that to her. Yet they had only to look around. It was the triumph of hope over experience.

'But it's not a good idea to get pregnant when you're nursing. And perhaps you're not. We'll have to wait a week or two and see. In the meantime it's more important than ever that we build up your strength, just in case. So will you agree to the free milk and dinners? I'll try to hurry the Committee.'

'All right,' Eva said reluctantly. 'But isn't there anything you can do for me . . . ? I mean . . .'

'If you mean can I get rid of the baby, the answer is "No". It's against the law, even if I were agreeable. What you really need is advice on how not to have babies so close together. But now isn't the time.'

'It's men that need the advice,' Eva said sharply.

'Men and women both,' Rose said. 'It's a partnership. In the meantime I'll give you a chit to collect some baby food from the clerk - and I'll ask the Health Visitor to drop in and see you in a couple of days, see if you're having any problems with it. You will come and see me again next week, Mrs Denby? I'm sure I can help you.'

But to what extent, she wondered sadly, when Eva Denby had left the room. If she *is* pregnant - and she's as likely to be right as not - how much can *I* do? She felt tired and helpless and wished the long, hot afternoon would end. But now she must face Doctor Stanton and the Committee. She wondered what they wanted of her.

Doctor Stanton sat behind his desk. Rose took the chair he indicated and found herself sitting directly opposite John Worthing, who was flanked on either side by the other two Committee members.

'Good afternoon, Doctor Rose,' the Chairman said. 'We've had a full and interesting report of the work of the clinic in the last six months - and of course your part in it - but we just wondered if you had anything you wanted to bring up? Any little matter?'

So what has he said about me? Rose asked herself. Do I need to defend myself? But against what?

'There is one thing,' she said. 'Could it not be made possible for the clinic doctors to sign the orders for free milk and dinners without having to wait for the Committee? It would make such a difference to the mothers.'

'I have naturally raised that point myself,' Doctor Stanton said stiffly. 'It's not new . . .'

'Then I underline everything I imagine you've said about it.'

'We have to remember it's the ratepayers' money we're squandering,' Councillor Rogers said disagreeably. 'They won't thank us for throwing it about.'

Rose looked at his waistcoat straining over his plump body, at his round, red face and heavy jowls. She doubted that he had ever been hungry.

'Come on, Albert, it's scarcely squandering,' John Worthing said. 'And it's not a king's ransom we're talking about.'

'We are the guardians of the rates,' Councillor Rogers said pompously.

'I think the doctors have a point,' the Chairman said. 'I'm agreeable to putting it to the full Committee. Of course we couldn't have just anyone signing the orders. It would have to be done by the Medical Officer.'

Which means I'll have to argue every case with him, Rose thought impatiently. But never mind, it was a forward step. And to give Doctor Stanton his due, he was reasonably fair-minded on that question.

'Anything else, Doctor Rose?' the Chairman asked. 'If not, then we won't keep you. Time we were off, gentlemen!'

She was back in her room, bringing the records up to date, when the door opened. She raised her head and saw John Worthing, his height and breadth filling the doorway.

'May I come in?'

Not waiting for an answer, he entered, and closed the door behind him. His physical presence, the air of cool arrogance which fitted him like a second skin, filled the room with an almost tangible excitement. Rose could not find her voice.

'I'm here to offer you a lift home,' he said. 'I'm dropping Doctor Stanton so it's on my way.'

She knew that she must excuse herself. Here and now was the moment to stop something which, if she allowed it, might overwhelm her. It would never do that to him, she judged. She felt sure he was always totally in control.

'I rather wanted to finish . . .'

He stretched across the desk and closed the file she was working on. 'Come on now,' he said. 'Everyone else has left. And you look whacked!' His lips curved in an amused smile, as if he read the reason behind her refusal. 'I'm only offering you a lift home!'

So he was. She was making too much of it. And she was hot and tired, disinclined to walk through the stuffy streets.

'Thank you,' she said. 'I accept.'

She put away her papers, doffed her white coat, took down her hat from its peg. It was a cream straw hat, narrow brimmed and trimmed with brown petersham ribbon. She pulled it down over her springy hair, stuck a hatpin through, and was ready.

In the car Doctor Stanton sat in front beside John Worthing while Rose sat in the back. She was not included in what little conversation there was, but that did not worry her. She was glad of a chance to relax. She was surprised when they arrived at Doctor Stanton's house first.

'I thought he lived further away from the clinic than I do,' Rose said when they had dropped him.

'So he does. I came a different way round. I'm going to drive out of the town and up on to the top of the moor beyond Barnswick, to get some fresh air. I hoped you might like to come with me.' His tone was casual. He kept his eyes on the road, not turning to look at her as he made the invitation.

'Oh but I don't think . . .' But her spirits rose sky high, even as she protested.

'I'm not forcing you. We shan't be long. Fifteen minutes there, ten minutes out of the car, fifteen minutes back. Do you the world of good.'

It would too. A breath of moorland air would be the next best thing to Faverwell. But ought she . . . ?

His dark eyes, creased at the corners with amusement, met hers in the driving mirror.

'I don't plan to kidnap you,' he said.

He's mocking me and I deserve it, Rose thought. How silly I'm being!

'I'd love it!' she said quickly.

She thought he might have invited her to sit in the front seat, but he did not do so, nor did he speak again. As they drove through the centre of Akersfield and took the road for Barnswick she studied him from behind. His hair was thick and dark, his shoulders broad. She wondered how men coped with worsted suits and stiff collars in weather like this, then wondered how he would look when he was not formally dressed. His hands on the wheel were as shapely as a woman's, out of character with the rest of his strong, squarish appearance.

They had left Akersfield behind now and were climbing the long, narrow hill which led to the moorland village of Barnswick and then, half a mile further on, to the moor. When they reached the crest of the hill he drew his car into the side of the road and stopped.

'Out you get,' he said. 'We'll walk a bit and do some deep breathing. Fill our lungs with decent air.'

He took her hand to help her out of the car. She freed herself as quickly as good manners allowed her to, afraid of the feelings which ran through her at his touch. They walked forward to the high point of the moor, the ground dipping away in front of them to the wide valley. It was a West Riding scene; softer, and with more trees than in her native dale. The hills were rounded, not as high, and the farms and clustered cottages across the valley were of dark millstone grit instead of the pale limestone of Faverwell. But the air was clear and bright and there was a breeze moving here on the tops.

'It's heavenly!' Rose said. 'Good to be away from chimneys.'

He made no answer and she searched for words to break the silence.

'Were you satisfied with this afternoon's meeting?' she asked.

'Quite. Incidentally, since I daresay you're wondering, Stanton didn't speak at all badly of you. But we're not here to talk about work, Rose – and that's enough.'

She looked up at him, surprised by the abrupt change in his voice.

'I wasn't entirely honest with you, Rose,' he said. 'I brought you here for something more than the view.'

She questioned him with her look.

'Rose, will you come and have supper with me? There's a place Ilkley way, only a few miles across the moors . . .'

There was an invitation in his eyes which said more than his words. With everything in her she wanted to accept it. And why should she not? she asked herself. But she knew the answer, and she must make it quickly if she was not to weaken.

'John, I can't. You know I can't.' The words were almost inaudible. She felt as if all her strength had gone into forming them.

'Why can't you, Rose? I'm only asking you to have supper.'

'When we started out you were only asking me to come up to the moor. And you know why I can't.'

'Tell me! Tell me why you can't have a meal with me. It's a little thing.'

'It might . . . lead on,' she said quietly.

'And you wouldn't want that?'

Why was he forcing her into making these admissions? And why did she not simply refuse to answer him? But already there was something in their relationship which ruled out dishonesty, even insincerity, between them. Or was that feeling only on her side? She had no way of knowing.

'I . . . couldn't allow it.' She sounded so prim, so cold. It was not how she felt. She wanted to take whatever this man offered, and to give to him in her turn.

'I've thought about you a great deal since New Year's Eve,' he said. 'There are things I want to tell you. If the opportunity hadn't arisen today, I would have made it anyway.'

What things? she wondered. But she would not allow herself to hear them. She must not let him weaken what little resolve she had left.

'Please don't say any more, John,' she begged. 'You have your marriage, I have my job. There's nothing more to be done.'

Hearing her own voice, she thought how calm she sounded – but inside she was weeping with longing.

'I shan't give up,' he said. 'Not yet.'

But he would in the end. She faced that. He would tire of her refusals and turn to someone else.

He took her hand, raising it to his lips, gently kissing the tips of her fingers. She wanted him to take her in his arms but he made no move to do so. How strong he was, she thought, how totally in command of himself.

'I must go,' she said presently, 'I have to go out this evening. If we don't leave soon I shall be late.'

'You're going out with Bairstow?'

'Yes.'

For one instant she saw jealousy flash in his eyes.

'He's not right for you, Rose!'

'We're going to the theatre,' she said. 'He's a good friend. I know what I'm doing.'

He smiled his sardonic smile. 'At least you had the sense not to offer me friendship,' he said as they walked back to the car.

In the front of the car, when they took the bends on the curving road, she felt her shoulder against his, and closed her eyes against the thrill which went through her body at the contact. She must not put herself in this situation again. It was more than she could bear – and dangerous.

'Promise me something,' he said as they turned into Victoria Street. 'Oh, it's nothing you can't do! Promise me that if you ever want anything – any kind of help – you'll come to me.'

'I promise,' Rose said.

There was no harm in it since she could not imagine such a thing ever happening.

Chapter Five

The weather continued hot. Doris Chalmers, the Health Visitor, came into Rose's room in the clinic fanning herself with the sheaf of papers she carried. Her round face was suffused with colour and there were beads of perspiration on her downy upper lip.

'It's too much in my job,' she complained. 'Walking up and down these hills all day. Anyway, I popped in to tell you I visited Mrs Denby yesterday.'

'How was she?' Rose said quickly. 'She hasn't been back to the clinic since her first visit three weeks ago.'

Doris Chalmers shook her head.

'Not good, I'm afraid.'

'The baby . . . ?'

'Baby Meg is much better. She's taking the supplementary feeding well and she's put on a bit of weight. It's Mrs Denby I'm worried about. It's pretty certain she's pregnant again. She's suffering morning sickness, which she tells me started early with her other two pregnancies.'

'I was afraid of this,' Rose said.

'She'll have to be persuaded to wean Baby Meg. But she's reluctant. And that slob of a husband is no help. He seems to work on the lines that if the one inside her is ignored it'll go away! But if she's going to carry this baby and keep herself going she'll need a sight better food and more rest than she's getting. She could do with a holiday, too. Fat chance of any of it!'

'We've got permission through for the free milk and dinners,' Rose told her. 'Could you call and tell her that and try to persuade her to come and see me?'

Doris Chalmers looked doubtful. 'I will when I can but I'm rushed off my feet. New babies everywhere. The fewer they can afford, the more they have!'

'Then I'll go myself,' Rose said.

Doris Chalmers pursed her lips, shook her head. 'Not allowed, Doctor. Not your province. Not that I'd mind, of course. Anyway you wouldn't like it much when you got there. Paradine Street stinks in this weather. Privies and middens; and dirty water and the Lord alone knows what else tipped into the drains right outside the houses. And the insides of the houses infested with bugs. Those houses were condemned before the war. It's time they were all pulled down.'

'It sounds as if it's a miracle they don't have an outbreak of typhus,' Rose said.

'That could be a blessing in disguise. Might make the authorities do something. Well, I'd best get going. I just thought you'd like to know about Mrs Denby.'

'Thank you, Doris,' Rose said. 'I wish I could do something. Does Mrs Denby have relatives nearby?'

'Her mother lives in Babcock Street. Mrs Foster's a decent woman but I gather she doesn't visit Eva. Can't stand the husband.'

'Perhaps you could ask her mother to persuade Eva to come back to the clinic,' Rose suggested.

'Not unless I was to meet her in the street,' Doris Chalmers said. 'I can't call on her.'

Throughout the afternoon Rose dealt with a succession of pregnant women, most of them young, but a few in their late thirties and early forties. Two of the women were carrying their tenth child and in appearance, she thought, they looked years older than her own mother.

They were a surprisingly cheerful lot. Every time the door opened she could hear the chatter from the landing where they waited. But talking to each one of them in the privacy of her room she found that close underneath the cheerful surface lay apprehension and worry, fear of how they would make out. Their lives – with few exceptions, for there were no better-class women amongst them – were close-patterned with unemployment, poverty, fatigue, bad housing. There was scarcely one who was not undernourished and she was constantly reminded of the girl from Paradine Street.

In between examining babies, advising mothers, pacifying fractious toddlers with jelly babies, vague thoughts flitted around in Rose's mind about what she could and could not do for Eva and the rest.

She would like to set up some sort of fund – she had no

idea how - from which such women could be sent for a few days' holiday. Akersfield had its own convalescent home at Morecambe Bay, but that was for people who had recently come out of hospital. Rose saw in her mind some place where these women could have a change of atmosphere, a short freedom from work and worry when they most needed it. But it was a dream and she was in no position to make it come true. In the meantime she must get permission from Doctor Stanton to visit Mrs Denby, get her back to the clinic.

When the afternoon session was over she knocked on his door, and entered. He did not look up from his papers.

'Yes, what is it?'

'It's about Mrs Denby.'

'Mrs Denby? Do I know her?'

'She came on the afternoon of the Committee visit. A new patient. I saw her because you weren't available. She hasn't been back since.'

'So?'

'I'm rather worried about her. She has a child of eighteen months, another of about nine weeks, and it seems she's pregnant again. And she's not a very fit woman.'

'I imagine not. What do you expect me to do about it? I remember now that free milk and dinners were agreed.'

'That's the point. I'm worried that she won't take them up. And I think we ought to keep an eye on her through this pregnancy.'

'I'm sure that would be wise,' Doctor Stanton agreed. 'But if she doesn't wish to come to us we can hardly drag her here by the hair of her head.'

'I thought if I went to see her . . . I thought I might persuade her . . .'

'That is not your job,' Doctor Stanton said coldly. 'I explained the rules to you on your first day with us. That, you will remember, is the job of the Health Visitor. Why have you not asked her to do this?'

'I have. I put the baby on supplementary feeding and Nurse Chalmers has visited twice. She's advised Mrs Denby to come back to the clinic, but to no avail.'

'Then I see little we can do. If this lady needs a home visit from a doctor then she should call in her own.'

'I doubt she's even got one,' Rose said. She matched his quiet tones with her own, trying not to lose her temper. 'Her husband has been out of work for some time now. It's likely she's not in benefit.'

'Do you know this for certain?'

'Not for certain. But I'm sure it will be true. Please, Doctor Stanton, all I want is to pay one quick visit – not to give any treatment in the home; just to persuade her for her own sake and the children's to attend the clinic. If she doesn't get good ante-natal care I'm afraid of what might happen to her.'

She recalled Eva's pale prettiness, and her own feeling when she had seen her that somewhere under the drab and worried exterior there was a person of character. She felt a deep pity for, and a sense of rapport with, Eva. She was determined to fight for her.

'I'm sure if you could see her you'd agree with me,' she pleaded.

'I daresay I would. I don't need to see her to believe you. It's a story all too common among our patients and I deplore it as much as you do, Doctor. But visiting them is out of the question.' He met Rose's troubled look with an expression so calm that she wanted to hit him. With great difficulty she controlled herself.

'If it's common,' she said, 'then isn't it time something was done about it? We're just patching up trouble instead of trying to prevent it. I know we can't do much about the bad housing and the drains and such, but as doctors there is some advice we could give them.'

And then suddenly she could contain herself no longer. Her voice rose and she spoke with passion.

'You know as well as I do that the infant mortality rate in Akersfield is a disgrace, in spite of anything we do here in the clinic. Isn't that partly because too many babies are born to women not strong enough to bear them? Women who breed like rabbits until they're worn out and prematurely old. Why doesn't someone *do* something? Why doesn't someone give these women some advice?'

She hated him because he remained unmoved in the face of her anger. She hated him for the reasonable tone of his voice as he replied.

'And who is this someone you're thinking of, Doctor? Are you setting yourself up, perhaps, as knowing what's best for everyone?'

'You know I'm not!' she retorted.

'We are not here to interfere in people's marriages. You in particular, since you are not married, can hardly have the answers. Nor are we here to run people's lives for them. We are doctors. Our role is to help the sick.'

'It would make sense to try to prevent sickness when we could,' Rose said sharply.

'And what do you think our ante-natal clinic is doing?'

'It's not enough,' Rose said stubbornly. 'There should be something, someone, so that women don't get pregnant when they don't want to.'

'Even if that is true,' he said, 'I repeat that it is not our job. It is a matter between man and wife. And now, Doctor, if there is nothing else . . .'

'There is one other thing.' In fact she had only just thought of it. 'I want to suggest to Mrs Denby that she goes and stays with my mother in the country for a couple of weeks. I'm sure my mother would have her. There will be no expense for anyone in the clinic . . .'

He interrupted her.

'Doctor, that is nonsense. Such an action is well beyond the scope of your job and if you persist in such a thing you could get yourself, and this clinic, into difficulties. Your job, let me remind you, is as Assistant Medical Officer to this centre. You are here to treat patients who present themselves, within the resources of the clinic. Your job does not go beyond that. Do you understand me?'

'Perfectly,' Rose said. 'But outside my job, as a private person . . . ?'

He sighed. 'I cannot govern what you do as a private person.' But he would like to, Rose thought. 'I strongly advise against such activities. Such actions can border on the political. As doctors, especially in the public service, we must never to be seen to have anything to do with politics.'

'Politics!' Rose protested. 'I'm talking about giving a woman who's not well a couple of weeks' holiday.'

'There is no knowing where things end,' Doctor Stanton said.

He walked to the door and held it open for her to leave. How right you are, Rose thought, walking past him with her head in the air. How very right you are! And he would never know that it was his calmness in the face of other people's troubles which suddenly fired her resolve.

In the first place, she decided, as soon as she was finished in the clinic and before she went back to her lodgings, she would visit Eva Denby.

She found Paradine Street without difficulty and a small child, playing on the street, informed her that Mrs Denby lived at number seventeen. Nurse Chalmers had not exaggerated. Rose doubted if anyone could exaggerate the awfulness of the place. The street was narrow, the paving stones broken. On each side of the street was a long row of mean little houses, with every so often an entry which led to the houses at the rear, for they were built back-to-back.

Rose walked through a dark passageway and found herself in a cobbled courtyard, down the middle of which a drain ran. On one side of the courtyard the three privies which served twelve houses stood next to the middens which spilled out rubbish, attracting a cloud of flies and bluebottles. On the other side the house doors mostly stood open. The privies and middens stank in the summer heat and Rose tried to hold her breath against the putrid smell. Children played on the cobblestones and two small boys, naked except for short, dirty cotton vests, sailed paper boats in the pool of water around the grating. One of them broke off to pee into the pool to make his boat sail faster.

Dodging the lines of washing slung between the houses and the privies, smiling at a group of women who stopped their conversation to stare at her, Rose knocked on the door of number seventeen. It was Eva Denby herself who answered the door, holding it open no more than an inch or two. Rose was shocked by the change in her appearance since she had seen her three weeks ago. Her face was chalk white, her fine eyes deeply and darkly circled, her lips colourless. There was a film of sweat over her forehead which Rose doubted had anything to do with the surrounding temperature, and she was as thin as a stick. She carried the baby on one bony hip and Dorothy clung to her skirt on the other side.

'Good afternoon, Mrs Denby!' Rose said. 'Perhaps you remember me? I'm Doctor Rose, from the clinic.'

'Oh yes.' She spoke in a dull, disinterested whisper.

'May I come in?'

Eva Denby did not move. 'My husband's in,' she said.

'Fine!' Rose said. 'I'd be glad to meet him. I'd like to come in if I may.' She had no wish to conduct a conversation on the doorstep, within sight and sound of several clearly interested onlookers. Also, she did rather want to meet Mr Denby.

Reluctantly Eva moved aside and Rose followed her into the house. She recognized the smell as soon as it assailed her nostrils. It was the characteristic odour of bug infestation and it pervaded the little room. She had met it often enough on midwifery training, visiting houses where at night the wallpaper could be seen to move and where nurses kept their hats on for fear of bugs dropping in their hair.

Rose's second thought was that Mr Denby, who rose slowly from his chair as she came into the room, was an extremely handsome and physically attractive man, not at all as she had expected him to be. He was tall, blond, with the looks of a Viking warrior and a physique to match. It was clear who was first in line for food in this house.

'Good afternoon,' Rose said to him. 'I'm Doctor Rose Stanton, from the clinic. I was around this way and I thought I'd drop in, see how your wife was. Quite unofficially, of course!'

'You were around this way, Doctor? Paradine Street?' He was sharp. He didn't believe a word she said.

'So how are you, Mrs Denby?' Rose asked.

'The Health Visitor came,' Eva Denby said defensively. 'She said the baby was doing all right.'

'I know. She told me.' She must somehow assure the girl that she was not here to accuse her of something. 'Nurse Chalmers was pleased with the baby. She said she was a bit concerned about you, though.'

'Did you say you were here unofficially, Doctor?' Jim

71

Denby looked her straight in the face as he asked the question. 'Not on behalf of the clinic?'

'That's right.' He was a slippery customer, this one. She didn't trust him, but that was unimportant as long as her visit didn't make trouble between husband and wife. 'But I would like to persuade your wife to come to the ante-natal clinic and that's why I'm glad to meet you. I'm sure you can persuade her.' She turned to Eva. 'I take it you were right about being pregnant?'

Eva Denby nodded.

Jim Denby smiled. 'Well now, Doctor, I wouldn't stand in the way of Eva attending the clinic if that's what she wants to do.'

'I was sure you would agree,' Rose said pleasantly. 'Just as I'm sure you'd want her to have the milk and dinners which the Committee have agreed she's entitled to.'

His face clouded at that. 'I don't like charity. I've never taken it and never will.'

'Oh but it's not charity,' Rose said swiftly. 'You've paid for it in the rates. It's nothing more than your due. I understand you fought in the war. What did you fight for if not for better things for your family. It's certainly not charity.'

'Well if you put it like that,' he said truculently.

'I do, Mr Denby.' It was her guess that he would take anything that was offered, providing his pride could be saved.

Rose turned to Mrs Denby. 'You could do with a bit of a holiday. How long is it since you had one?'

Jim Denby burst out laughing; a strong, uninhibited laugh which reminded Rose sharply of the way John Worthing had laughed on New Year's Eve. Strangely, this man had some of the same strong, masculine attraction which was also John Worthing's; an almost animal sexuality. She could understand why Eva had first fallen for him. Apart from that, of course, he was nothing like John Worthing.

'Holiday, did you say? The likes of us don't have holidays, Doctor! Some say being unemployed is one long holiday, but I suppose that isn't what you meant?'

'Not at all. But I thought it would do your wife a world

of good to get away for a week or two's rest and change. You want this new baby, perhaps a son, to be strong and healthy, I'm sure?'

'If he's anything like his Dad, he will be!' He drew himself up to his full height, thrust out his chin and his chest. 'There's nothing weak about his Dad, I can assure you Doctor Rose!'

His eyes challenged her. He had used her first name deliberately, she knew that. He was thrusting his sexuality at her, lacking the sensitivity to know how he revolted her.

'We once went on a half-day *charabanc* trip to Knaresborough,' Eva Denby said. Her face was alight, her voice suddenly and astonishingly animated. 'Afore we were married. Do you remember, Jim? It was lovely! All those trees and the river and everything!' Then she stopped speaking as suddenly as she had started, and turned away.

'Where would *we* get the money for a holiday?' Jim Denby asked.

'I don't know. I'd think about it. But it would be nothing to do with the clinic.'

'I understand, Doctor. Quite unofficial, as we said before!' He closed one eye in a wink. I can't stand him another minute, Rose decided. She turned to Eva.

'So you'll come to the ante-natal clinic next Monday?'

'I'll see that she does, Doctor,' Jim Denby said. 'Have no fear.'

Well if she comes it will have been worth it, Rose thought, taking her leave. She could put up with the husband for the sake of his wife. Also, she would write to her mother this evening, see what could be done about a holiday. She should have a reply before next Monday's clinic.

Rose slipped into the dining room and took her place at the supper table. The other boarders, including Alex, were already seated. Aside from Alex she knew none of them well. They were friendly, but seemingly had their own pursuits. They included two schoolteachers, a man who worked in the Surveyors' department in the town hall, a buyer from one of Akersfield's department stores. Mrs

73

Crabtree was delighted with the standing of her boarders and to capture a doctor, albeit a woman doctor, had been the final accolade.

'You look as though you've been hurrying,' Laura Browning, one of the schoolteachers, said.

'Yes. I had a call to make after work.'

Rose met Alex's questioning look, but this was not the time to tell him what she had been up to. After supper they walked upstairs together.

'I'll give you a cup of coffee,' she said.

They had long given up the habit of standing chatting on the threshold of each other's rooms and several times a week she either gave him coffee or took it in his room. If Mrs Crabtree had any thoughts about this she kept them to herself.

'I have something to tell you,' Alex said.

'And I have something to ask you!'

'Go and put the kettle on. I'll join you in a minute,' he said.

When he came he was bearing an unopened bottle of whisky.

'A celebration!' he said.

'Really? What this time?'

He was one for celebrations, always finding something worth commemorating.

'No really, I mean it. It's really special this time. I've been promoted, Rose! Standing before you, you see the new Assistant Editor of the Akersfield *Record*!'

'Oh Alex, I'm so glad!' Rose's pleasure was genuine. He was good at his job; keen and ambitious. It pleased her to see him so obviously happy.

He poured generous glasses of malt whisky.

'I knew you'd be glad,' he said. 'Let's drink to it!'

'It's a big step up, isn't it?' Rose asked.

'More money, more responsibility – and next in line for the Editor's job when the old man goes – though that won't be for a long time yet.'

'Is that what you really want – to be Editor?'

'I suppose it is,' he said. 'Eventually. To run the whole shoot. But what were you going to ask? I'd say it was a pretty good evening for asking.'

'It's an idea I have. I don't know whether it would work. I'd like your opinion.'

She told him about Eva Denby, about her visit to Paradine Street.

'A holiday wouldn't solve her problems,' she concluded. 'But it would give her a bit more strength to face them. I think I can do something for her if only her husband lets me.'

'Wait a bit,' Alex said. 'Something rings a bell. What's her husband's name?'

'She called him Jim.'

'James Denby, Paradine Street. I remember now. I've come across him in court. He's a petty criminal, but clever with it. I'd steer clear of him if I were you, Rose.'

'Then I'd say she needs help all the more,' Rose said. 'The thing is, she's only one of many. I see them all the time. I thought if I could get a scheme going, some sort of fund to send these women for a few days into the country or to the seaside, give them some good food and a taste of pleasure, it might make a world of difference to them.'

'They'll still have to come back to the Paradine Streets of this town,' Alex said thoughtfully. 'That could make life seem worse than before.'

'But you're wrong,' Rose contradicted. 'They'd have something to look back on. You should have seen Mrs Denby's face when she talked about the half day in Knaresborough. She was transported.'

Alex shrugged. 'So how would you set about it?'

'The trouble is, *I* couldn't. Doctor Stanton made it quite clear that I mustn't put a foot wrong. I don't agree with him, but he's my boss and he could make things awkward. So I have to find someone else who likes the idea and will undertake to get it off the ground. I thought of you, Alex!'

She smiled up at him as though she was handing him a precious gift.

'Me? You can't be serious, Rose! I can't do that any more than you can. However much I might sympathize with your mothers, in my job I can't take sides.'

She was astonished by his reaction.

'You mean now that you're Assistant Editor,' she said bitingly. 'Does your new job mean you're going to sit on the fence for the rest of your life?'

'Don't be silly, Rose! It has nothing to do with me being Assistant Editor. It would still be the same if I was the most junior reporter. On a newspaper we publish the news. We don't make it.'

She felt suddenly deflated. It had seemed a wonderful idea and she had felt so sure of Alex's cooperation.

'Then you won't help?'

'I didn't say that, Rose. Of course I'll help. When you find someone to take up the idea I'll get the *Record* to give it plenty of space. That'll be a tremendous help.'

'But I don't know anyone,' Rose objected.

She stood up, walked across to the window, looked out on to the street. 'Oh well, I suppose I'd better do what I can to fix up Mrs Denby with my mother. That seems to be about my limit. So if you'll excuse me, Alex, I'd like to write my letter. I could catch the late post.'

'Rose Stanton, you amaze me!' Alex said. 'I never thought you'd give up so easily. We'll think of something. Write your letter. We'll take it to the post and then go for a walk.'

'I'm sorry,' Rose said. 'I'm too tired to walk any further than the post box. It's been a long, hot day.' But longer and hotter in Paradine Street, she thought. 'But I am really pleased about your promotion, Alex,' she added.

He left her, taking the whisky with him, but when later she walked downstairs on her way out to post the letter he came out of his room. 'I'm coming with you,' he said. 'I've thought of someone. I can't imagine why I didn't think of him right away!'

Out in the street it was cooler, and there was a slight but refreshing breeze.

'Who?' Rose asked.

'John Worthing.'

'I couldn't possibly ask John Worthing,' Rose said quickly.

'Why ever not?' Alex looked at her in astonishment. 'It's the kind of thing he could do. And he likes you so you're halfway there.'

There was no way she could explain. She tried to push away the feelings which even the mention of his name had stirred in her.

'He's a generous bloke,' Alex persisted. 'And he can afford to start it off with a bang. He's rich. He manufactured khaki cloth for uniforms right through the war. Made a packet.'

'Why wasn't he in the army?'

'He has a foot injury from when he was a kid. He could never have marched.'

'So he's a war profiteer?' Why did she speak as though she wanted to hear something bad about him?

'Not the way you mean it,' Alex said. 'Yes, he made a lot of money, but he made it fairly. His cloth was good stuff. Some of the cloth which went into uniforms was so bad that it fell to bits in the rain and the mud in France. There was nothing like that about John Worthing's product. And he was generous with his money, gave a lot of it away. He'd probably start you off with a good donation and lend his name to the fund.'

'I don't want to take money from him,' Rose said stubbornly.

'I don't understand you. The money would be for the fund. But if you want to give up the idea . . .'

She couldn't. She thought of Eva Denby in Paradine Street, thought of the women she had seen that afternoon, and knew she couldn't. She would approach John Worthing. 'Promise to come to me if you need anything,' he'd said.

She telephoned his home next day. A woman answered.

'Who is speaking?' she asked. She had a gentle, slightly petulant, cultured voice. Mrs Worthing, Rose had little doubt. She wondered what the other woman looked like, there at the end of the telephone. She sounded tall, slender and elegant.

'Doctor Rose Stanton.'

'Just a minute.'

The silence seemed to last forever but in the end John Worthing came to the phone.

'I'd like to see you,' Rose said hesitantly. 'Whenever it suits you. It won't take long.'

His reply was terse, almost as if she was a stranger.

'Saturday. Twelve-thirty. I'll pick you up at Victoria

Street.' He rang off without another word.

At twelve twenty-five she was looking out of her window, watching for his Daimler to turn the corner into Victoria Street. She wished she had arranged to meet him away from Mrs Crabtree's prying eyes, but his manner on the phone had given her no chance to do so. The Saturday morning clinic had dragged on until noon, so that she had had to take the tram back home and had had time only to wash her face and change into her best dress of striped Macclesfield silk. Thank heaven she had now had her hair cut. The style suited her, with the sides curving forward on to her cheekbones and a fringe showing under the same straw hat which must see her through this summer. Yesterday evening had been spent in re-trimming it with pink Petersham ribbon to match her dress. She was annoyed with herself that she cared so much how she looked for this occasion, but there was no denying the truth of it. She wanted John Worthing to find her attractive – though she intended, all the same, that it should be no more than a business meeting.

At half-past twelve exactly the long, black limousine rounded the corner. She was downstairs and waiting on the pavement by the time it stopped outside number fifteen. John looked serious and unsmiling as he held open the door for her. As she took the seat beside him her heart thumped so loudly that she thought he must hear it. In less than a minute they were away. As on the previous occasion, he drove through the centre of Akersfield, though now it was thronged with Saturday shoppers, and took the road towards the moors. He drove in silence, his eyes fixed on the road ahead. Rose wondered why he did not ask her what it was she wanted. She felt that she was sitting here under false pretences.

'Where are we going?' She had to break the silence. Was he angry with her because she had telephoned him at home?

'Ilkley way. I haven't waited for your agreement this time. Since you asked to see me I've taken it that whatever it was about didn't preclude you eating. I've booked a table at the Heifer.

78

He sounded neither angry nor pleased. His concentration seemed to be on his driving, which was fast and skilful. When it seemed that he had nothing more to say to her, Rose studied his profile, noted his aquiline nose and strong jawline, the curves of his full, yet firm, mouth, his strongly-marked dark eyebrows and uncommonly thick lashes. It was not a Yorkshire face. Somewhere in the past, she wondered, was there Middle Eastern blood? And everything worked together in his appearance. What he wore enhanced his strong good looks. The worsted of his dark suit was the finest, the velour of his grey trilby hat the smoothest, but a silk tie in reds and blues lifted the conventionality of his appearance, gave him the touch of flamboyance which suited him, added to his slightly foreign air. He took off his hat and handed it to her.

'Chuck it on to the back seat!'

She held it on her lap, finding a strange comfort in the feel of it, surreptitiously stroking the underside of the brim with the hand furthest away from him. It was almost as though she was stroking his own, dark hair.

He drove up through Barnswick and out again on the moorland road, travelling fast, not another car in sight.

'Don't you want to know what I want to see you about?' Rose asked him at last.

'Yes,' he said. 'But not until we've eaten.'

The Heifer Inn was on the bank of the river, close to the bridge. As they sat at their table, in an alcove by the window, they could see the clear brown, peaty water rippling over the pebbles. They ate fresh, local-caught trout, new lamb, strawberries, meanwhile making desultory conversation about matters of no importance, as if they were polite strangers. It was unbearable. Is this what I wanted? Rose asked herself. Had he absolutely ceased to care about her? Had he already – the thought stabbed her – found someone else who was prepared to be more generous than she was? But why bring her here at all? He could easily have summoned her to his office.

'We'll take coffee in the garden,' John Worthing told the waiter.

Not until they were seated in the shade of a tree and the waiter had served them and left them, did he say 'And now

79

what's it all about?'

It was a relief to be able to speak something other than pleasantries. Rose told him of the scheme she had in mind. She thought for a moment, just at first, that he looked disappointed, and she wondered what he had been expecting from her. But the look passed and as she unfolded her ideas with mounting enthusiasm he listened intently.

'I'm sure it would work,' Rose said. 'And it would make such a difference to the women I'm thinking of.'

'I like the idea,' he said. 'Of course there are details to be gone into - like do you want to buy a house in the country or at the seaside, or do you want to use existing boarding houses and have the mothers stay there. That kind of thing.'

'If we wait until we have enough money to buy a house, then we might have to wait a long time,' Rose said. 'We could work towards that, but it would be best in the first place to send the mothers to established boarding houses. That way we could make the money work right from the beginning . . .'

She broke off, conscious that for the first time that day he was smiling at her. She was glad to have lightened his mood, though she had no idea how.

'It's your enthusiasm,' he explained. 'It's a pity you can't run this thing yourself. Your enthusiasm would have people bending over backwards to help you.'

'Well I can't,' Rose said. 'You know my job won't allow it.'

'I do know. So I will. At least I'll start it off. I'll make a donation of a hundred pounds. It's not a fortune, but it's enough to do a bit of good, and not too much to arouse curiosity.'

His eyes met hers, and with relief she saw in them, for the first time that day, the admiration which he had been so quick to show on previous occasions.

'I'll have a word with the editor of the *Record*,' he said. 'He can publish the idea and start a subscription list.'

'What about the Health Committee?' Rose asked. 'Will they be awkward?'

'It's nothing to do with the Committee. They don't

employ me. In fact I'll wager they'll chip in, especially if they can do it publicly. But don't worry, your name won't be mentioned.'

'I don't know how to thank you,' Rose said.

'Yes you do. But I'm not looking for thanks.'

There was a silence between them, which he was the first to break.

'Let's go for a walk,' he said suddenly. 'There's a path along the river bank, on the other side of the bridge.'

The path was stony, and so narrow and overhung by trees, that most of the time they had to walk in single file. When, about half a mile along the bank, they came to a gate which led into a field, John held it open and motioned Rose through, into the meadow which lay on the other side.

'I didn't bring you along here to walk behind you, conversing with the back of your neck,' he said. 'The grass is as dry as tinder here, so we can sit down. I want to talk to you.'

He sat down first, in the shelter of the wall, then took her hand and pulled her down beside him. She landed off balance, so that she fell against him. At once his arms were around her, holding her fast.

'Please John . . .'

He stopped her words with his kisses; searching, passionate, demanding kisses. After her first protest she gave in to him. But it was more than that, much more: she responded with a passion to match his own, her demands were no less than his. She had never known, until now, the feelings he released in her. It was as if she had suddenly been born; a new person, eager, aware, wanting to receive, longing to give. It was she who wanted no boundaries, he who suddenly pushed her from him and sat up. Rose lay outstretched on the ground, looking up at him, not understanding the abrupt change in his manner.

'I can't do this!' he said roughly. 'I didn't intend it. I didn't bring you here for a quick roll in the grass. I brought you here to talk to you. I told you on that evening three weeks ago that there were things I wanted to say to you. I brought you here to make you listen.'

Rose sat up. Her hands shook as she fastened the

buttons of her dress. She was trembling from head to foot and she felt ashamed, not so much from what she had done as from what he might think of her. I didn't come for a roll in the grass, either, she wanted to say. It was the first and last time with him. It had to be. But the agony of that decision, swiftly taken, was almost more than she could bear. If he came back to her now, only touched her with one finger, would she be able to keep to it?

'Please listen to me, Rose,' he said.

She didn't want to listen. She was afraid that what he had to say might take away her resolve. She opened her mouth to protest, but no words came.

'You know my situation, Rose. My wife is ill. She's been an invalid since our daughter was born. I married her when she was eighteen and I was twenty. I knew almost at once that it was no good, but by then the baby was on the way. It was my fault. I was wrong for her from the start, but I'd persuaded her into marrying me. I can't ever give her what she wants from me but I owe her a debt.'

'John, you mustn't say this to me,' Rose interrupted. 'You can't want me to hear it.' Her heart ached for him; it hurt her to see this strong man shedding his pride.

'I do want you to hear it, Rose,' he insisted. 'I want you to know where we stand. I'm serious about you. There's no way I could ever leave Diana, not while she needs me. She depends on me totally. But you must know how I feel about you, Rose. It began the ninute I saw you in the Committee room. I went away thinking about you. When I met you at the party on New Year's Eve you'd scarcely been out of my thoughts.'

It can't be happening, Rose thought. This green meadow, the sound of the river, the peace of the afternoon – and in her heart a turmoil which shattered everything. He was saying the things which with all her heart she wanted to hear, but could not take.

'I'm certain you feel the same way about me,' he said. 'Don't deny it.'

'I don't deny it,' she said softly. 'How could I? But there's no future in it.'

'Not the future we both want. I know that, Rose. Not what I would give you if I could. But something, surely?

Something worth having. I love you, Rose.'

He pleaded with her as she could not have believed so arrogant a man could plead.

'That is infinitely worth having,' Rose said. 'I'm proud that you do. But I can't agree to the kind of relationship I know we both want, I as much as you. You know this has to be the start and the finish.'

He gave her a long look. She saw the hardness come back into his eyes, saw the proud lift of his head, wanted to take back everything she had said and to be in his arms again. She felt herself to be utterly defeated.

'Very well, I believe you, Rose - for the moment. But you'll find I don't give up easily. You'll change your mind. You will be mine in the end, you know!'

'We mustn't see each other again,' Rose said helplessly. It sounded trite, banal.

'Don't be ridiculous! That's impossible in Akersfield.'

'Then we must do the best we can.' She felt lifeless, as if nothing mattered any more. 'In the circumstances we must scrap my holiday scheme.'

'So you're willing to sacrifice these women for your own comfort? I don't believe that.'

'I wish I hadn't asked you,' she said. She wished she had never thought of it.

'I'm glad you did. There's nothing I wouldn't do for you, Rose. I mean that, in spite of everything.'

Except break up your marriage, she thought. But if he offered to do that, would she let him?

Once again he read her thoughts as if he was inside her head.

'If my wife were as strong as you are, I would leave her. As it is, she can't manage without me.'

But I must, Rose thought. For the rest of my life I must live without you. She wondered how she would bear it.

He held out a hand, pulled her to her feet. When she was standing before him he kissed her gently, no passion. Her lips were cold.

'It's you I love,' he said.

A shiver ran through her as they walked back along the river bank towards the car.

Chapter Six

On Monday morning the postman brought Rose a letter from her mother. 'Your lass and her bairns will be welcome,' Mrs Stanton wrote. 'Emily will lend her a pram and she's looking out some baby clothes. I am sending you a parcel with some oatmeal parkin and a nice cheese.'

Rose smiled. She had been the recipient of such parcels all the time she had been in Medical School. Her mother constantly feared that, away from home, she would not eat enough. An unfounded fear, Rose thought, getting up from Mrs Crabtree's breakfast of bacon, eggs, sausages, bread and marmalade and lashings of hot, strong tea.

She was pleased, but not the least bit surprised, by the reply to her request. Her mother, in spite of her taciturn ways, would always give help where it was needed, and with the minimum of fuss and palaver. Rose knew that at the Ewe Lamb Eve Denby would be cared for by both her parents, cosseted even, in a quiet way which would not embarrass her. Now she must persuade the wretched husband to let his wife go, and that might not be so easy.

Rose wanted to give Alex the good news but for the last two days he had been visiting his aunt, in Manchester. She wouldn't see him until tonight. She had been surprised by how much she had missed him over the weekend. It had taken his absence to show her close they had grown, what good friends they had become since she had come to live at Mrs Crabtree's. They were always there for each other to turn to. She suspected that on Alex's side the feeling was one of more than friendship, but it was not so for her. Her feeling for John Worthing - a feeling she did not want, which she passionately desired to tear out of herself - made that impossible.

She had wanted to see Alex when she returned from lunching with John Worthing on Saturday, her mind in turmoil, her spirits low. She badly needed his everyday sanity, the calmness of their friendship, but he had already left.

Unable to bear her own thoughts she had taken herself off to the cinema on Saturday evening, watched a film of which she afterwards remembered nothing, and on Sunday she had taken an early tram to Saltaire and walked vigorously over Shipley Glen. The outing had refreshed her body but it had done nothing to quieten her mind. She was glad when the weekend was over and she could get back to work.

On Monday afternoon it was the ante-natal clinic again.

'It's going to be a busy one,' Nurse Butterworth said. 'It's amazing how this clinic has grown.'

'It's good that more women are catching on to the idea of ante-natal care,' Rose said. 'The trouble is that most of these women ought to have been taking more care years ago, not just in the few months before they have the baby. Look at the state of their teeth, for instance!'

'Terrible!' Nurse Butterworth agreed.

It was a sad fact that there was always a procession of women from the ante-natal clinic to the dentist on the floor above, where most of the treatment was wholesale extractions. 'A tooth for every child,' Nurse Butterworth continued. 'But some of 'em lose the lot! But what can you expect? They've been badly fed from the cradle.'

Halfway through the afternoon Mabel Pearlman brought in another file.

'Mrs Denby is here,' she said. 'I told her she wanted the Infants' clinic, but she said not. I just can't believe it!'

'You should,' Rose said. 'You've seen it all before.'

'I've seen too much,' Mabel said. 'I'm never going to get married. I can tell you that for certain!'

Rose laughed. 'You'll change your mind. Most women do.'

'Even you, Doctor Rose?' Mabel asked cheekily.

The words went deeper than the girl could know. In her heart Rose knew that with part of her she envied every one of these women who came with their swelling bellies, and she coveted the tiny infants she so carefully tended. But such thoughts were an indulgence she did not often allow herself.

'I couldn't do my job if I were married,' she replied.

It was not quite true. She couldn't stay in this job but,

married or not, she would always be a doctor. She had won that for herself and no-one could take it away from her. There was nothing against her setting up in practice if she could afford to do so. She recalled Gerald's words, that married to him she wouldn't starve while waiting for patients. It was the first time she had thought of Gerald in months. She knew now that whatever she did in the future, Gerald would not be part of it.

'So Mrs Denby will have to be seen by Doctor Stanton,' Mabel said. 'Seeing she's new to this clinic.'

'I suppose so,' Rose said.

But if luck was with her Doctor Stanton would pass Mrs Denby back as she had already treated her in the Infants' clinic. Would she unwittingly mention that she had been visited by Rose? Oh well, if it happens I'll simply have to deal with it, Rose thought. She hated her fights with Doctor Stanton. And now, she realized, she would have to visit the Denbys again to make arrangements for the visit to Faverwell.

She was pleasantly relieved when, towards the end of the afternoon, Mabel Pearlman showed Eva Denby into her room. 'Doctor Stanton has seen Mrs Denby,' she said. 'He said you should take over.' It seemed there were to be no repercussions.

'Sit down, Mrs Denby. How are you?' Rose said.

'I'm all right.'

It was the standard reply from most of the mothers. It meant that they were surviving, that they had learned to take whatever came. To find out more she had to question them closely.

She examined Eva. Her chest was not too good and she had the all-too-common pallor of skin and fingernails and the slight breathlessness of anaemia. She was also far too thin, each rib clear enough to be counted, her hip bones prominent under the inadequate covering of flesh.

'We'll have to try to build you up,' Rose said. 'By the way, I've had a letter from my mother. It's all right about the holiday!'

She had expected the girl to be pleased but she was taken aback by the sudden glow in Eva Denby's face. It was as if someone had lit a torch inside her.

'I'm glad you're happy about it,' Rose said. 'I can't discuss it here. It's not clinic business. I was thinking of visiting you tomorrow evening but perhaps you and your husband would like to come to see me instead?'

The light went out of Eva's face as suddenly as it appeared. 'It's no good, Doctor,' she said. 'He won't let me go.'

'Not let you go? You mean not let you come to see me?'

'Not let me go on holiday. He says he can't manage.'

'Can't manage? But you'll be taking both children with you. I've arranged that.'

'It's his dinners. There'll be nobody to make his dinners. And do his washing.'

There is no point in losing my temper, Rose told herself quickly. It won't help this poor, silly girl. I shall have to tackle that pig of a husband.

'Well, anyway, ask him to bring you to see me tomorrow evening. At about seven-thirty. Fifteen Victoria Street. Do you know where that is?'

'Yes I know it,' Eva Denby said.

'Will your mother look after the children while you come?'

Eva nodded.

'Very well then. And if you don't turn up I shall come to Paradine Street on Wednesday after clinic. Now this is what you are to do about the free milk and dinners . . .'

Rose had been home no more than a few minutes when there was a tap on the door and Alex entered.

'How did your weekend go?' she asked.

'Fine. And what about yours? What did he say?'

For one moment she was bewildered. The events of the day, her meeting with Eva Denby, had momentarily driven John Worthing out of her thoughts. But not really out of her mind. He was never quite that, only waiting in the wings; and now he came on stage again, as dominant as ever. She saw the dark, lively eyes, which sparked with passion when he looked at her, saw the full-lipped, sensual mouth, the shapely hands, heard the deepness of his voice - as if he was standing there before her.

'What did he say?' Alex repeated the question. 'About the fund?'

'Oh, the fund! He liked the idea. He said he'd back it; establish a fund and start it off with a hundred pounds.'

'Why, that's wonderful, Rose! You'll have the whole scheme going in no time. You could even fit in some holidays this summer.'

'I suppose so.'

'What do you mean, you suppose so? What's wrong? You don't look all that pleased.'

'Of course I'm pleased,' Rose said.

'You surely haven't gone off the idea? You were so keen.' Puzzled, he sought her face for an answer.

'Of course I haven't. Why would I do that?'

'I can't imagine.'

'There are several details to be settled,' Rose said. 'Where the mothers are to go not being the least of them. But I don't suppose I'll be involved in that.'

'I expect you will be,' Alex said. 'Once the fund's been set up I don't see that Doctor Stanton or anyone else can prevent you supporting it in your spare time. It's a good scheme.'

Providing it went ahead successfully it would be better not to be involved, Rose thought. If she was to know any peace of mind she must avoid John Worthing.

'My mother says she'll have Eva Denby and her children,' she said, changing the subject. 'But Mrs Denby now says she thinks that husband of hers won't let her go. I've asked them to come and see me here tomorrow evening. I thought I might do better with him on my own ground.'

'If he should come alone, call me in,' Alex said. 'I don't trust him as far as I can throw him.'

'I can deal with him,' Rose said firmly. 'He might scare the living daylights out of his wife but he doesn't frighten me.'

Until she heard the ring on the doorbell at half-past seven, followed by Mrs Crabtree's loud voice, with its overlay of refinement, and Jim Denby's rough, but somehow attractive tones, in reply, Rose had doubted whether the Denbys would come. She had warned her landlady of the impending visit, said that she would have to see them in her own room since other boarders were using the sitting room. Now Mrs Crabtree stood in her doorway, the Denbys behind her.

'Two *persons* to see you,' she said frostily. She did not like this kind of visitor and she hoped that Doctor Rose wasn't going to encourage such people often.

'Thank you Mrs Crabtree,' Rose said. 'Mr and Mrs Denby, please come in.'

Against the comparative comfort of her room they looked so shabby. It had not been as noticeable in Paradine Street, where everything was dilapidated and seedy, but here they looked dreadful. Mrs Denby's navy serge dress, clearly a hand-me-down and a poor one at that, fitted where it touched. It was hot and cumbersome for the summer evening and seemed to weigh her down. Her shoes were trodden over at the sides, scuffed at the toes. I must look out a summer dress or two, Rose thought.

Jim Denby was equally shabby, his jacket and shirt frayed, his trousers thin at the knees; but somehow his personality rose above his appearance. How splendid he would look, properly dressed, Rose found herself thinking. And how she disliked him. He stood there, cap in hand, but there was arrogance in his attitude.

'So what's all this our Eva's been telling me, Doctor,' he asked, taking the offensive.

'Well I expect she's been telling you that my mother has invited her to Faverwell for a fortnight's holiday. My parents keep an inn there. Naturally I wanted to see you about it also, though I knew you'd want her to go.'

It was humbug, but she had discovered on her visit to Paradine Street that it was the way to deal with this man. She was sure he could take no end of flattery. She saw the quizzical look Eva Denby gave her. She knows what I'm up to, Rose thought.

'So who's paying for all this?' he asked. 'Train fares, board and lodgings?'

'That will all be taken care of. You don't need to worry about that. All we have to think about is getting your wife well again. Once you're in work, if you want to repay the train fare you can do so.'

'Oh I should want to do that, Doctor,' he said swiftly. 'Naturally I'd want to do that!'

Never in this world, Rose thought.

'A pub,' Denby continued. 'Now that sounds very nice. Not that I'd want my wife going into a pub, not unless I was with her, you understand.'

'I understand perfectly,' Rose said. 'But I'm afraid that wouldn't be possible. Your wife would have my room. It has only a single bed. My mother will borrow a cot for the baby and perhaps Dorothy will have to share her mother's bed. But Mrs Denby won't be in the bar at all. I assure you my mother will look after her very well indeed.'

'Well I don't know . . .'

'You realize your wife is far from well, Mr Denby?' She spoke forcefully, looking him straight in the eye.

She sensed at once that she had touched a nerve. She saw the beginning of fear in the eyes which had been so bold in meeting her. It was the fear of someone who knew that death was no stranger to Paradine Street, and that it did not always wait for people to grow old.

He really is worried, Rose thought. Though most likely he was worried about what *he* would do if his wife were to be really ill. She pressed home her advantage, hating herself for playing on his fear. But after all, there was substance in it. The sanatoria were full of young men and women who would die from tuberculosis because they had lived in places like Paradine Street, where germs grew and multiplied, and they themselves were too run-down and weak to resist the infection. Eva Denby had no more immunity than some of those, and she was far from fit.

'It would be difficult for you, with Dorothy and the baby, if your wife were to be ill,' she said. 'It's not easy for a man, looking after things.'

She hated herself for the sympathy in her voice which this man took to himself. But if it was the only way . . .

'She could go on Saturday week. I'd make all the arrangements, get the train ticket and so on. So that's all right then, is it?'

She spoke as though he had already agreed. He gave in.

'I want whatever's best for my wife. Whatever's best.'

'Good! I knew you would!' She tried not to show her relief.

'And you say this has nothing to do with the clinic? It's all off your own bat?' he said.

'Quite!' But remembering Doctor Stanton she did not feel as confident as she sounded.

'Very well then,' she continued. 'I'll call and see you in a few days' time when I've made all the arrangements. I'll get the train ticket.'

'Now if you give me the money, there's something I could do for you,' Jim Denby offered quickly. 'No trouble at all and save you the time.'

And no chance at all, Rose thought. He'd never get as far as the booking office.

Eva, from first to last, had not spoken, but as Rose showed them out she turned to her with a smile of singular sweetness, a smile which reached to her beautiful eyes.

'Thank you, Doctor!' she said.

On the following Saturday afternoon Rose went again to Paradine Street. She passed the same women sitting in their doorways, the same small children playing by the drain. It took her all her time not to say something to the mothers but she doubted whether it would do any good. In any case, where else were the children to play?

Jim Denby opened the door of Number Seventeen.

'Come in, Doctor,' he invited.

It was dark, coming from the bright sunlight into the room – such a shabby little room with its stone-flagged floor with one meagre, rag rug in front of the fireplace. It was not until she stood in the room that she realized that Eva was not there.

'I had hoped to see your wife, Mr Denby. There are one or two arrangements . . .'

He had somehow manoeuvred her into the middle of the room and placed himself between her and the doorway. With his great physique he towered above her, so close that the aggressive masculine smell of his body filled her nostrils. She was not afraid, she told herself. It was his way of imposing himself on her simply because she was a woman. He wouldn't dare to try anything on, not with all those women outside who had seen her come in.

'Eva's gone to her mother's,' he said amicably. 'But that's all right, you can tell me.'

'It's nothing important,' Rose said quickly. 'Mrs Denby's mother lives in Babcock Street doesn't she? I can walk that way and perhaps catch your wife there.'

'Hot weather to be walking the streets, Doctor. And not really your kind of streets at all. Not what you're used to. You should be careful coming into these parts on your own. Why, even the police only come in pairs!' His voice mocked her. 'It could be . . . awkward for the likes of you.'

'I'm sure I'm quite safe,' Rose said firmly. 'Doctors go anywhere.'

'Lady doctors?'

'Even lady doctors. And I assure you, I'm not in the least afraid.'

She challenged him deliberately with her boldness, with the direct look she gave him. He was not to know that her knees were trembling, her throat dry. He took a step towards her, raised his hand and touched her shoulder. She tried not to shudder as she felt the strength and heat of his hand through her thin blouse.

'You're really much too pretty to be a doctor!' The sudden, soft intimacy of his voice was more alarming than any of his blustering. 'That pretty red hair! I daresay you're a fiery one, given the right place!' It was clear to her what he thought the right place was.

Rose took a deep breath, managed to speak normally, ignoring his words.

'Well, I'll be off then, Mr Denby. I'll see your wife another time.'

She tried to side-step him but now his hand gripped her shoulder and she could not pass.

'Please let me go,' she said. 'This is rather silly.'

'Silly is it?' he said. 'You're the one who's silly, Doctor. Poking your nose into other people's business, coming down here with your posh ways. My Lady Bountiful throwing us a few scraps. What difference do you think *you* can make in the end? What can *you* do about this stinking, rotten existence? You'd draw the line at sharing it wouldn't you? When you leave here you'll be glad enough to go back to your fine room, your well-filled table.'

He spoke quickly, the words running together in a long, low growl. He was too intent to hear the door open and see the woman standing there.

'Could your Eva let us have a cup o' sugar?' she said.

Jim Denby turned at the sound of her voice and Rose slipped past him.

'Oh, I didn't know you had company!' the woman said.

Yes you did, Rose thought. You watched me come in. But thank heaven for your curiosity.

'Pardon me, but aren't you the lady doctor from the clinic?' the woman asked.

'That's right. And I'm just on my way.'

She'd like to know why I'm here, what my business is - and no doubt she'll somehow find out. It was impossible to do anything by stealth.

Rose decided to walk to Babcock Street. She had no wish to make a return visit to Paradine Street.

The whole area through which she now made her way was broken down and nasty: mean, rubbish-strewn streets, cracked pavements, houses which if they were not soon pulled down must surely fall down. There was nothing green. Not even grass or weeds would grow between the cobblestones here. Jim Denby's words rang in her ears. She shuddered at the remembrance of his touch but his words ate into her. 'What can you do about this stinking, rotten existence?'

In Babcock Street a woman told her where she could find Mrs Foster. The door was open and, standing on the step, Rose could see into the house. The room was basically like the one in Paradine Street, but altogether brighter, cleaner. And since there was no bed in view Rose assumed that Mrs Foster also had the bedroom upstairs, whereas in the case of the Denbys, the Health Visitor had informed her, the upper room was occupied by an old man who scarcely ever left it.

She knocked and called out, 'May I come in?'

Mrs Foster came to the door, Eva behind her.

'Why, it's Doctor Rose from the clinic!' Eva said.

'Step inside, Doctor,' Mrs Foster said. 'Pleased to meet

you, I'm sure. Our Eva's told me about you.'

Rose was surprised and heartened to see that in these surroundings Eva Denby was different; still thin, pale, worried, but with more life and without the dumb despair which darkened her face when she was with her husband.

'I've been to Paradine Street,' Rose said. 'Your husband told me you were here.' At the mention of Jim Denby, Rose saw the hunted look come back into Eva's eyes.

'I came to say, would you be at the railway station next Saturday at two o-clock? I'll have your ticket for you and see you on to the train. Can you manage that?'

'She'll manage it all right. I'll see to that!' Mrs Foster promised. 'It's very good of you, Doctor. Very good indeed of you to take all this trouble.'

I guess *she* knows why I'm not parting with the ticket until the last minute, Rose thought. She knows as well as I do that if Jim Denby gets his hands on it he'll as likely as not sell it back and get the money.

'It's just what our Eva needs,' Mrs Foster went on. 'A couple of weeks away from everything. What she's going to do with three bairns and only the dole, I'm sure I don't know.'

'The dole's run out, Mam,' Eva said. 'We've been on relief for a month now.'

The three women stood silently for a minute. There were no words for their feelings. 'Well, there it is,' Mrs Foster said at last. 'As I said to Eva, I'd have been glad to take little Dorothy while Eva went away, to make things easier. But he wouldn't let me.'

'The fresh air will do Dorothy good,' Rose said.

She turned to Eva.

'All you have to do, Mrs Denby, is get off the train at Grassington and someone will be there to meet you. Either my father or my brother-in-law. Oh! I've brought you a couple of summer dresses and a few other bits. I hope you don't mind.'

Eva took the parcel from Rose and opened it on the table.

'Oh Mam, just look here! Two lovely dresses – and a petticoat and a bodice! And look at this!' She held up a string of pink coral beads which Rose had included in the parcel. She turned to the small square of mirror on the mantelpiece, holding the beads against her neck, then turned again to Rose.

'Oh Doctor, they're beautiful! Aren't they beautiful, Mam?'

Her eyes shone, her face was animated. This is how she used to look, Rose thought. No wonder that awful man wanted her, though how could she have fallen for him? But she remembered his good looks and his powerful masculinity. He had no doubt swept Eva off her feet.

'What size shoes do you take?' Rose asked.

'Fives.'

'A pity. Mine would be too small.'

'I'll see our Eva has a decent pair of shoes to go in,' Mrs Foster said. 'Don't you fret, Doctor. I'll manage it somehow. The Insurance man can wait, for one!'

That evening Alex came into Rose's room waving a copy of the Akersfield *Record*.

'Look at this, Rose!'

She took it from him and read:

MOTHERS' HOLIDAY FUND
ENTERPRISING MOVE BY LOCAL COUNCILLOR

Councillor John Worthing, a well-known local benefactor, today deposited the sum of one hundred pounds with the Penny Bank to launch a fund whose aim will be to send young mothers, especially those whose husbands are unemployed, on holiday.

'We shall not have to look far to find these needy mothers,' Councillor Worthing declared. 'In these days there are far too many of them, in Akersfield and elsewhere.'

The Councillor, ever ready to help a good cause, appealed to the people of Akersfield to support this fund by sending donations, large or small, either to the Penny Bank or to the Akersfield *Record* itself.

'The *Record* has done him proud,' Alex said. 'That'll set the fund off to a good start.'

95

'Councillor Worthing has done Akersfield proud,' Rose said quietly.

She had neither seen nor heard from John Worthing since their lunch together. It was better that way, she told herself. Better just to read about him in the newspaper.

'If I'm to be ready by seven-thirty I must make a start,' she said. Alex was taking her to a tennis club dance.

He looked at her keenly. There was something not quite right.

'You don't sound yourself, Rose. Promise me you're not getting too involved. The Denbys . . . the Fund . . . all those women you worry about in the clinic.'

'Do you expect me to be indifferent?' Rose asked. 'Shall I tell you what that awful Jim Denby said to me? He said "You'd draw the line at sharing it, wouldn't you?" I can't bear the man, but he was right.'

'I should hope so,' Alex said. 'You can't afford to get in too deep. You have realized that since the moment you started to train as a doctor. You have to keep your distance from these things. It's the same with me. I have to report no end of things I dislike, I come across injustices all the time, but I can't let myself get entangled in them or I'd not do my job properly. That applies to you, Rose.'

Rose shook her head. 'I don't see it like that.'

He took her hands in his, drew her towards him.

'I really do want your happiness, Rose. I'd do anything for you. You know that, don't you?'

'Yes. And it means a lot to me.'

'I wish you felt about me as I do about you.'

'I wish I did, dear Alex,' Rose said. And it was true.

Eva Denby, carrying the baby and accompanied by her mother, who had Dorothy by the hand, was at the station early. She was relieved that Jim had decided not to come, but not surprised. He hated his mother-in-law and on this occasion Mrs Foster flatly refused to be left out of the party. She would not feel secure about this holiday until she had seen Eva safely in the train and the train pulling out of the station, without Jim Denby. She prayed to God that he would make no attempt to visit Eva in Faverwell.

The two women sat on a bench in the station forecourt.

It was exciting just to be here, to watch the luckier citizens of Akersfield, those who had somehow managed to hold on to jobs in spite of everything, the straw-hatted men and women with their large suitcases and carpet bags, the children with their buckets and spades, on their way to or from the seaside. Mrs Foster felt that she could have spent the day in the station, happy simply to be part of the scene. Eva was more intent on watching for Doctor Rose and felt a great relief when she saw her walk into the station, accompanied by a tall, fair man. She waved her hand and Doctor Rose spotted her through the crowd and came across.

'This is Mr Bairstow,' she said.

Alex had insisted on accompanying her in case, he said, Jim Denby turned up and started any awkward business.

'A lovely day for the start of your holiday,' Rose said. 'Now here is your ticket. And this is something for the journey; sandwiches, and some fruit and chocolate.'

Eva took the paper bag from Doctor Rose. She would have liked to have started on it there and then but for the sake of politeness she put it in the top of the carpet bag which contained her clothes and the children's for the holiday. Although her mother had given her some dinner before they left Babcock Street, she was still hungry. She was always hungry, as though she had some ravenous beast inside her, waiting to be fed. But it was not a wild beast, it was a baby, which, try as she might, she did not want. She was ashamed of the fact that she could offer it no welcome.

She was also ashamed of the carpet bag, which had a hole in one corner. How wonderful it would have been to have carried a suitcase, even a cardboard one; but no-one she knew had such a thing because very few of her acquaintances had ever been on holiday for more than a day.

'Thank you, Doctor Rose,' she said.

'I think the train will be in,' Rose said. 'Platform three. Why don't we get you settled?'

They all four, plus the children, trooped on to the platform. It was all excitement, all marvellous, even the snorting engine which let off steam just as they passed, frightening little Dorothy half to death so that her cries and the engine's noise echoed together against the station's high glass roof. Eva breathed in the steamy smell and vowed that she would never forget it. When, some minutes later, she waved good-bye to everyone, felt the bump as the train moved, watched the party on the platform getting smaller and smaller as they receded into the distance, it was with the most tremendous sense of adventure, all her troubles for the moment forgotten.

Mr Bairstow seemed a nice fellow. He had pushed a brand new copy of *Peg's Paper* into her hand before the train left. Was he Doctor Rose's Young Man? She doubted if anyone in the world was good enough for Doctor Rose.

When the figures on the platform were no longer visible and the train was steaming its way through the suburbs of Akersfield, she took out the paper bag and began to eat, spreading her handkershief over her lap so that no crumbs should soil the pretty, pink-flowered dress which Doctor Rose had given her. From time to time her hand strayed towards the coral necklace around her throat.

Chapter Seven

Heaven must be something like Faverwell, Eva thought. Her mother reckoned heaven was a big garden with lots of lawns and with the Black Dyke Mills Band somewhere in the background, playing 'The Lost Chord' and selections from 'The Gondoliers': three nice meals a day waiting for you when you went in from the garden, and an occasional glass of Guinness in the evenings.

Eva, pushing the pram slowly along the road which ran by the river, could now disagree. The baby, propped against Mrs Stanton's snowy-white pillow; Dorothy, who was forward at walking but did not yet talk, tottering beside the pram; Bess, the Stantons' ancient sheepdog who had taken upon herself the guardianship of this new family, walking at the same easy pace: the high green hills, and the river itself, rushing over the stones here, but dark and still down by the bridge – what better combination could heaven offer? And there was no mill smoke to blacken everything it touched, no coal carts, no rubbish spilling in the road.

The only thing was that once you got to heaven you presumably stayed there, but in her case she would have to go back to Paradine Street. And to Jim. Not only that, but the child she was carrying would inevitably make its appearance, bringing more trouble with it. She had almost stopped being sick in the mornings now and after ten days in Faverwell felt better in her body, but nothing stilled, completely, the fear and apprehension in her mind.

'We'd best turn back now,' she said to Dorothy. 'We mustn't be late for dinner. Would you like a ride on the pram then?'

Although Dorothy seldom spoke, she understood every word that was said to her. Now she stood in the road, holding out her arms to be lifted up.

'I wonder what's for dinner?' Eva said.

Every day it was something delicious. Ham and new potatoes; a meat-and-potato pie running with gravy; a forerib of beef with Yorkshire pudding, and potatoes roasted around the joint. And to follow, treacle tarts, gooseberry pies, apple charlottes, jam rolls. And then later in the day the teas! Ox tongue, tinned salmon, potted meat, currant pasty, stewed fruit, sponge cakes: the kind of food you got only at funeral teas in Akersfield. Eva's mouth watered in anticipation and remembrance. She swung Dorothy into the pram and stepped up her pace along the road back to the Ewe Lamb.

'Just in nice time!' Mrs Stanton said, opening the door to them. 'It's shepherd's pie.'

'I wondered if you'd like to give me a hand with the church brasses this afternoon,' she said when they were sitting down to heaped plates. 'The little lass can have her nap and Mr Stanton'll keep an ear open. We'll take the babby along wi' us.'

'I'd be more than willing,' Eva said.

She had done whatever she could to help Mrs Stanton but she had not been allowed to do any heavy work; nothing more strenuous than dusting, mending, polishing the glasses in the bar – that sort of thing.

Eva had seldom been inside a church except for one or two christenings and, even rarer, weddings. It was cool and dim, quiet and still, smelling of summer flowers. Through the clear glass windows she could see the green fells and the blue sky behind.

'Now,' Mrs Stanton said briskly, 'Candlesticks or lectern, which is it to be for you?'

The lectern, it appeared, was the big, brass eagle on which the bible stood.

'I'll tackle the lectern,' Eva said.

Her mother would have enjoyed this, she thought, setting to work. Mrs Foster's favourite household task was blacking the grate and the fireirons and polishing the brass rail and knobs on the fender. But Babcock Street seemed a long way away. Eva rubbed hard at the massive bird, giving extra strength to the breast feathers, and the sun streamed in through the window, changing the brass to pure gold.

'You're making a real good job of that,' Mrs Stanton

said. 'It was about the only job I could get our Rose to do when she was a little girl.'

It was pleasant to think of Doctor Rose doing this. None of the other mothers in the clinic would know that much about her. It made her seem, just for the minute, almost a friend.

When she had finished the lectern, the eagle shining gloriously, reflecting her own face - and Mrs Stanton was still at work in the vestry on what she called the plate - Eva sat at the back of the church, Baby Meg asleep in a basket in the pew beside her. She desired so much to pray, but the words would not come. And she knew that the reason they would not come was that what she wanted to pray for was not right. Dear God, she wanted to say, please take away the baby in my body. But she was afraid to say it. Supposing her request angered him and he punished her by striking at Baby Meg or Dorothy? Vengeance is mine, saith the Lord. I will repay. She could not put the children at risk.

If only there was something she *could* do! But she had no idea what. If she had mixed more with the women in Paradine Street, shown herself readier to join in the gossip, they would have advised her what to do in such circumstances. Eat a pound of parsley, some said; but that must be a pillowcase full - and where would she get hold of it anyway? And if it didn't work, then what about the baby? That much parsley could turn the blood green!

'There! All done and dusted,' Mrs Stanton said, emerging from the vestry, taking off her pinafore. 'I was just thinking that you'd said you'd like to walk up Faver Fell. If you want to do that tomorrow I'll look after the bairns. Mind you, you mustn't expect to climb to the top, not in your condition. It's quite a hill. But lovely views, even from halfway up.'

It was something Eva had wanted to do from the day she had arrived in Faverwell and seen the green hillside rising up behind the village. 'Thank you. I'd like that,' she said.

The following day she set off after breakfast, Mrs Stanton pressing a packet of sandwiches into her hand.

'For biting on,' she said. 'It's hungry work, walking. Keep to the path. I'll expect you back for dinnertime and if

101

you're a bit late I'll keep your dinner in the oven.'

The track was clearly defined. Around Eva as she walked the black-faced sheep cropped the grass to a green sward. Some of these sheep would be Mr Bishop's. He and his wife, Doctor Rose's sister, had been very kind to her. Everyone in Faverwell was kind.

At first the slopes were gentle, short grass underfoot, but then they became steeper, with rocky outcrops and areas of scree over which she had to scramble as best she could. In her mind she had determined to reach the top, but it was hard going. Up and up she climbed, keeping her eyes firmly on the summit, not allowing herself to look back. But in the end, though she was no more than a few hundred yards from the summit, her heart pounding and no breath left in her, she knew she had to stop. She would sit awhile, eat her sandwiches, and then try again.

The view from this height was stupendous. The river wound its way up the dale, here and there disappearing under a bank of trees. The cattle in the fields looked like toy farmyard animals and the village itself like a child's plaything. A rare motor car moved like a small, black beetle along the twisting road. In all her life she had never seen a view like this. Also the sandwiches, homecured ham spread with Colman's mustard, were first class.

She had just eaten the last crumb, licked her fingers, when the pain started; too soon and too fierce to be indigestion. She knew at once that she would never reach the top of the fell and, seeing the long hillside which stretched down before her, her disappointment was mingled with worry as to how she would get to the bottom. Then the pain went away as suddenly as it had come and she set off at once down the slope.

But within minutes it was back again. Sweat broke out in great beads on her forehead and ran down her face. The pain came and went, though never leaving her for long. Sometimes it tore at her so badly that she had to lie down on the grass, biting her knuckles so as not to scream. Whenever it eased she went forward a few yards. Nothing more than blind instinct and an overwhelming desire to reach some haven, got her back eventually to the Ewe Lamb. As she went in the door she felt the blood trickle down her thighs.

'George, get Doctor Harper at once!' she heard Mrs Stanton say. And then she was in Doctor Rose's bed, with the deep blackness of the pain and the sound of the rushing beck coming together to drown her. Mrs Stanton's voice, a long way away and perhaps some time after, for it was dusk in the room, said, 'I'm afraid she's lost the baby.'

Rose was getting ready to leave the clinic after what had been a busy day when the telephone message came through.

'I'm speaking from the post office,' her mother said, shouting because she was not used to the telephone and could not believe that anything other than the full use of her lungs could carry her voice as far as Akersfield. 'Can you hear me?'

'Perfectly! Is everything all right?'

'No it isn't,' Mrs Stanton said. 'Well, I suppose it is now, in a sort of way . . .'

'What do you mean, Mother?'

'It's Eva. She's had a miscarriage. She won't be able to travel back to Akersfield on Saturday. You'll have to tell her husband.'

Shall I ask Alex to go with me? Rose wondered when the brief conversation was over. She did not fancy another encounter with Jim Denby. But it was her responsibility; why should she involve Alex? She would go to Paradine Street right away and get it over with.

In one way she could not feel too unhappy about the miscarriage. Nature had, not for the first time in Rose's experience, found her own solution. But she abominated the worry which had gone before, the unfruitful pain, the waste of a life, though hardly formed. Women who had suffered miscarriages had told her that they were affected in mind and spirit as much as in their bodies, and for a long time after the event. Some even said that the pain was worse than that of giving birth. Eva would recover, but she was not in a condition to do so easily. She needed to take things quietly for a while, to be built up again. That much she must, at all costs, get across to Jim Denby. But at least she didn't expect him to be unduly upset at the loss of the baby.

She was wrong about that. Facing him across the table, which was littered with the dirty pots and pans and detritus of what looked like every meal since Eva had left, she saw the quick anger flare in his face as she broke the news.

'This is your doing!' he shouted. 'I hold you responsible for this! I never wanted my wife to go away. I knew she wasn't fit.'

'I'm sorry,' Rose said. 'I truly am. I'm sorry Eva has had to go through this. But going to Faverwell wasn't the cause. On the contrary, it might well have prevented it. But she was clearly not strong enough to carry the baby. Nature has its own way of dealing with some situations, you know.'

'That's a load of rubbish! She carried the other two, didn't she? She had no trouble at all until *you* started interfering. If she'd stayed at home, if she'd never gone near your bloody clinic, this would never have happened. I don't . . .'

'Mr Denby,' Rose interrupted. 'It could have, I assure you. It was always on the cards.'

He was not listening to her. He had stopped shouting and was looking at her intently, a sharp, calculating expression on his face. There was a moment of charged silence as they looked at each other. Rose felt a *frisson* of apprehension. When he spoke his voice was quiet and incisive.

'As I remember it, Doctor, you did all this off your own bat? Nothing to do with the clinic, didn't you say?'

'That's right.'

'Aye, I thought so. So I should think your employers'll be none too pleased. You might get into a deal o' trouble - sending a patient away, causing her to lose her baby!'

'I've told you, it is not at all like that . . .'

'It's exactly like that, Doctor. And it doesn't sound too good, does it? After all, you didn't know my wife, except through the clinic. You'd never have met her otherwise. Now our Eva said there was another doctor up there, a man who was the boss . . .'

'Doctor Stanton is head of the clinic.'

'That's it. Doctor Stanton. But of course he doesn't have to know ... well, not *your* part in it anyway.' Jim Denby's voice was silky smooth. 'She could have had the miscarriage right here in this place.'

'Which is exactly what I've been saying!' But thank heaven for Eva's sake that she hadn't. It was a hell-hole.

'But she didn't, did she, Doctor? She had it right in your mother's house. Well now, I can see I'm going to be put to a lot of expense over this. There's the question of money to go and visit my wife. I can't leave her alone in her hour of trouble, can I? And I can't go empty handed. Flowers, chocolates ... And then when I bring her home there'll be extra foods, little comforts ... Yes, a lot of expense. It could easily come to fifty pounds. Oh yes, quite easily. But worth it, wouldn't you say?'

Disbelief and fierce anger struggled in Rose. She could have leaned across the table and struck him, wiped the leer from his slack mouth, the cunning from his eyes. But she forced herself to speak calmly.

'That's blackmail, Mr Denby. I could go to the police, you realize that?'

'But you won't, will you, Doctor?' he said softly. 'It wouldn't be very nice for my Eva, wouldn't do her any good at all if you was to go to the police. We have to think of her, don't we?'

He was clever all right. But Rose had no intention of letting the slimy creature get the better of her.

'For the sake of your wife I shall not go to the police,' she said. 'Not this time. But if blackmail is your game you've picked the wrong person. I don't respond to threats, Mr Denby. I shall give you enough money to visit your wife in Faverwell, and to take something to cheer her up. That is all, and not a penny more.'

She opened her purse, took out a pound note and a ten shilling note and laid them on the table.

He stared at her defiantly.

'Thirty bob for the life of a bairn! So you reckon that's all it's worth?'

'I reckon it's all you're getting,' Rose retorted. 'Your wife lost the baby because she wasn't fit to carry it, because she should never have been made pregnant. I hope you see to it that she's not made pregnant again, not until she's fit and ready.'

His fair skin flushed scarlet, his blue eyes bulged and blazed with anger. He raised his hand as if he would strike her and she was glad of the width of the table between them. But it would never do to let this man see that she was afraid.

'You interfering bitch!' he shouted. 'You foul-mouthed virgin! What do you know about anything?'

'Enough to see the results!' Rose cried. 'It's men like you . . .'

'Men like me,' he broke in scornfully. 'You know nowt about men like me - nor any others for that matter. I knew that when I first clapped eyes on you. I know when a woman's never had a man. You live through other people. You know nowt yersen. I could give you a lesson you wouldn't forget in a hurry!'

'If you dare to lay one finger on me I *shall* go to the police!' Rose threatened. She was sick with fear. She felt powerless against him. But something . . . perhaps it was her refusal to show fear, she would never know - changed his attitude.

'Get out then,' he said savagely. 'Get out! And don't think you've heard the last of this. You haven't, not by a long chalk!'

She left quickly, head held high, looking neither to left nor to right as she passed the inevitable group of women. She knew she ought to go and break the news to Eva's mother but as yet she didn't feel able to. She was trembling from head to toe, as much from anger as from fear. Foul-mouthed virgin he had called her. Her anger lasted all the way to Victoria Street, where she met Alex, also on his way in.

'What's wrong?' he asked.

A few minutes later he brought a tot of whisky up to her room.

'Get this down you,' he ordered. 'You look all in. Why didn't you let me go with you? I'd have dealt with him!'

'I *did* deal with him,' Rose pointed out. 'And really, I

don't need whisky.' But she sipped it gratefully all the same. Inside herself she knew that it was not Jim Denby's threats - frightening though they had been at the time - which had upset her most. It was the other things he had said. He had said out loud things she preferred to bury in her own heart.

Though Denby meant it as an insult, to be called a virgin was, to Rose, the least of his taunts. In his eyes it denoted a woman who was of no worth at all; sexless, too sterile ever to flower. That was not true of her. It *was not true*! The feelings John Worthing had so quickly aroused in her were the proof of that. She knew herself to be as able to love, as capable of sexual passion, as any other woman. But even had the man she loved been free, her job at the Welfare Centre precluded marriage. In accepting it she had knowingly relinquished her chance of wifehood, motherhood. She complied with the rules, unwillingly, since there was little she could do about them. Yet Doctor John Stanton was doubtless considered a better doctor because he had a wife and five children.

But it was the other things John Denby had said which had given her a jolt. 'You live through other people. You know nothing for yourself.' Could that be true? Would it always be so?

That was the way it was for a vast number of women. The war had robbed them in their thousands of husbands, lovers, the possibility of bearing children. Since there were not enough men to go around they would go through life dry virgins, denied the experience which most people thought made a true woman. They would seek fulfilment in work, suppress their sexual emotions, expend their maternal feelings on other people's children. Could she be content with that? In spite of herself, the blatant masculinity of that lout of a man had challenged her afresh.

'Anyway,' Alex said. 'Put him out of your mind. I've got pleasanter news.'

It was more easily said than done. Jim Denby had made her face more than she wished to.

'Do you want to hear it?' Alex asked.

'Of course! I'm sorry.'

'John Worthing's giving a garden party. He does it every year for some charity or other. And I've been sent two tickets. But that's not all. Guess what the profits are going to?'

'Not the Mothers' Holiday Fund?'

'Right first time!'

She wondered, for a moment, why John Worthing had not sent an invitation to her. Perhaps he had assumed, correctly as it happened, that she would not attend alone, but that the sending of two tickets to Alex Bairstow would bring her.

'Where's it to be?'

'At his own home. He lives on the outskirts of Akersfield. A house called Moorgate – well you know that, you telephoned him there. It's a big place. Standing – as the advertisements say – in its own grounds. You'll like it.'

'I'm not sure I want to go,' Rose said.

She wanted to with all her heart. She wanted to see him again; she wanted to see him in his own setting. But could she bear it, this glimpse of intimacy?

'You must go,' Alex said. 'No question about it. If only because it's for your project. Besides, anyone who is anyone will be there. It's your chance to meet Akersfield society. Also, if it means anything to you, it would give me the greatest pleasure in the world to take you there.'

'Thank you, Alex. I appreciate that. And I'll think about it,' she promised.

'In the meantime,' he said. 'If we don't go down to supper it'll be all over. I'm not allowing you to miss a meal just because you feel a bit down.'

The ante-natal clinic was in full swing, the waiting benches on the landing crowded. It seemed to Rose that half the women in Akersfield were pregnant. She was busy examining a patient when she heard the unmistakeable voice of Jim Denby, loud and strong, in full spate.

'Right, Mrs Fletcher,' Rose said. 'You can get dressed now. Please excuse me. I'll be back in a minute.'

He was standing on the landing, shouting, a flustered Miss Pearlman trying unsuccessfully to quieten him.

'I demand to see the Chief Doctor,' he yelled. 'I know

my rights. I demand to see him at once!'

As Rose came out of her room he swung around and pointed an accusing finger at her.

'She's the one!' he shouted. 'Doctor Lah-di-dah Rose! She's the one who lost my wife her baby!'

He turned towards the waiting mothers, who had at once ceased their conversations, not wishing to miss such a promising diversion.

'Don't let her near you, any of you! Don't you take the risk! Otherwise that little lot you're carrying . . .' His eyes swept their burgeoning figures '. . . might never live to know you.'

He was unsteady on his feet, lurching a little as he spoke, and his words were too carefully enunciated. Also, Rose doubted not at all, this was how he had used the money she had given him to visit Eva in Faverwell. What a fool she had been to put the cash in his hand.

'You're drunk, Jim Denby!' one of the mothers called out. 'I know you.'

'I've had a drink,' he said carefully. 'Which I don't deny. I had it to console myself. This woman . . . this woman who calls herself a doctor . . . has robbed me of my bairn. She's an interfering bitch! Don't you let her come near you!'

Two dozen pairs of eyes swung around to Rose. They half believe him, she thought. They're wondering what I've done. They're wondering if I've given her some terrible treatment which I'm about to force on them ! She could see the apprehension beginning in their eyes.

'Mr Denby, you must calm yourself,' she said firmly. 'You can't come in here upsetting everyone like this. You know you're talking nonsense.'

'Nonsense is it? Well I'll see your boss and we'll see if *he* thinks it's nonsense.'

'Shall I tell Doctor Stanton?' Miss Pearlman asked. 'What shall I do?'

At that moment Nurse Butterworth came out of Doctor Stanton's room. She positioned herself squarely in front of Jim Denby, arms akimbo. He swayed a little towards her.

'Now my man, what's all this about?' she demanded.

'You can't come in here making this sort of noise!'

'Oh yes I can,' he said belligerently. 'And I don't want any truck with you. I want to see the doctor. The real doctor, not this one.' He pointed at Rose. 'She's the one who lost my wife her baby. She's the one . . .'

Nurse Butterworth cut him off. 'We've heard all that rubbish. Anyone can hear you a mile off. You can go in to Doctor Stanton now and he'll give you ten minutes. Not a second longer. And I wouldn't stand too close to him if I were you. He doesn't care for the smell of drink.'

All eyes followed him as he went with Nurse Butterworth – and then turned to look with curiosity at Rose.

'I'm sorry about that, ladies,' she said. 'Don't let it worry you. The explanation is quite simple. I'll be ready for my next patient in five minutes.'

Back in her room she sat behind her desk, her head in her hands, taking deep breaths to try to calm herself. It was all nonsense, of course. No-one was going to take much notice of a drunken oaf. She pulled herself together, stepped out on to the landing and called for the next patient . . .

'Mrs Porter!'

There was an uncomfortable silence and then a woman said, 'She's left, Doctor. She went home.'

Rose discovered, going through the list, that six of the women had left. It was unbelievable! Was her reputation as a doctor so slight that a drunk in a rage could undermine it like this?

Her next patient in was the woman who had recognized Jim Denby.

'I know him for what he is, Doctor,' she said. 'A bastard if ever there was one – if you'll pardon the language. All wind and water, but a nasty piece of work. I've tried telling that lot out there but some of 'em only take notice of whoever shouts loudest. And of course they're worried about their babies,' she added frankly.

Miss Pearlman knocked and popped her head around the door. 'Doctor Stanton would like to see you as soon as you've finished with this patient.'

110

It might have been her imagination, but it seemed to Rose, as she crossed the landing to Doctor Stanton's room, that the benches were even emptier. When she went in Jim Denby was seated opposite to her boss.

'This is her,' he began. There was triumph in his face and in his voice.

'Thank you Mr Denby,' Doctor Stanton said. 'I have noted all you've said.' He turned to Rose.

'Mr Denby has made certain accusations, Doctor. To get matters into perspective I would be grateful if you would answer one or two questions in his presence.'

'Certainly Doctor.' But why did he not see her alone? Why was she not allowed to present her side, as Denby had his? Also, she badly wanted to sit down. Her knees were trembling. Jim Denby occupied the only visitor's chair and she was obliged to stand.

'Quite simply,' Doctor Stanton said, 'is it true, as Mr Denby states, that you arranged for his wife to go away to your parents' home, that you paid for her to do so?'

'Yes but . . .'

'We won't go into the reasons just now. And is it true that while there, Mrs Denby has suffered a miscarriage?'

'Quite true. But in my opinion . . .'

Doctor Stanton held up a hand, silencing her.

'We will discuss all that later, Doctor. I wanted to verify, or otherwise, Mr Denby's statements. I won't keep you any longer, Doctor. I'll see you later this afternoon. Just now we have a busy clinic.'

Less busy than you believe, Rose thought. Why would the man not allow her to put her side? But perhaps he had a point. There could be no reasoning in Jim Denby's presence.

Denby followed her out, a yard or two behind her as she crossed the landing. 'You'll not get away with it!' he shouted. 'I'll make you pay for this, Madam! I'll see the papers get hold of this!'

Yet it is not the loss of the baby he is making me pay for, Rose thought. She was to pay in another way because she had refused to succumb to his blackmail; and because, somehow, she had interfered with his masculinity, had dared to suggest that he went easy on his wife.

At the end of the clinic she presented herself to Doctor Stanton again. He faced her with a stern, cold expression.

'It is true, is it not, that you knew Mrs Denby only as a patient in the clinic? You were not acquainted with her otherwise?'

'Quite true,' Rose agreed. 'What I did was a private thing.'

'I must differ with you about that,' he said. 'However, allow me to continue. I wish first of all to know why I was not informed of Mrs Denby's miscarriage. I understand you yourself were acquainted with the fact twenty-four hours ago.'

'You were not here,' Rose pointed out. 'You left to attend a meeting before my mother telephoned with the news. And you were not on duty this morning. Of course I would have told you at the first opportunity. How could I do otherwise?'

'But in your own good time, I imagine. While I, together with everyone in the clinic, I am sure, have to hear it from her husband. The fact that he is an odious creature does not alter the fact that he would seem to have right on his side.'

'It is not as clear cut as that, Doctor . . .'

'On the contrary . . .' He was getting into his stride now, really enjoying himself, Rose thought. He's been waiting all these months for an opportunity like this. He's not going to let me down lightly.

'. . . On the contrary, it seems particularly clear cut to me. In the first place, had I been consulted, which I was not, I would have cautioned against Mrs Denby going away from home at a time like this. I would have said she was not in a fit state to travel. In fact - reluctant though I am to agree with Mr Denby - I have to say that I believe that if Mrs Denby had stayed at home in Akersfield she would not have lost her child. You can see for yourself the gravity of this position.'

'But it's not true!' Rose cried. 'It's a hundred to one that Mrs Denby miscarried because she was too weak to bear another child so soon after the last one. She conceived when her baby was only three weeks old and her elder child eighteen months. Perhaps it's just as well she did miscarry.'

'How dare you say such a thing?' Doctor Stanton demanded. 'It is not for us . . .'

'I dare more,' Rose interrupted. 'I dare to say that as doctors we evade our responsibility by not advising women in Mrs Denby's position how to avoid having too many children. I say we have a duty to do just that.'

'Then you are in the wrong profession. Birth control is not, and never has been, part of any doctor's training. It does not lie within our orbit.' His voice was cold, measured. The flat calm of his statements goaded Rose more than a display of feeling could ever have done.

'That's false reasoning!' she cried passionately. 'It's not long ago that most doctors thought anaesthetics were wrong, that patients were meant to bear pain. That didn't mean doctors were right – and most of them now think differently. It will be the same with contraception.'

'Not in my clinic,' Doctor Stanton said. 'And may I remind you, Doctor, that you are working in *my* clinic. You are not independent, though I daresay you would like to be. You are responsible to me for any actions which affect our patients. So far I have to say that, although I do not question your medical skill, you have been a disruptive influence. One could hardly describe today's incident as other than disruptive!'

It was no use. She would never get through to him. She wished, for a moment, that he *had* been allowed a say in the choosing of his assistant. None of this would have happened, and half-a-dozen pregnant women who needed medical care would not have walked out and abandoned it. He had yet to learn about that.

'What do you propose to do?' she asked quietly.

His answer surprised her.

'Nothing. Unless the husband takes this further I shall do nothing. If more unpleasantness occurs, why then, I shall have no option but to place the matter before the Committee. By the way, I gave the man a pound to go to see his wife. I consider we owe him that much. And it might be that that will serve to quieten him. You may re-imburse me or not, as you wish.'

She could not help it. In spite of the deep disturbance within her, Rose smiled a wide smile.

'Of course I will re-imburse you, Doctor. But don't think the money will take Jim Denby to see his wife. His concern doesn't stretch that far. It will go straight into the till of the nearest pub, where the thirty shillings I gave him obviously went!'

Chapter Eight

Three days later, when Rose returned in the late afternoon from the clinic, Mrs Crabtree stood in the hall, waving a copy of the Akersfield *Record*.

'There's a bit in here about your clinic!' she said, her voice high with excitement. 'Have you seen it? "Akersfield Mother Loses Baby" . . .'

'Could I borrow that for a moment?' Rose said abruptly. Without waiting for a reply she snatched the paper from her landlady's hand and ran up the stairs.

Mrs Crabtree was disappointed. She had hoped to relate the story and have a nice discussion about it with her favourite boarder. Not that Doctor Rose's name was mentioned, but Mrs Crabtree distinctly remembered that a Mr and Mrs Denby had called a few weeks back. She hadn't liked the look of them at the time and she flattered herself that she was seldom wrong about people.

In her own room, not stopping to take off her hat and gloves, Rose began to read; and as she did so the sick feeling which Mrs Crabtree's words had given her increased. It seemed incredible that this could be happening. The report had a prominent position in the 'Letters to the Editor' section – a part of the paper which, Alex had told her, people sometimes read more avidly than the news because it was a better source of local gossip.

Dear Sir, (she read)

In view of the recently launched Holiday Fund for Mothers, readers of the *Record* will be concerned to hear that a young mother, recently despatched on just such a holiday (though not by the fund), suffered a miscarriage and lost the child she was expecting.

'She is too ill to return home,' her distraught and grieving husband told me. 'I am convinced that this would never have happened if my wife had not been sent away. She was clearly not fit to travel.'

If this is to be the result of sending mothers on

holiday we should think twice about the Mothers'
Holiday Fund. Leave well alone, I say.

Mrs Denby, at the time she was sent away, was
attending Akersfield's Infant Welfare Clinic.

Yours faithfully,
P. Blamires, Esq.

It was unbelievable! Rose had dismissed Jim Denby's
threat that he would go to the newspaper as an idle one,
or in the remote chance that he did so, that the *Record*
wouldn't entertain him. So who was this P. Blamires who
had taken up the cudgels on his behalf?

She was so unutterably tired of it. Since their stormy
interview Doctor Stanton had scarcely spoken to her and
he had made a point of seeing as many patients as possible
himself, handing next to no-one over to her. Of the six
women who had walked out, only one had returned, and
two more had left since. There was clearly no doubt in
Doctor Stanton's mind as to where the blame lay, and it
seemed that Nurse Butterworth shared his view. She was
professionally polite, but no longer friendly. Only Mabel
Pearlman seemed to be on Rose's side. In the last few days
Rose had been grateful for the encouraging smiles she had
received from Mabel and had forced herself to drink all the
extra cups of tea which the girl, it being her way of giving
comfort, had sneaked in to her.

She took off her hat and gloves and threw them on the
table. She picked up the paper again and was re-reading
the letter when she heard Alex's knock. When he came in
she realized by the look on his face that he knew all about it.

'Why didn't you warn me?' she demanded. 'You could
at least have warned me. Or you could have stopped it.'

'I didn't know,' Alex said. 'The Old Man keeps "Letters
to the Editor" close to his chest. But in any case it's not
something I could have stopped.'

'Not stopped? Why ever not? It's ridiculous. It's not
even true!'

'But the facts stated in the letter *are* true,' Alex said
gently. 'Mrs Denby *did* lose the baby. She *had* been
attending the clinic. The opinions are those of the
writer . . .'

116

'And Jim Denby – though he knows they're false.'

'And of Denby. But people are allowed to express opinions. That's the whole basis of the column. That's why people read it.'

'So who is P. Blamires, Esquire?' Rose asked. 'Aside, that is, from being a mouthpiece for Denby?'

'He's the mouthpiece for a good many people in Akersfield,' Alex told her. 'He's a respectable citizen who is more than willing to write letters to the paper for those he reckons can't do it for themselves – especially if the letter are going to stir things up. But what he writes is usually interesting to the reader so more often than not it gets published.'

'And never mind the harm done!'

'There won't be much harm done, Rose,' Alex assured her. 'It'll all blow over quickly. In a day or two there'll be a letter about something different and all this will be forgotten.'

'But already some of the women have decided not to come to the clinic,' Rose pointed out. 'This will make it worse. And they're women who need to come. They'll miss more than the medical care. They'll miss the free milk and dinners they desperately need.'

'It doesn't say the clinic sent her.'

'The inference is clear enough. Though of course no-one sent her. She went of her own free will, and glad to go.'

Alex took both her hands in his. 'I can see you've had a bad day. I'm sorry, Rose. Let's go out somewhere after supper. We could make the second house at the Empress. Cheer you up.'

Rose pulled her hands away from his, though in her heart she wanted nothing as much as to lay her head on his broad shoulder and have a good cry. She was sick of it all.

'Every day's a bad day now. I'm doing no good to anyone. I doubt if I've done any good to Eva. Perhaps you were right when you warned me that she'd have to go back to Paradine Street. By the way,' she said, 'I've decided to go to Faverwell to see her on Saturday. I doubt if her husband will be going.'

A thought struck her. 'I wonder,' she mused, 'if P.

Blamires also gave him some money to visit?'

'Let me take you there,' Alex said quickly. 'I can borrow a car and we'll drive up.'

'If you like.'

'And the second house at the Empress tonight? Florrie Forde?'

'I'm sorry,' Rose said, 'I'm not in the mood.'

It would be hellish in the clinic tomorrow. She couldn't hope that Doctor Stanton wouldn't have seen the letter. She wondered if John Worthing had seen it, and what his reaction would be.

She was at the clinic early next day but Doctor Stanton was there before her. So was Mabel Pearlman, her face troubled as she greeted Rose.

'He says will you go into his room right away, Doctor Rose.'

'I will.'

'I saw the letter in the paper,' Mabel said. 'If you want to know, I think it's rubbish.'

'Thank you, Mabel,' Rose said.

She went into her room, took off her hat, put on her white coat and went to face Doctor Stanton.

'I need hardly tell you why I want to see you,' he said tersely. He did not look at her as he spoke, but fixed his pale eyes on a point somewhere behind her left shoulder. 'I have had both the Chairman and Councillor Rogers on the telephone. They are considerably disturbed and distressed, as am I. There is no doubt that your ill-considered action, private though you might have meant it to be, will harm the welfare service which the Health Committee and myself have built up with such care and patience and which was at last beginning to bear fruit.'

'But that's not fair!' Rose cried indignantly. 'I don't like it any more than you do when a woman loses her baby, but you know it's not uncommon, especially among our kind of patients. It's incredible to me that so much is being made of it.'

'It may seem incredible to you, but it is happening, and in the glare of the press. With the agreement of the Chairman I have composed a letter, which Miss Pearlman will take at once to the offices of the *Record*, stating categorically that the clinic had no part in sending Mrs Denby away. For the sake of the clinic the letter does not mention you in any way, and for the same reason it has been decided that nothing else shall be done in the matter. You are fortunate this time that you will not be asked to appear before the Committee, but you are specifically requested not to grant an interview to any reporter who might approach you from the *Record*. That will be all, Doctor. We have a busy morning ahead.'

He bent his head over the papers on his desk. She was dismissed.

She had a patient with her, was examining a baby whose legs were thin and rickety, whose buttocks and groin were covered in an angry rash, when the telephone rang.

'I'm going to give you some cream,' she told the mother. 'Apply it every single time you change the baby, and change him often. Don't leave him in a wet nappy. This rash is very irritating to the child.'

The telephone rang again and she picked it up, speaking sharply into it. She disliked being interrupted when she was busy with patients.

'Yes?'

'John Worthing. Are you busy?'

She caught her breath at the sound of his voice, felt the heat in her face, the trembling of her hands; hoped the woman with the baby, who was listening with undisguised interest, would not notice.

'I have a patient with me.' She tried to keep her voice steady.

'I won't keep you.' His voice was sharp, businesslike. 'I've heard all about your bit of trouble. I just wanted to say "Don't worry". It will pass.'

'Thank you.'

'Are you coming to my garden party?'

She had not, until now, made up her mind; but hearing him she knew she could not keep away.

'Yes,' she said.

'Good!' He rang off. She turned back to the baby's mother. 'I think we might try some cod liver oil,' she said with an effort. 'It will help your baby's limbs grow straight and strong.'

Saturday morning was free, since once every six weeks she did not have to assist in the clinic on that day. Immediately after breakfast they set off in the car Alex had borrowed – a small, navy-blue Morris two-seater with an open top and dicky seat.

'I'm thinking of buying it,' Alex said. 'I can get it for twenty pounds. What do you say?'

'If that's what you want.'

To buy, or not to buy, a secondhand car was of no moment. She was too dispirited to care. Doctor Stanton's letter had been published in the *Record* and there had been no repercussions so far, but the atmosphere between herself and Doctor Stanton was icy. He had stepped up his policy of keeping as many patients as possible to himself, so that all week she had been left with not enough work to do and with too much time to think. It was the subtlest and most efficient way of punishing her and she was sure he knew that.

'I'm hoping a trip to Faverwell will cheer you up,' Alex said, driving out of the town. 'You've been a bag of misery this week.'

'I'm sorry,' Rose apologized. 'And I daresay Faverwell will do the trick. Anyway, I'll try to be more cheerful.'

'You don't have to be for me,' Alex said. 'You don't have to put on a show.'

It was true. He was understanding and accepting, and she was grateful for it. She wondered if, sometimes, she did not take advantage of his good nature.

It was another warm, sunny day. She was glad to have the car hood down, to feel the breeze as they drove through the dale. The limestone walls glistened in the sun. The long, hot summer had all but dried the river in parts, exposing its pebbly bed. The river meadows were golden with what would be a good second crop of hay. A second crop, not possible every summer, made all the difference to winter feeding the stock. Between Grassington and Faverwell Alex slowed down, driving leisurely on the traffic-free road. Rose breathed in the country air and felt better for the sights and smells of the dale.

The Ewe Lamb looked busy. Since the war cycling had flourished and at this moment there were a dozen or more bicycles propped against the walls of the inn while their owners drank beer in the bar parlour and ate the packed lunches which they had brought with them.

'You're a sight for sore eyes, and no mistake!' George Stanton said, breaking off serving to greet his daughter and to shake hands with Alex. 'Your mother's been looking forward to seeing you. Go through to the back. I'll bring you a pint in a minute or two, Mr Bairstow.'

Mrs Stanton's greeting was less effusive but Rose, knowing her mother's ways, could tell that she was glad to see them and that she took to Alex.

'Eva's gone into Grassington with our Emily and Christopher and the children,' she said. 'They thought it might make a change for her. She should be back any time now.'

'How is Eva?' Rose asked.

'Much better. Almost well enough for home. But I'm feared you'll find she doesn't want to go.'

'You'd understand that, Ma, if you saw where she lived.'

Mrs Stanton frowned. 'I do understand, Rose, but there's nothing for her here. You know that. Besides, she's a married woman.'

'Has her unspeakable husband showed up?' Rose enquired.

'No. Nor written. But I think she's written to him.'

'So much for his concern,' Rose said.

Ten minutes later the party from Grassington returned. Eva's face lit with pleasure at the sight of Rose.

'You're looking well,' Rose told her. In spite of her recent miscarriage, Eva looked a little plumper, rounder in the face, and her skin had a degree of the clear healthiness which characterized Rose's own complexion. But she had a worried look.

'While you, on the other hand,' Emily put in, 'don't look all that blooming. It seems to me the city air doesn't agree with you.'

Rose shrugged. It was not the city air which got her down but she had no intention of going into that. 'I'm all right,' she said. 'A bit tired, that's all.'

After lunch Rose took Alex on one side. 'I'm going to take Eva for a walk,' she said. 'Find out what's on her mind.'

Emily and Christopher had taken their daughters back to the farm for the midday meal. Rose thought Emily looked a little more cheerful, but then farmers and their wives usually felt better when the summer was good.

'Let's go for a walk, Eva,' Rose said.

'Leave the bairns with me,' Mrs Stanton said quickly.

They walked down to the river.

'We can cross by the stepping stones when the water's low,' Rose said. 'In the winter you can't even see them. The winter here is long, cold and wet.'

They climbed up from the river bed on to the far bank and began to walk along the path towards the dale head. At first Rose talked of general things – the weather, Eva's children, her own two nieces. She liked Eva Denby; she wished they were just two women, friends, taking a country walk. But there was more to it and the subject had to be broached.

'Eva,' Rose said, 'You really are much better, aren't you?'

'Oh I am, Doctor Rose. I am! You're mother's been ever so kind to me. Everyone in Faverwell has been kind to me. I've never been so happy in my life.'

'I'm glad,' Rose said. 'Look, let's sit here for a while. I hate to say it,' she said when they were seated, 'but it is time you were thinking about going back home, Eva. No-one wants to rush you, of course, but . . .'

She saw the instant fright in Eva's eyes, saw the girl's hand clench until the knuckles showed white, heard the entreaty in her voice as she interrupted.

'Oh no, Doctor Rose, I can't go home! Please don't make me!'

'I'm not . . .'

'I've thought it all out. I know I can't stay and be a burden on Mrs Stanton, but I could take a job in service, somewhere where I could take the children with me. They're ever such good children!'

Rose shook her head. 'There isn't anywhere, Eva. Unemployment in the dales is as bad as it is in the towns.

No-one has the money to take on extra help. And with a small child and a baby, however well-behaved . . .'

'Then I'll get a job in Grassington!' Eva cried. 'There's more jobs there.'

'I'm afraid you'll find it quite impossible,' Rose said sadly.

'Well I'm not going back to him! I'm never going back to him. You don't know what it's like, Doctor!'

'I can imagine,' Rose sympathized.

'You can't really,' Eva said. 'Begging your pardon, and I don't mean to be cheeky, Doctor, but you can't imagine what it's like. You have to go through it to know.'

Tears welled in her eyes, rolled down her face. She lowered her head and sobs tore at her body. Rose put an arm around her, felt the thin shoulders shaking.

'I'm sorry, Eva. I'm truly sorry. Perhaps it was wrong of me ever to suggest you coming here. Perhaps I've only made things more difficult for you?'

Eva raised her head.

'Oh no, Doctor Rose, don't ever think that! I've had the happiest time of my whole life here. And if I have to go back I'll never forget it.'

'Perhaps you could come here next year,' Rose suggested. 'I'm sure my mother would welcome you.'

'Oh no I couldn't'. Eva spoke with hopeless conviction. 'He won't ever let me come again. You see I haven't told you everything.'

'What do you mean?'

'I haven't told you I've already written to him to tell him I'm not going back, not ever. He'll have had the letter this morning. If I have to go back to him now he'll make me pay for that.'

She started to cry again. 'What am I going to do, Doctor?'

'I don't know, Eva,' Rose confessed. 'I don't know.'

She felt herself to be the last person in the world to help in any situation which involved Jim Denby, though Eva did not know that she had no intention of adding to her troubles by telling her what had happened while she had been away.

'Cheer up,' she said. 'We'll think of something.'

But of what, she had no idea.

'Perhaps we should be getting back now,' she said. She got to her feet and held out a hand to Eva. As they walked back along the river bank Rose put an arm around Eva's shoulders, trying to comfort her.

When she and Alex drove away from the Ewe Lamb on Saturday evening Rose's spirits had not improved. Remembering last Christmas she realized that this was the second time Faverwell had failed to work its magic on her. But the fault was in herself and the thought troubled her. Faverwell had not changed and her family were as supportive as ever.

'A good place,' Alex said. 'A loving family. I envy you your background.' His own parents had died when he was still at school. His only relative was his aunt in Manchester.

'I *am* to be envied that,' Rose acknowledged.

But the thought of Eva Denby's troubled face would not leave her. She had put the girl in a situation which was worse than the one from which she had tried to rescue her, and she could think of no way out of it.

'I feel helpless,' she told Alex. 'With part of me I wish I'd never started it. And yet I suppose I'd do the same thing again.'

'And you will,' he said. 'But you won't always come up against a Jim Denby.'

'What do you suppose he'll do about Eva's letter? She's got to face him.'

'He'll make her pay,' Alex said. 'My guess is by making her pregnant again. And I doubt if he'll stop at making his wife pay.'

'You mean he'll be after my blood?' Rose said.

They drove in silence for a while and then, just short of Grassington, Alex, without warning, pulled into the side of the road and turned off the engine.

'Is something wrong?' Rose asked quickly, unused to the ways of cars.

'No,' he said. 'I simply want to talk to you. Not about the Denbys, or anyone else. This time it's just you and me.'

There was an air of suppressed excitement about him. She knew at once what he was going to say and she did not want to hear it.

'Alex. I don't think now is . . .'

He interrupted her.

'Please listen to me, Rose!' The determined look on his face, the force in his voice, were new to her.

'Rose, will you marry me? I love you and I want you. I want you for my wife. Give me the chance and I swear I'll make you happy.'

He took both her hands in his own firm grasp, as if he was afraid she might somehow escape him. She was moved by the excitement and longing in his eyes, the eagerness in his voice.

'I can't,' she said, faltering, not because she was unsure, but because she did not want to hurt him.

He was not in a mood to accept refusal.

'Yes you can,' he said eagerly. 'All you have to do is say "Yes". Oh, I know what it will mean! Don't think I haven't considered it. I understand that it will mean giving up the clinic, and I know how much that means to you. But there are other things you can do. We can rent a house. You can set up a private practice . . .'

'That's not what I want . . .'

'Wait!' he commanded. 'Let me finish. I know the usual kind of private practice isn't all that you want, and I understand the difficulty, in any case, of waiting for patients to come to you. But you could also open up a surgery, say a couple of days a week, in the area where you want to work - Babcock Street for instance. You could rent a room, work right among the women you want to treat. You'd no longer be tied to the clinic, subject to Stanton. You'd be a free agent. I'd help you in every way, Rose. I'd deny you nothing!'

He was alight with enthusiasm, gripping her wrists so tightly that she was sure he must leave marks on them. She hated herself for she knew she was going to kill his fervour.

She shook her head. 'I truly appreciate everything you offer me. I wish I could accept. But it won't do, Alex. It all sounds tempting, and professionally it's what I'd like -

especially the women's clinic. But I can't return your love, Alex, and I can't marry you as a business proposition. It wouldn't be fair. What would you get out of it?'

'I'd get you,' he said. 'I want you.'

'But I don't love you,' Rose repeated. 'Not in the way you love me. I can't pretend I do.'

'I know that, I'm willing to take the gamble. You do care something for me?'

'Of course I do. A great deal. You know that. You're the best friend I have - the one I turn to.'

With all her heart she wished she could love this man. With an equal love on her side, marriage to him could be a pleasant thing. They were in so many ways compatible. And to the pleasure of marriage and children, which she had always known she desired, she would be able to add the satisfaction of a job which she wanted with all her heart to do; to practise among working women without the restrictions which at the clinic seemed constantly to tie her down.

But Alex Bairstow, for all the liking she had for him, could not raise in her one hundredth part of the excitement, the longing, the soaring of the spirit which even the sound of John Worthing's voice over the telephone aroused in her. The spark was missing; there would be no fire in such a marriage. While John Worthing existed she was trapped by him. She did not want to be, but that was the way it was.

'Then I'd settle for that,' Alex said. 'Friendship is a pretty good foundation. So is need. I need you; you need someone - so why not me?'

She leaned forward and kissed him on the cheek.

'It's still "No", Alex. I'm honoured and I'm grateful, but I can't take so much and give so little.'

He shook his head. 'Let me be the one to worry about that!'

'No,' Rose said. 'I can't.'

Still holding her wrists, he looked at her steadily, searching for a sign of hope in her face. But there was none. He let go of her and got out of the car. He cranked the engine with the starting handle and when the engine leapt to life he got back in again.

'Promise you'll tell me when you change your mind,' he said.

Rose could think of no circumstances under which she would do so.

On the following Monday Rose was met once again by a wide-eyed Mabel Pearlman, bursting with news.

'That Mr Denby was here again on Saturday. Shouting and bawling something awful, he was, and in front of all the mothers. You should have heard the things he said, Doctor Rose.'

'I'm quite pleased I didn't,' Rose said shortly. 'Could I have this morning's case files, please, Mabel?'

Mabel bit her lip, looked away.

'I can't. That is, I've been told . . .'

'What do you mean, Mabel?'

'It's just that . . . well, Nurse Butterworth said that Doctor Stanton said that I wasn't to hand out any files until later, until you've seen him. It's not me, Doctor,' she added quickly. 'It's just what I was told.'

'I see,' Rose said. 'Is Doctor Stanton in yet?'

'He's been here the past hour.'

So it was to be a near repetition of last week's scene, Rose thought. But when, a few minutes later, she stood in front of him, she realized that it was to be much worse. Afterwards she could not remember everything he said in his cold, cutting voice; but some words stood out, echoed round and round in her head.

'We are accused – *you* are accused, by your unwarrantable interference, not only of being the cause of his wife losing her unborn child, but of breaking Mr Denby's marriage to the extent that he has now lost his wife and his other two children. He lays this directly at your door.'

'That I did not do,' Rose said vehemently. 'He has driven his wife away himself, by his own intolerable behaviour! Ask her!'

'She is unfortunately not available,' Doctor Stanton said dryly. 'But he is. He has shown me the letter he received from his wife. He has said that unless I report you to the Health Committee he will take that letter to the editor of the Akersfield *Record*. And he makes it quite plain that he will have no compunction in involving this clinic as well as yourself. He will state - and he will do it through the man Blamires who knows how to use words - that you and this clinic have used undue influence over his wife.'

'How dare he!' Rose cried. 'And how can you believe him? Surely you cannot allow him to dictate what you must do?'

'He dares because he is in a strong position,' Doctor Stanton said. 'He speaks of damages, though whether that will hold water one cannot tell. What is quite certain is that he can damage this clinic, and that I am not prepared to risk. I have therefore no alternative but to report the whole matter to the Chairman of the Committee. You will be summoned to appear before them in due course.'

'I see. So it's to be my word against his?'

'There is little need of his word. His wife has lost the baby, and now he has her letter. She goes so far as to say that but for you, but for the time she has spent away from Paradine Street, she would never have had the courage to leave him.'

'She has not left him,' Rose said. 'I know for a fact that she will be returning - more's the pity! And now may I have my files for this morning's patients? Miss Pearlman informs me that you are holding them.'

'Ah yes,' he said smoothly. 'In fact, Doctor, you will not need them. The Chairman has agreed with me that until this matter is cleared up - he hopes to arrange an emergency meeting of the Committee in two or three days' time - it would be best for all concerned if you did not see patients.'

Rose was summoned to appear before the Committee on Wednesday afternoon. The intervening hours were the longest of her life. The town hall clock was striking three as she walked into the room where nine months earlier she had been so delighted to receive her appointment. John Worthing, sitting as before to the right of the Chairman, raised his head and looked long and directly at her as she seated herself in the big chair. Longing to hear from him, wondering why he had not communicated with her, she had this morning succumbed to temptation and telephoned his office. He was in London, his secretary said. He would be back in time for this afternoon's meeting. In the look he gave her now, though his face was stern, she felt sympathy. But in the long faces of the rest of the Committee she could detect none at all.

The meeting began as predictably as she had expected. After all, she had been through it all with Doctor Stanton, though she hoped that the Committee would be less chilly than her immediate boss.

'Why did you take this action without consulting your superior officer?' Councillor Rogers barked. He treated her as though he was conducting a court martial. She disliked him more than ever.

'I've already explained that I considered there was no need to do so . . .

'You considered there was no need to inform the Head of the clinic?'

'None,' Rose said. 'I had mentioned to him that I wanted to visit Mrs Denby, mainly to get her to come to the clinic. I thought she badly needed the help we could give. I understood from Doctor Stanton that such a visit could not be made as part of my duties and for that reason I visited her in my own time. The idea of offering her a holiday was a secondary one and every part of that was a private matter. The clinic was not involved.'

John Worthing spoke for the first time.

'I find that a reasonable explanation.' His tone was mild. He's trying to play it down, Rose thought. She wondered if he knew what she was going through.

It was too good an opportunity for the Chairman to miss. He cleared his throat, sat upright, clasped his small, fat hands in front of him and spoke.

'All of us who have the privilege of serving the public, of serving Akersfield, realize that we can have no private lives. Our deeds can never remain hidden. What we do, we do in the full light of day, the glare of the footlights!' He leaned towards Rose, shaking his head regretfully. 'We belong to Akersfield. Doctor Rose!'

She wanted to laugh at the absurdity of it all. She wanted to scream. She couldn't believe it was happening to her.

You mean I've been bought, body and soul, for three-hundred-and-seventy-five pounds a year?' she blurted out. 'Is that what you're saying, Mr Chairman? Because if it is I want to tell you here and now that in my case it's just not true! I was engaged to do a job. I've done it. Even Doctor Stanton can't deny that. But neither this Committee nor anyone else is going to buy my private life!'

The Chairman flushed puce. He seemed likely to suffer a stroke at any second. There was a swelling murmur of disapproval, disbelief, among the men around the table. Only John Worthing remained silent, his eyes never leaving Rose.

'How dare you, young woman!' Councillor Rogers demanded.

'I dare all right!' Rose flared. 'I'm being pilloried because you - this committee - can't stand up to a man you know to be wrong. I'm your scapegoat because you're afraid of the newspapers. You'll all feel better when you can say you've chastised me. Why don't you just tell Jim Denby to go to hell?'

The Chairman struggled to speak.

'My dear young lady . . . I had hoped that a few words from the Committee . . . there is no need whatever . . .'

'I understand perfectly,' Rose interrupted. 'I can see that you've already decided against me. If Denby can be told, officially, that I've been reprimanded, then everything will be settled. Well you can go further, gentlemen.

You can tell Mr Denby, and anyone else you wish, that I've resigned my job! I'm giving my notice here and now. And if I hear the slightest suggestion that I've been dismissed, or have in any way harmed the clinic, then I shall fight. I'm not afraid of Denby, or of a dozen like him!'

She could not believe her own ears. How could she be saying these things? How could she be throwing away her job like this? But she knew, as clearly as she had ever known anything in her life, that she could not continue to work with Doctor Stanton.

'Doctor Rose, are you sure you know what you're saying?'

John Worthing's voice, clear and incisive, cut through

130

the buzz of astonishment which ran around the meeting. Rose looked directly at him, no longer seeing anyone else in the room.

'I'm quite sure, Councillor Worthing.'

It was with a great effort that she kept her voice steady. She was terrified that she would break down.

'Then you're a little fool!' he snapped. It was as if for him also there were only the two of them. No-one else mattered.

For a second, which seemed an eternity, they held each other with their eyes, across the width of the table. But it was no use. He could not help her, and suddenly she could stand no more. She picked up her handbag, pushed back the chair, and ran out of the room. She ran through the empty waiting room, down the long flight of stairs, and was running across the lobby when John Worthing caught at her from behind, jerking her to a standstill, swinging her around to face him.

'Stop it! What in the world do you think you're doing, Rose? There's no need for this!'

They faced each other angrily.

'Let me go!' Rose shouted.

'I've told you,' he said. 'It will all blow over! Now go right back in there and make your peace. I promise you it will be all right. They had no intention of doing anything very terrible, you know.'

His tone was quieter, but she was not to be mollified.

'I'll do no such thing,' she said, pulling away from him. 'I'll die first!'

His anger flared again.

'Don't be such an exasperating little fool!'

She was stung by his sharpness when what she craved was sympathy. Had he no understanding at all?

'What will you do?' he demanded. 'Where will you get another job?'

'I don't know. Most likely not in Akersfield if they have anything to do with it. I don't know and I don't care!'

'Rose, don't do this,' John Worthing pleaded.

She was aware that other members of the Committee were now walking past them in the lobby, that she was attracting attention. The glances they gave her were not so

131

much hostile as curious, wondering if there was something further to be learned about this young woman who had flown off the handle so unexpectedly, so divertingly.

'I'm going, John,' she said. 'Please don't follow me.'

For the rest of the week she went in to the clinic but was given no work to do. She was quite sure that her resignation had pleased Doctor Stanton, but they did not discuss it. She felt numb, unable to decide what she should do next. She felt certain that there was no work for her in Akersfield and that she would have to leave the town. It surprised her that the thought of leaving Akersfield was so painful to her. She had known it such a short time. But in her heart she knew it was not Akersfield, much though she had grown to like it, but those whom it held which bound her so closely.

Saturday was the day of John Worthing's garden party, to which she now no longer wished to go.

'There'll be all the wretched Committee there,' she said to Alex. 'I never want to see them again.'

'Face them,' Alex said. 'It's the best thing. In any case they'll be lost in the crowd. Anyone who's anyone in Akersfield will be there. Apart from all that, you promised me.'

'Very well, I'll go for you,' Rose said in the end. And she would see John Worthing again, perhaps for the last time if she was to leave Akersfield.

Saturday was also the day fixed for Eva's homecoming. Rose had been to see Eva's mother, who had told her that she intended to meet Eva at the station.

'She can come back with me to begin with, but she can't stay here,' Mrs Foster said. 'We've only got the one small bedroom. I don't know what's to become of her, I'm sure!'

'I'll come to the station, too,' Rose said. 'I want to tell her myself that I'm leaving the clinic. I'd rather you didn't tell her why, Mrs Foster.'

'I won't,' Mrs Foster promised. 'Though I daresay *he* will! It's a sin and a shame you're going. You're just what we need here. Not just young mothers with babies, but lots of women around here could do with someone like you to turn to.'

132

It was a chastened and apprehensive Eva the two women welcomed at the railway station, though physically she seemed stronger and the children were blooming with health. She was clearly upset at the news of Rose's departure from the clinic. 'I shan't go if you're not there,' she said.

'You must, Eva,' Rose urged her. 'It's important for the baby.'

They parted outside the station, Eva to go with her mother, Rose to get ready for the garden party.

In spite of her protestations that she did not want to attend the garden party, Rose had purchased a new dress – flowered voile, with floating panels around the skirt, which was a daring eight inches above the ankle. Skirts were getting shorter all the time. And, going the whole hog, with money she could now ill afford to spend, she had also bought a new hat of Bangkok straw, trimmed with a large, squashy pink rose. She rubbed a *papier poudre* leaf over her nose and chin to take off the shine, pinched her cheeks and bit her lips to bring the colour into them, and was ready when Alex arrived.

'You look wonderful!' he said.

'You don't look so bad yourself,' Rose told him.

He was wearing a pearl-grey suit and, in keeping with the occasion, a straw boater with a coloured band.

She was surprised by the size of John Worthing's house – a many-gabled, mid-Victorian building – and by the extent and beauty of the grounds around it. There were close-mown, undulating lawns, flower beds and pergolas, trees and shrubberies, even a small lake.

'I had no idea it would be like this,' she said to Alex.

'I told you, he's a rich man. And a man of taste.'

Alex seemed proud to have her on his arm as they moved around, taking pleasure in introducing her to people. He seemed to know everyone. Rose acknowledged greetings, exchanged pleasantries, conscious that all the time her eyes were scanning the throng for a sight of John Worthing. They had been at the party almost an hour when, rounding a corner, she came face to face with him – she on Alex's arm, he with his wife on his.

'So there you are!' John Worthing said. 'I was beginning to wonder if you hadn't come.' Rose met his look, saw the admiration in his eyes, followed quickly by a look of enquiry. There had been no word between them since the afternoon of the committee meeting and she wondered if, after all, he did not care that she was going out of his life.

Then she realized that Mrs Worthing was looking at her.

'Allow me to present my wife,' John said. 'Diana, my dear, this is Doctor Rose Stanton.'

'My husband has spoken of you,' Mrs Worthing said.

Her voice was cool, clear, light; no trace there of local accent, only the very best education. Rose wondered what John had said about her. There was a polite reserve in Mrs Worthing's manner which gave nothing away.

'You have a lovely garden here,' Rose said.

'Yes, it is nice, isn't it? It was a wilderness when we came here. My husband and I made it - or, rather, planned it - together. It was great fun, wasn't it darling? It still is. There's always something to be done.'

Mrs Worthing was, as Rose had pictured her, tall and elegant. She was too thin, even for the current fashion, and there was a nervousness about her which showed in the restless movements of her slender hands and the unquiet expression on her fine-featured face. Behind the flimsy curtain of her impeccable manners, Rose sensed a turbulence of emotion. Though it was impossible to judge on so short an acquaintance it seemed to her that Mrs Worthing's invalidism might be more nervous or mental than physical. But she was beautiful, charming, and quite clearly in love with her husband.

'Do go and have something to eat,' Mrs Worthing urged. 'They're serving refreshments in the marquee. Perhaps we shall see you both later.'

With a quick pressure on her husband's arm she bore him away. Rose, her arm still through Alex's, watched them until they were out of sight.

'She's attractive,' she acknowledged.

'They say she was a beauty when John married her,' Alex said. 'I must say, she's looking in better health than I expected. Let's hope it lasts. But John, nice fellow though he is, doesn't help her.'

'What do you mean?'

'Women! You'd think with a lovely woman like that he'd never stray. In fact he's well known for it. Of course he always returns to her in the end. I daresay, underneath, he's as much in love with her as she is with him.'

STOP! Rose wanted to shout. Stop, stop, stop! He was driving knives into her. Suddenly she saw so many things, saw what must be the truth of it all. She had been a silly, romantic fool! She was no doubt one in a long procession of John Worthing's spare women. Of course it wouldn't matter if she left Akersfield. Someone else would take her place. Did he take them all to the Heifer for lunch? Has he a *penchant* for redheads, she wondered bitterly, or am I at least different in that respect? But in no other, she thought.

'I don't know what women see in him,' Alex said. 'Perhaps as a woman you could tell me?'

He was not being consciously cruel. That was not in Alex.

I could tell you all right, Rose thought. I could tell you that he moves the heart, lifts the spirits, stirs the senses, as no other man has ever done for me – or ever will: that the sight of him and the sound of his voice make me tremble.

'I haven't the slightest idea!' she said brightly. 'Shall we go and find some food? I'm starving!'

After they had eaten, though she scarcely tasted the delicious food, or the pale, China tea in delicate cups, they walked around again, patronizing the sideshows; knocking down coconuts, dipping into the bran tub, guessing the weight of a cake. It was fun. In spite of herself she began to enjoy it. Alex was a good person to be with.

'You realize all this money's going into your fund?'

That was something else she would have to abandon when she left Akersfield. Although she was not known as the instigator, she recognized that she would always have been closely connected with the project, would have done everything she could for its success. She felt that in abandoning the fund she was somehow casting aside all those mothers who needed it.

'I'm sorry I shan't see it in action,' she said. 'I feel almost more guilty about that than about anything.'

She had still not the slightest idea where she might be, even in a month from now. She had started at once to look for jobs, but so far there was nothing. Perhaps she would have to go back to Faverwell - but what would she do there?

'You could be here,' Alex said. He took her arm, drawing her close to him as they walked. They were exploring the perimeter of the garden now, away from the stalls, the tents, the sideshows. When they came to a bench, set under an oak tree, they sat down.

'Rose,' Alex said quickly, 'I'm asking you again. Will you marry me? In spite of all you've said before, I know we could make it work. Look how much we've enjoyed this afternoon. A large part of marriage must be like that - I don't mean garden parties, but liking the same things, enjoying being together.'

She turned towards him. He was so good, so sincere. How much simpler life would be if she could fall in love with Alex, marry him and live happily ever after. But it was not simple.

'I would be afraid, Alex,' she said. 'I would be afraid that I'd take so much more than I could give. I do care for you - but not in the way I'd want to if I were your wife.'

Not in the way that she would care if it were John Worthing sitting beside her. For a brief moment she hated John; that he had ever encouraged her, caused her to love him more than she might have, bound her to him by enticing him into admitting it. But, she told herself firmly, there were no bonds which she could not and would not break if she made up her mind to it.

'I understand all that,' Alex was saying. 'You've never been less than honest about it.'

Oh yes I have, she thought. But she had no intention of telling him the whole truth, risking further hurt to him.

'I'm prepared for that,' he said. 'I won't expect from you what you can't give. I promise that, Rose.'

They fell silent. Into Rose's mind came all the advantages of marrying Alex. She would stay in Akersfield.

She would set up her own practice and – more important – be free to open a clinic where she could, among other things, help women to plan their families. She would be able to continue with the Mothers' Holiday Fund. But none of these things, important to her though they were, mattered if she could not also make Alex happy. She tried to put it into words to him.

'. . . I would *have* to believe that there was a chance, a good chance, that we could be happy together, before I gave way to the other temptations,' she said. 'If that sounds somewhat cold-blooded, then I'm putting it badly. It's because I care for you as much as I do – and respect you utterly – that I would have to feel that there was a likelihood that we'd make a go of it.'

'But there is, Rose!' Alex said eagerly. 'I'm sure of it! Rose, say you will! I love you so very much.'

She hesitated – but not for long.

'I will marry you, Alex,' she said.

Held closely in his arms, returning his kisses, she vowed to herself that she would be a good wife to Alex. She would learn to love him as he loved her. She would forget her feelings for John Worthing as though they had never existed.

After a while, Alex's arm still around her, they went back to the big lawn. Through the crowd Rose saw the Worthings moving towards them. They were still arm-in-arm, she looking up at him with a proprietary air, he smiling down at his wife. Alex spotted them at the same time.

'Let's tell our host and hostess,' he said quickly. 'It's their party. They should be the first to know.'

As a jubilant Alex broke the news, his arm possessively about her, Rose looked at John Worthing. The eyes which met hers were as black as coal, as hard as flint.

'And when is the wedding to be?' Mrs Worthing asked pleasantly.

Rose turned away from John Worthing's icy regard and looked up at Alex. She was glad she had promised to marry him. It was going to be all right. They would be happy together.

'Quite soon,' she said. 'As soon as possible.'

PART TWO

Chapter Nine

When Rose walked into the Babcock Street surgery at nine o-clock in the morning Mrs Foster was still there, hard at work scrubbing the lino-covered floor. She sat back on her heels, surprised to see her employer.

'Good-morning, Doctor. I didn't expect you this early, otherwise I'd have finished.'

'It's all right, Mrs Foster,' Rose said. 'I know surgery isn't until ten, but if I'm going to be absent for a week or two there are a few things I must see to.'

'If you'll pardon me saying so, you shouldn't be here at all today. You should be at home, resting. That's what you'd tell your patients to do.' Mrs Foster's voice oozed disapproval. She plunged her hands into the bucket of water, wrung out the floorcloth, mopped the suds from a square of floor so that Rose could get by.

Rose contradicted her. 'It *isn't* what I tell my patients, Mrs Foster. I tell them to keep going normally until labour starts – but not to get overtired. It helps to be occupied.'

Mrs Foster grunted. 'Well mind how you walk over this wet floor, Doctor. We don't want any accidents, do we?' She stood aside while Rose picked her way to the back room.

'I know you don't approve of me working right through my pregnancy,' Rose said, 'but I assure you it's quite all right. I'm as fit as a flea.'

'It's not for me to approve or disapprove,' Mrs Foster said primly. 'But after what you've been through . . .'

'Don't worry, everything's going to be all right this time,' Rose assured her. 'I feel pretty good.'

But in fact she felt tired, her body heavy and awkward now that her time was near. She was thankful that the hot summer had given way to a cool September. That, at least, made things easier.

'You've waited a long time for this baby,' Mrs Foster said.

Rose did not need the reminder. So much had changed since that October day, almost two years ago now, when she had gone into the church in Faverwell on her father's arm and come out on Alex's, irrevocably, and a little frighteningly, bound to him.

She had wanted the quietest possible wedding; no fuss, preferably in a registry office. In spite of the honesty of her intentions, she had this uneasiness about making her vows in church, feeling that her forthcoming marriage was somehow not real, afraid that she might thereby mock God. Surprisingly, Alex had strongly backed her parents' desire for a church wedding.

'Why disappoint them?' he said. 'Anyway, I want to turn around and see you walking down the aisle in all your glory!'

She gave in. Since from the first moment of their engagement she had known there were things she could not give Alex, whenever she could she gave freely, and with all the affection she could command.

They were married in a church packed with relatives, friends, customers of the Ewe Lamb – and with her two small nieces as bridesmaids. She wore a dress of pale cream chiffon, trimmed with silver lace on the skirt, embroidered with seed pearls at the neck and on the short sleeves, which fell like petals from the shoulders. Alex's eyes shone with love and admiration at the sight of her, but there were tears in her own. The wedding dress hung at the back of the wardrobe now, draped with a piece of sheeting. She never looked at it.

'All done and dusted,' Mrs Foster said, standing in the doorway, drying her hands on her apron. 'I'll be off then, Doctor.' She adjusted the round, black hat which she wore all the time, even when she was scrubbing the floor.

Rose took a half-crown from her purse and handed it to Mrs Foster. It was more than the going rate for cleaning the two tiny rooms, plus a lavatory at the back, but Mrs Foster's need was great. Also, Rose felt certain that a little of the money found its way to Eva Denby in the form of food.

'So you won't be wanting me for the next week or two,' Mrs Foster said. 'What with the surgery being closed.'

Rose laughed. 'It's not as cut and dried as that! The baby's due today, but you know what first babies are. It could be another fortnight before it decides to appear. I shall keep on here as long as I can and get back as quickly as possible. In the meantime I'd be grateful if you'd pop in here and keep an eye on things. If there's any post, for instance, you could bring it to my home.'

Mrs Foster's face brightened. 'That I'll do with pleasure, Doctor. Only don't you be coming back to work too soon, now!'

'Dear Mrs Foster,' Rose said. 'How many of the mothers you know around here have the luxury of two whole weeks' rest, with a nurse in attendance, after their babies? Did Eva, for instance?'

'That she did not!' Mrs Foster replied. 'Two days, more like! Thank God she's never got in the family way again. No thanks to Jim Denby, you can be sure of that!'

Rose herself thought it strange that in the last two years Eva had not conceived. She had not been to the Babcock Street surgery for the birth control advice which Rose gave to other local women. She was doubtless too afraid of her husband to defy him on that, though from time to time she surreptitiously set foot in the surgery with the children, simply in order to see Rose. Perhaps the miscarriage Eva had suffered in Faverwell had left her unable to conceive, but Rose had had no opportunity to examine her and she knew she had not been back to the clinic.

'Well I daresay Mr Bairstow'll be glad when it's all over,' Mrs Foster said, lingering, wanting to chat. 'Men aren't a mite of good at times like this – begging his pardon of course!'

'I suppose he will,' Rose agreed.

'They like to get back to . . . well, you know what I mean, Doctor. The married bit. It's not much cop for them, the last few weeks, is it?'

It wasn't much cop for the wife, Rose thought; but that wasn't true for her, and she knew it. In spite of being so big and awkward, she had felt a freedom in these last few weeks such as she had not known since her wedding night. It seemed to her that everything that was wrong in their marriage had started then, from the moment the uniformed page boy had shown them to their room in the hotel in Scarborough, where they were to spend a three-day honeymoon.

While the boy deposited their suitcases and received a

generous tip from Alex, Rose had stood there, seeing nothing but the large double bed which, with its deep, frilled valance, its rose-coloured bedspread, its rails and knobs of gleaming brass, dominated the room. There was scarcely space for the other bits of furniture, which seemed to have been added as afterthoughts. The bed was everything.

She had wanted, instantly, to run and run and run: out of the room, down the wide stairs, out of the hotel, across the dark cliff tops; anywhere to escape that voluptuous, threatening bed.

She did not do so, of course. She remained where she was, seemingly rooted to the thick, crimson carpet. She heard the page boy leave and then she heard Alex turn the key in the lock. Only her utter stillness, her rigidity as he came behind her and put his arms around her, betrayed her feelings – but he did not even notice. He swivelled her around towards him and kissed her long and tenderly. Then with equal gentleness – she could not complain on that score – he took off her hat and tossed it on to the dressing table, removed her jacket, letting it fall to the floor, and began to unfasten the buttons of her dress.

She moved, twisting her body out of his embrace.

'Not now, Alex!' she protested. 'It's after seven o-clock. We have to go down to dinner.'

'We don't have to go down to dinner,' Alex said. 'We can skip it.'

'But I don't want to skip it!' She managed a smile. 'I'm really quite hungry!'

'So am I,' he said. 'But not for food! Rose, we've waited a long time for this.' He picked her up and lifted her on to the bed. 'You're a wee bit of a thing,' he remarked. 'You weigh next to nothing!'

It was true that he had waited patiently to possess her. Throughout their short engagement he had been loving but restrained, kissing her often, declaring his love in words, but not fondling her even as much as John Worthing had done on that afternoon which now belonged to another world. It had seemed to her that Alex was not a sexually demanding man, that he knew nothing of the kind of passion which showed in John Worthing's every glance, sounded in his voice.

She was wrong; utterly mistaken. From the moment Alex laid her on that soft, wide bed, removed the last of her satin underwear, he was caught up in a passion which knew no bounds; his hands on her breasts, his tongue probing her mouth, then his face, bristly because he needed a shave, buried in the softness of her belly; and all the time the endearments pouring out of him in a frenzied, incoherent stream.

When he started to enter her, he said, 'I won't hurt you, Rose. I promise I won't hurt you!'

'Let him hurt me!' she found herself praying. 'Let him hurt me so that I can pay for the wrong!' She drew in a long breath, arched her neck in sharp pain as he pierced her, but she did not cry out. When his climax came she turned her face away from him and the tears ran down her cheeks on to the pillow.

She should not have married him. She should have listened to the voice which had told her over and over again that there was only one man she should ever marry. And now it was too late, there was nothing she could do. But at least Alex must never know. She would see to it that he did not. In their daily lives it would not be too difficult. They were good friends, compatible. It was this which had deceived her into thinking that marriage with him could work. In bed she would be acquiescent, she would give him all the affection she had for him, and more. He need never know.

They had missed dinner.

'There's no point in dressing,' Alex teased her. 'It would be a waste of time! I'll order a tray to be brought up - and a bottle of wine.'

It embarrassed her that the waiter saw them both in their dressing gowns so early in the evening, but Alex was nonchalant about it.

'I daresay he knows we're on honeymoon,' he said. 'They won't really expect to see much of us downstairs.'

After the meal he had made love to her again, with as much ardour as if it was the first time. It was physically less painful to her, but she could not respond. She lay quiescent and let him do what he wanted. Caught up in his own mounting desire, he seemed not to notice her, and when it was over he fell quickly asleep, his head uncomfortably heavy on her breast. When she felt sure, by the depth of his breathing, that he would not easily waken, she moved from under him and turned away, occupying a narrow space on the edge of the bed. She faced the fact that from now on it was the furthest she would ever be from him. She would never sleep alone, never again be free.

Sleep did not come. After an hour or two she got quietly out of the big bed and went to the window, drawing back the curtains a little. The night was dark. She could hear the strength of the sea, but it was not visible. She stood there a long time, listening to the waves beating against the cliffs. Eventually the first streaks of a hesitant grey dawn broke over the sea. Another day. Perhaps it would be better. She would think of a way. She began to shiver with cold, and crept back into bed, moving carefully so as not to waken Alex.

And then as she lay there, straight as a lamp post, the tears came, racking her whole body with deep sobs, so that Alex stirred in his sleep, and then awakened. At once his arms were around her and he was holding her to him.

'What is it, my darling? What's wrong?' He held her against him, stroking her hair.

'I'm sorry,' she said. 'It's just that . . . well, I couldn't sleep. I don't know what came over me. I'm sorry, Alex.'

'I'm sorry,' he said. 'I've been selfish. I didn't realize you hadn't been satisfied. I'll do better, I promise. You're so wonderful, Rose. Everything's going to be marvellous. You'll see!'

His hands were moving over her body, caressing her breasts, stroking the curves of her buttocks, the length of her thighs. And then he was on top of her and inside her again. It was growing daylight now and she closed her eyes against the sight of the room, which she hated, and knew she would never forget.

As her husband's passion mounted, his arms gripping her in a frenzy, the face she saw before her closed eyes was that other face; that dark, foreign-looking face with the aquiline nose, the sensual mouth, the eyes dark with desire. The hands moving over her body were John Worthing's hands. It was then that her own passion was stirred.

'Was that better?' Alex asked when it was all over.

I have just committed adultery, she wanted to cry out! She felt that the sin must be visible on her, like a brand; that in the now full light of day Alex must see it on her face and in her eyes.

'Don't look so worried, my dear one,' he said. 'It *will* come all right. We must give ourselves time, that's all.'

It would never come right. She knew that for certain. But for his sake she must hide the knowledge. The pretence that everything was fine was the least she could offer him. In trepidation, she wondered how long it would be before he saw through her pretence.

Within weeks of their honeymoon she found herself pregnant. In her own mind she was convinced that the child had been conceived in that first early morning when in spirit she had been in John Worthing's arms. She was a stranger to herself in those first few weeks of pregnancy: wretched, constantly sick; torn by a guilt which turned into an obsession that the child would look like John Worthing. She knew that it was a totally foolish thought but she could not shake it off.

'I hate to see you like this,' Alex said. 'You're clearly not suited to having children. Perhaps we shouldn't have any more?'

'Do we want an only child?' Rose asked.

'I don't mind if we don't have any,' Alex admitted. 'I just hate to see you like this. And there's another thing.'

She knew what he was going to say. It had been inevitable from the beginning. But she did not want it put into words. While it was not mentioned, it could somehow be glossed over.

'Please, Alex!'

'No, Rose. It has to be said. I know you don't want me to make love to you. It's become quite clear to me, though I know you try to hide it. I'm assuming it's because you're pregnant . . .'

'Of course it is!' Rose broke in quickly.

'. . . But it's not easy for me, Rose. I try not to bother you, I try to be gentle . . .'

'But you are, Alex,' she protested. 'Please don't blame yourself. Sometimes it happens to women when they're pregnant. It will pass.'

Once she had had the baby, she promised herself, she would really try harder. She would make it up to him. But for the present she seized gratefully on the excuse he had given her.

The excuse was short lasting. At three months, exhausted by nausea and vomiting, she miscarried. At once, all her apprehensions about the baby were swallowed up in a deep disappointment as she realized how much she had wanted this child. And as the weeks passed and the winter gave way to spring it became clear that there was to be no improvement in her relations with Alex. She became adept at refusing him. She was ashamed of the dozens of ways she found to say 'No'. When she was too ashamed to say it yet again, she gave in to him. But now there was more than apathy on her part. As Alex assuaged himself at her body she felt an aversion to his nearness. She tried to dissemble her feelings, but more and more often she failed to deceive him. In the end he turned on her.

'What is it about me?' he cried. 'Am I so loathsome that you have to turn away in disgust? Am I so cruel that you have to weep every time I make love to you – which God knows isn't often? Tell me what it is!'

'It isn't you, Alex. It's me. And I don't know why!'

But she did know why, though there would never be any way she could tell him of this other man who came between them whenever Alex took her in his arms.

'How long is it to go on?' Alex demanded. 'You're over the baby. What's the excuse now?'

'I haven't one,' Rose said. 'I do try, Alex. I really do try!'

He turned round on her angrily.

'Do you think it pleases me to know that my wife has to *try* to bear it when I make love to her? That she *tries* not to find me repellent?'

For ten days after that occasion he had not come near her. They had slept in the same bed, not touching. It was during that time that she found she was pregnant again.

'Perhaps it will be better when we have the baby,' she said to Alex.

But that was not to be, either. In August she miscarried for the second time. Afterwards she lay weak and desolate, convinced that the loss of her babies was a judgement on her. Though he tried, Alex found it impossible to comfort her; nor could he find solace for himself in her. It was then that he started to drink.

Rose tried to tell herself – and it was true – that he had always drunk a lot. But that had been a different kind of drinking. Then it had been part of being happy – a few drinks to celebrate. Now he was driven by unhappiness and frustration, and she knew that it was her fault.

Except for one occasion, he did not get drunk, nor did he ever drink much in the daytime, and never enough to affect his work. He sat at home in the evenings with the whisky bottle to hand, morosely sipping. Or he went out to drink, which was worse because she was not there to try to stop him when she thought he had had enough.

It was on a night early in January that he came home drunk. She had gone to bed and, hearing him come upstairs, pretended to be asleep. He had pulled the bedclothes off her and shaken her shoulder.

'Wake up!' he shouted. '*IF* you're asleep, which I doubt!'

She sat up immediately.

'I'll go and make some coffee.' She made to get out of bed but he pushed her down again.

'I don't want coffee!' he said. 'I want you! I want my wife! And why do I want my wife? Because I'm celebrating!'

'Celebrating?'

'Bloody well celebrating! I've been made Editor! Editor of the *Record*. The Old Man's going to Sheffield, and from now on it's all mine. So lie down in that bloody bed and I'll show you just how a normal man celebrates with a normal wife – which you're not, and never have been – but I'll show you just the same!'

'Please Alex!'

She had seen him in drink before, muddled, over-amorous, but always amiable. This time he was a different man. The gentleness and consideration which, though less in evidence over the last year, had always been part of the real Alex, were gone.

'Please Alex!' he mimicked her. 'Please Alex, not

tonight! Well I'm going to show you, Madam!'

His eyes were tormented, as if something against his will was driving him to hurt her. He tore back the bedclothes and came on to her, violent, demanding; making love with the vengeance of a man who had been frustrated beyond endurance. There was no thought in her mind this time of that other man. Her thoughts were on her own pain, and the shame that they must both feel when this was over.

It was thus that the child she was carrying now, had carried this time to full term, had been conceived.

In spite of its beginnings, she wanted this child. She had kept fit and well through most of her pregnancy and now she looked forward to its birth.

With Alex there had been no repetition of that drunken scene. He had been ashamed, but his shame had put an even greater distance between them.

'What can I say, Rose?' he apologized. 'I was drunk. It's inadequate to say I'm sorry.'

'I understand,' Rose said. 'It's best that we forget it.'

But she never would, and for him her pregnancy, the sight of her swelling body, was a daily taunt.

If her salvation was in the child she longed for, Alex's, Rose thought, was in his work. His job as editor of the *Record* brought him new responsibilities in which he immersed himself. She thought that perhaps his increased work load absorbed his sexual energy, in the way that her own work, and her pregnancy, filled her mind. He was drinking – she knew the signs; but steadily, not to excess. And in his new job, encountering more people, meeting deadlines, it was part of the everyday scene.

'I'll be off then, Doctor,' Mrs Foster repeated. 'All the best, I'm sure.'

'Thank you. Of course you never know. I might still be here when you look in on Thursday!'

As Mrs Foster left, Rose unlocked her desk drawer and took out a small card index file. She kept the minimum of paperwork on the patients who came here since she had sensed early on that they did not like having things written down about them. She had also simplified every routine so

150

that on the three mornings a week when she was there, patients could walk in off the street and be sure of seeing her. They paid a minimum of a shilling a visit, more if they could afford it. When she thought it might cause hardship, she took no fee.

She quite expected a rush of patients this morning since it was known in the district that her baby was due and that she would soon be unavailable for a week or two. She did not have to wait long. Five minutes after the door had closed noisily behind Mrs Foster it opened again, clanging the bell which made her premises sound like the corner shop they had once been.

'Come straight through!' Rose called.

The visitor was Eva Denby.

'Why, Eva! Your mother left not five minutes ago!'

'I know. I met her. She's taken the children. I wanted to see you.'

Two more years of Paradine Street, of unemployment and near starvation, of Jim Denby's hectoring and bullying, had added ten years to Eva's appearance. She was twenty-three, and in her pale, drawn listlessness, looked thirty-five. Rose guessed that, like many a mother who came in here, she lived largely on tea with skimmed condensed milk, and bread-and-margarine.

'How are you?' Rose asked.

'I'm all right.' The usual reply. She was quite clearly anaemic, too thin, and her pretty face was spotty. But her eyes were alive, questioning; anxious and hopeful at one and the same time.

'What do you want to see me about?' Rose asked. 'Won't you sit down?'

Eva perched on the edge of a chair as if ready at any second to take flight.

'I don't like to ask you,' she said. 'You've been good to me. I don't like to keep on . . .'

She paused, not knowing what to say.

'Are you . . . not well?' Rose asked tentatively. 'Are you pregnant?' was what she meant. Eva shook her head.

'It's not that. Though the Lord alone knows why. He uses me every night of the week, so why don't I get pregnant? Sometimes I think God has made me barren because I

151

wanted to lose that child. I get so afraid that I'd almost like to find myself expecting again.'

'Then what . . . ?'

Eva took a deep breath and suddenly the words rushed out.

'They're building some new houses Marton Green way. Council houses, to rent. They have three bedrooms and a bathroom, and a lavatory by the back door, one to each house. And a garden where you can grow things and the children can play. They say they have electric light, which is a bit frightening, but I daresay you could get used to it . . .' Her voice trailed off. She looked apprehensively at Rose. 'I've never slept in a bedroom since I was married,' she said. 'Just in the living room, me and the kids and him. I'd like to have a bedroom.'

She didn't add that she had never lived where there was a bathroom, or a lavatory not shared. There was nothing unusual about that.

'It sounds wonderful,' Rose said. 'Do you think, then, that you might get one of these houses?'

'That's just the trouble,' Eva said. 'There aren't enough. And some people have six children; we only have the two. They take notice of that. But if you was to put in a word . . . you know a lot of people . . . Oh, I wouldn't ask, Doctor Rose, I wouldn't trouble you, only I can't bear to go on living in Paradine Street for the rest of my life. If only we lived somewhere decent I'm sure Jim would be better! I'm sure he'd change!'

Fat chance, Rose thought. But presumably miracles could happen.

'I don't know what *I* could do, Eva,' she said. 'Has your husband been to the town hall?'

Eva's face shadowed.

'He says it's no good. He says you have to know someone.'

'He wouldn't thank *me* for interfering.'

'He wouldn't know it was you,' Eva said swiftly. 'If you was to put his case to the town hall . . . if someone was to come and see where we live. If only someone *saw* it, *smelt* it!'

Rose nodded. 'I agree. Though I can't imagine that the

Housing Committee doesn't know about Paradine Street.'

She knew, while she was speaking, whom she could ask. But from loyalty to Alex, from a true desire to make their marriage work, she never saw or spoke to John Worthing unless she had to. The only occasions she could not avoid were the meetings of the Committee of the now thriving Mothers' Holiday Fund, of which she had been a member for more than a year. Even there she kept a polite distance from him.

'I'll think about it, Eva,' she promised. 'I'm not sure what I can do. Could you afford the rent with Jim still out of work?'

'The rent is . . . what do you call it if the Council helps . . . if you're out of work?'

'Subsidised.'

'That's right. For a little while. And they say Marton Green is a lovely place. Right on the edge of Akersfield. Almost in the country. Ever so clean.'

'It's a long way from most jobs,' Rose pointed out.

Eva shrugged. 'What does that matter if you haven't got a job? All Jim has to do is to walk to the Labour Exchange. He has plenty of time to do that.'

'Well, I'll try to speak to someone,' Eva promised. 'But don't build on it, will you?'

Eva's face flushed with pleasure.

'I can't thank you enough, Doctor! I'm sure if you do it, it'll all turn out all right. And I hope everything goes well with the baby. I truly hadn't forgotten that.'

Rose, getting up to see Eva to the door, suddenly thought, 'My baby will be born today.' The doorbell clanged as she stood up. 'Ask whoever it is to come straight in, will you, Eva?'

Yes, though there was no sign of it yet, she was quite sure that the child would be born today.

Chapter Ten

Though at the moment her shape made driving uncomfortable, Rose drove herself home in the little two-seater which Alex had given her for a wedding present. It was the same car in which he had taken her up to Faverwell when Eva Denby was there. She had quickly learnt to drive and after two or three lessons from Alex drove herself everywhere, at what he complained was far too high a speed.

'Home' was now number fifteen, Beechcroft Road, not very far from Mrs Crabtree's. They had stayed with Mrs Crabtree for a few weeks after the wedding, until Alex had found the house in Beechcroft Road at a rent they could afford. Drawing up at the gate she saw, as always, Alex's other and most wonderful present. It was attached to the iron gate, a highly-polished rectangle of brass, the September sun glinting on the engraved letters which never failed to delight her. 'Dr Rose Bairstow, MB, ChB.'

Her afternoon surgery was due to start at two o-clock, though even now, nearly two years after she had put up her plate, it was still not certain that anyone would attend. She had a modest number of regular patients, almost all of them women and children, but while some days she waited in vain for a patient to ring her bell, she guessed that they were streaming into Doctor Henry Lewthwaite's surgery at the other end of the road. Only Doctor Patel, with his plate in the next road, would have fewer patients than she; but he was an Indian practitioner which was worse, even, than being a woman.

Since she could not afford to engage a locum for the period of her lying-in she would have liked to have made an arrangement with Doctor Patel to deal with her patients then, but she knew that there were those to whom he would not be acceptable. Reluctantly, she had asked Doctor Lewthwaite to help her out, and he had willingly agreed. How many patients, she wondered gloomily, might stay with him permanently?

Annie, the little maid-of-all-work, met her in the hall.

'There's a lady in the sitting-room, Doctor. She's just arrived.'

'Then will you tell her I'll be free in about ten minutes? And could you get me a quick cup of tea and a sandwich? I haven't eaten.'

'A cup of tea and a sandwich is no sort of meal,' Annie said disapprovingly. She prided herself on speaking her mind.

'I know,' Rose apologized. She often found herself apologizing to Annie. 'I'll have something more substantial later.'

She ate the sandwich and drank the tea quickly, then asked Annie to show in the patient. On the whole, the patients who made up her private practice were as predictable as those in Babcock Street, though the underlying causes of whatever ailed them were different. She did not deal here with women who lived in hovels, could not afford to eat properly, and had too many children. Her patients in Beechcroft Road were mostly middle class. More often than not she saw them in their homes, because that was how they liked it, especially if there were children to be treated. She sent them quarterly bills and hoped they would not make her wait too long for payment. It was this money, because Alex refused to take it for household bills, which paid for the rent of Babcock Street and also went towards paying off what remained of the debt to her father.

The patient Annie showed in was a new one. She was tall, slender to the point of thinness, expensively dressed in the new autumn shades of russet brown and forest green, with a fringe of pale gold hair showing beneath her velour hat. Rose judged her to be about her own age. As she sat down she peeled off immaculate beige kid gloves to reveal delicate hands, the manicured nails buffed and polished to a rosy pinkness. Rose pushed out of her mind the sudden memory of Eva Denby's swollen hands as she had stood before her this morning, twisting them in embarrassment. If the woman before her was ill, she had as much right to her help as any of the Babcock Street women.

'Good-afternoon, Doctor.' The woman's voice was low, well-modulated, would have been attractive but for a note of discontentment. 'My name is Gwen Mayfield. Mrs Gwen Mayfield.'

'Good-afternoon,' Rose said. 'What can I do for you?'

Mrs Mayfield sighed. 'I don't know that you can do anything. No-one else has. And now that I'm here I'm not sure why I bothered to come. Maybe I'm not ill. I only know I feel awful.'

It was not an unusual opening nor, as Rose skilfully persuaded the woman to talk, was her story an uncommon one. Mrs Mayfield was a widow, her husband, a Major in the West Yorkshire Regiment, having been killed in November nineteen-eighteen, less than a week before the war ended.

'He was killed at Amiens,' Mrs Mayfield said. 'The thing is, he should have been on leave. If he hadn't volunteered to put it off . . .'

She shrugged. There was no hint of self-pity in her. It was just one of those things.

'Have you any children?' Rose asked.

'No. We'd been married only a few months. I suppose we would have had children later.'

And maybe you wouldn't have been sitting here now, Rose thought. You'd have been enjoying a full life, too busy to include me. She suspected that she was not the first doctor this patient had been to. Women like Mrs Mayfield, with time and money to spare, went the rounds.

When Rose had asked all the questions, she examined Mrs Mayfield. She could find nothing wrong with her except that she was far too thin, her lace-trimmed, *crepe-de-chine* underwear hanging loosely on her.

'Have you been losing weight?'

'Oh yes, I've tried to. One can't look at all decent nowadays if one is fat. I've been banting.'

It was really too stupid. Her Babcock Street patients were emaciated because they couldn't afford food, while in her home surgery she was constantly up against patients who starved themselves in pursuit of the breastless, hipless, boyish figure which was currently fashionable.

'That won't do,' Rose said firmly. 'That way you'll continue to be listless, tired, not able to sleep or concentrate.'

'I hope you're not going to lecture me, Doctor,' Mrs Mayfield said. 'I'd hoped you'd simply give me some magic tonic, or a bottle of pills . . .' She made languid gestures with her hands, as if conjuring something out of the air.

'I shan't give you anything of the kind,' Rose said. 'I believe you when you say you feel awful, but the remedy's in your own hands. You must eat properly and, in my opinion, you should try to find something interesting to do with your life. That's where your cure is.'

The woman was suffering from acute boredom, Rose reckoned, which brought depression in its wake. But she would not thank her for saying so.

'There *isn't* anything interesting,' Mrs Mayfield said. 'All these interminable tea parties, charity concerts. It's so tedious. I've practically stopped going to anything.'

'You don't think of taking a job?' Rose asked.

Mrs Mayfield stared at her.

'Take a job? What in the world could I do? I'm not trained for anything. I'm a married woman . . . well, I was. I don't actually *know* anyone who goes out to work. Except of course . . . well, you're different, aren't you? And then there are clerks and shopgirls. You don't mean that, surely?'

'No,' Rose said. She couldn't imagine it. Besides, there were not enough of those jobs for the people who really needed them. 'What about voluntary work?'

'You mean . . . flag days? Or visiting old ladies?' She sounded doubtful.

'Something more demanding,' Rose suggested. 'More regular.'

'Like what?'

'On the spur of the moment I'm not sure,' Rose admitted. 'But there must be something. For instance, I've just recently formed a Club for working-class mothers. Somewhere where they'll meet and talk, learn how to cook nourishing meals out of next to nothing, how to sew, how to look after their children's health. That sort of thing.'

How terribly dull she made it sound! How worthy! It was not at all how she intended it to be.

Mrs Mayfield looked at her in astonishment.

'I could never do that! I can't boil an egg!'

'You wouldn't need to. We can get experts to do all that.

What we need is a person of intelligence to organize it, to contact speakers, look after the accounts.'

She felt quite sure that underneath her airy manner Mrs Mayfield was intelligent. At the moment what she lacked was drive and purpose.

'Anyway, you could teach them how to look nice, how to make the best of themselves. I think that's important.'

For the first time since she had walked into the room a glimmer of interest showed in Mrs Mayfield's face. 'I daresay I could,' she said thoughtfully.

'Well, there it is, Mrs Mayfield,' Rose said. 'I'm by no means suggesting that this particular job is for you. I don't know you well enough for that. But think along those lines; start to eat properly and find an interest in life. And don't think that I don't sympathize with you, because I do. But no-one else can do these things for you.'

Mrs Mayfield stood up, drew on her gloves, smoothing down each finger. 'I'll think about it,' she said. 'Well, he said you'd sort me out, and you did!'

'He?'

'John Worthing. Councillor John Worthing. Didn't I tell you it was he who suggested I should come to you?'

The questions raced around in Rose's mind. What was Mrs Mayfield to John Worthing? Was she one of his reputedly many women? Perhaps a special one? She was a young widow, undeniably attractive. But he would not, could not be so cruel as to flaunt her if that was the case. He was simply sending her a patient because he thought she needed them. It was nothing more.

'No, you didn't say.'

'I thought I had,' Mrs Mayfield said. 'He spoke highly of you.'

'Thank you.'

Rose showed her to the door.

'When are you having your baby?' Mrs Mayfield asked.

'Today,' Rose said firmly. 'I'm having it today.'

As Mrs Mayfield was about to leave, Alex came in, almost bumping into them in the small hall. The three of them stood there, so that Rose had to make polite introductions. She was taken by the quick interest in Alex's face as Mrs Mayfield held out her hand to him. A pang of jealousy like a small pain shot through her, but the jealousy was not to do with Alex. If this woman has an effect on Alex, who is not susceptible, a cold voice inside her asked, what does she do to John Worthing?

'I'll see you again, Doctor,' Mrs Mayfield said.

As Rose closed the door on her she wondered which was preferable, that she should not set eyes on Mrs Mayfield again, or that she should know where she was, what she was doing? In any case, the choice was not hers to make.

'I have to go out again,' Alex said, following Rose into the sitting room. 'An editorial meeting.'

She was used to that. They spent more time apart than together, but because she was fully occupied with her work she did not mind.

'Alex,' she said. 'Do you know anything about new Council houses being built at Marton Green?'

'Yes. They've started on them. Why do you ask?'

'Eva Denby came in today. She's desperate to get one. It certainly would be a new life for her if she could.'

'She'd still have Jim Denby,' Alex said. 'Strange, though, how he's kept out of trouble these last two or three years. It must be his longest clear run since he was in Borstal, aged fifteen.'

'Do we know anyone? Eva's quite right in thinking it's who you know that counts.'

'Well I can't do anything,' Alex said. 'Not in my position.'

'Ah yes! I keep forgetting how high the editor sits above we ordinary mortals,' Rose said.

A fleeting look of annoyance crossed Alex's face. He sometimes wondered if Rose took his position seriously.

'Ask John Worthing,' he suggested. 'You're bound to be seeing him at the Holiday Fund meeting.'

'Perhaps I will.' Alex had echoed her own earlier thoughts. She had no wish to ask a favour of John Worthing, but Eva needed all the help she could get.

'Try not to be too late. And don't drink too much,' she said to Alex. 'I'm having the baby today.'

He looked at her in surprise. 'Or the next day or the next. How can you know?'

'I just do,' Rose said. 'I feel it in my bones.'

'I'll be back as soon as I can,' he promised. 'But you know how these things go on.'

She was sitting quietly by the first fire of the autumn, skilfully darning the toes of her silk stockings. She watched the coal glow and spark and the flames lick against the fire back. And as the flames leapt, suddenly the pain leapt in her body; sharp, insistent, consuming.

When her daughter was born, a few minutes before midnight, Alex was not yet home. She was glad that he was not, for in the hours of her labour, at the times when the pain had been the greatest, it was not Alex she had wanted to hold her hand, to give her comfort; it was not his name she had wanted to cry out. She had been unfaithful to him even in the fact of giving birth to his child.

When he did come, she by this time lying tidily in bed, the baby in its crib by her bedside, she saw that he had been drinking – and knew that it was because here was the situation he could not face. The child in the cot was the living reminder of that night nine months ago. The torment was in his eyes as he forced himself to look at his daughter. Would he be reminded every time he saw her? Rose wondered. And what would it do to the child?

As Alex bent to kiss Rose, his breath smelling of whisky, they were two people racked by their differing shame, crying out to each other, though not aloud, for forgiveness.

Rose lay flat on her back in bed, her abdomen tightly bound. She had been ordered to stay in this position by Nurse Dobson, who at this moment was tiptoeing around the bedroom in the most irritating fashion. She steadfastly refused to let Rose sit up, except on necessary occasions like feeding the baby, or washing her own hands and face in the enamelled bowl set on the bed table.

'At all other times, Doctor, you must lie flat!' Nurse said. 'I'm sure you know that as well as I do. We want everything to go back into place, don't we? And we don't want to lose our figure!'

Rose sighed. 'It's so difficult to read, lying down like this. Especially the newspaper.'

'But we shouldn't be reading, should we?' Nurse Dobson

said brightly. 'We should be having a little nap, building up our strength. And concentrating on *pleasant* thoughts when we're making milk for our baby! Not strikes and politics and murders which, with all due respect to your husband, is all we get in the newspapers these days.'

'Sometimes my husband complains that there isn't enough news,' Rose said. 'A nice juicy murder is meat and drink to the *Record*. Better still if it's a local one.'

Nurse Dobson tut-tutted her disapproval. 'I blame the war for all this unrest. Nothing's been the same since. Except babies, of course!' Her expression lightened as she surveyed the sleeping infant.

'What a little darling she is! Is she going to have her mother's red hair, I wonder? Of course it's usually dark when they're born.'

'Can't I hold her?' Rose pleaded. 'Just for a few minutes?' She longed to cradle her daughter in her arms, to examine yet again the tiny hands and feet, the rosebud mouth, the miracle of the pearl-like fingernails, each one perfect.

Nurse Dobson looked shocked.

'My dear Doctor, we can't have that! There's at least an hour to go before it's time for you to hold her. We must keep to the routine. Babies know, you know!'

Does my daughter know that I long to cuddle her? Rose wondered. **Does she know that she's the most beautiful, the most wonderful, the most loved . . . ?**

'We must begin as we mean to go on,' Nurse Dobson said firmly. 'As a doctor you must know that.'

Little did Nurse Dobson know that this was not how Rose meant to go on. She could hardly wait for the nurse to depart, which she was to do at the end of a fortnight instead of the usual month because Rose had flatly refused to keep a nurse for so long. When the child was a little older she knew she might have to hire some help to look after her, but for now, and for as long as she could, she intended to keep her daughter close. When she went back to the Babcock Street surgery she meant to take the baby with her. It would lie there in a Moses basket while she attended to her patients. She had it all worked out.

'Now I'm going to leave you,' Nurse Dobson said. 'You're to be a good girl and lie still and try to sleep.'

When the nurse had left the room Rose raised herself on one elbow and began to read the *Record*. The woman was quite right, of course. It *was* full of politics and crime: the likelihood of another General Election, the threat (as the *Record* saw it) of the Labour Party, the utterances of Trade Union leaders, the fear of the new Russia. A jeweller in Bradford had been robbed; an Akersfield woman had been knocked down by a car travelling at the disgraceful speed of forty miles an hour.

She turned the page and learned that skirts and hair were even shorter and that Oxford undergraduates were wearing trousers measuring as much as thirty-two inches around the bottom of the legs. Also that a greengrocery chain was selling a rabbit, plus four potatoes, two carrots and an onion, for tenpence. 'Ways with Rabbits' might be a good subject for the Mothers' Club.

She almost missed the 'Letters to the Editor' - she was uncomfortable in this half-sitting posture and afraid that Nurse Dobson might return at any minute - until her own name leapt out at her from the page.

'It is with pleasure that all readers of the *Record*,' (she read) 'will wish to congratulate the editor and his wife, Doctor Rose Bairstow, on the recent birth of their daughter. It is good to know that Doctor Rose does not follow the advice she so freely hands out on "How Not to have Babies". May we hope that, having now experienced the delights of motherhood herself, we shall hear no more of the opinions which are a threat to family life and abhorrent to all decent people.'

She sat bolt upright, flinging the newspaper to the floor - then went dizzy and had to lie down again. The effrontery of people! The letter was signed M. B. Taylor, so there was no telling whether it was from a man or a woman. But it was not, by a long way, the first brickbat she had received, and as her dizziness passed, so did the sharp edge of her fury. At Babcock Street, and occasionally here in her own home, she had a steady stream of abusive letters, some signed, many anonymous; many of them grounds for libel if she had

162

chosen to go so far. 'Destroyer of homes', 'Dirty beast', 'Disgrace to Womanhood', 'Purveyor of Filth,' were among the milder epithets which had been hurled at her. At first she had been shaken by so much animosity but now, on a personal level, it did no more than niggle her. What surprised her most was that there was always a fair sprinkling of letters from women.

It did not surprise her in the least that Alex had allowed the publication of this latest letter. He could well have suppressed it but he would have thought that quite wrong, even though the subject of the abuse was his own wife. It had not taken her long to learn that he was an editor first and a husband second. Well, now she would approach him as an editor and he would have to publish her reply.

Nurse Dobson came back into the room. She stood by the bed, straightening the counterpane, mitreing the corners, tucking it in tightly at the foot.

'There now, have we had a nice little sleep?' she asked. Not waiting for a reply, she picked up the newspaper, re-folded it, and put it on a table. 'We just have time for a lovely bed bath and a nice beaker of Benger's Food before it's time to feed baby!'

'I don't want a bed bath,' Rose said. 'I want a pencil and a sheet of writing paper.'

Nurse Dobson looked at Rose in shocked disbelief. She was not an easy patient, but then doctors never were, and being a lady doctor she was worse. But this was too much - unless it was the onset of puerperal fever!

'A pencil and paper,' Rose repeated, sitting upright. 'I'll have my bed bath some other time. Better still, I'll get up and have a proper bath. Right now I have to write an important letter.'

Nurse Dobson was bereft of speech. She did what her training told her to do, which was to advance on Rose, push a thermometer in her mouth, take hold of her by the wrist and, consulting the watch which hung from her starched bosom, take her patient's pulse.

Rose removed the thermometer from her mouth and handed it back. 'I don't have a temperature, Nurse. I'm perfectly well. Now if you don't fetch me a pencil and paper I shall get up and find them for myself!'

Nurse Dobson knew the answer to that. Keep the patient calm, keep her in bed. Without another word she left the room, and returned five minutes later with pencil and paper.

Alex came home earlier than usual. He greeted Rose, and then bent over the cot, gently touching the baby's cheek with one finger. Rose could not conceal her surprise. It was the first sign of interest he had shown in the child.

'I intend to try, Rose,' he said quietly, answering the question on her face.

Rose put out her hand and touched him. 'I'm glad, Alex. She needs a father as well as a mother. She's just going to be bathed. Stay and watch.'

Annie had built up the bedroom fire for Nurse Dobson until the room was like a hothouse. Nurse had allowed her to bring in jugs of hot and cold water, though she herself mixed the contents in the baby's bath, testing the temperature with her elbow.

'That will be all, Annie,' she said. She suffered the presence of mothers and fathers because that was the cross she had to bear, but little maidservants were another matter.

'You can stay and see her bathed if you want to,' Rose said, seeing Annie's disappointed face.

Alex sat beside the fire, silently watching Nurse Dobson's ministrations. From the bed, Rose tried to see the expression on his face, but his back was to her and he did not turn around.

When the baby was clean and fresh again, liberally sprinkled with talcum powder on what Nurse Dobson referred to as 'all her little parts', tightly bandaged around the abdomen in a clean binder and swathed in a long flannel petticoat and a nightie, with a matinee coat on top, Nurse Dobson handed her to Rose.

It was the moment Rose had been waiting for. She wanted to hold the child close, crush her in an embrace, never let her go. It might be true that her baby needed a father, but not just now, not at this moment. Now she's mine, Rose exulted. She's all mine!

'Have you decided what we're going to call her,' Alex

asked, coming over to the bed, reminding Rose of his presence. 'Is it to be Heather or Jenny?'

'Jenny, I think. It has a warm sound.'

'I agree.'

Rose unfastened the front of her nightgown, eased out a breast swollen and veined with milk, and offered it to the baby. It was accepted greedily. It was, Rose thought, watching the baby suckle, the most exquisite sensation she had ever known. Alex, bending over the two of them, reached up a hand and tentatively touched Rose's breast. She tried not to flinch. She wanted to be alone with the baby.

'I have to go back to work,' Alex said.

'Before you go, there's something I want you to read,' Rose told him. 'Only not just now.' She wanted nothing to interfere with this moment.

'We're going to banish Daddy now!' Nurse Dobson said playfully. 'Only Mummies and Babies allowed at feed times!'

An hour later Alex returned to the bedroom. Rose handed him the letter she had pencilled. When he came to the end, he handed it back to her.

'I can't publish it, of course.'

'Not publish it? Whyever not?'

'You know perfectly well why not.'

'You published the one today. I understand why you did even if I don't agree with you. In a way, I suppose I don't mind. It's all publicity. But why can't I reply to it?'

'Because you're my wife,' Alex said. 'I would be abusing my position if I let my own wife have the last word. I'm sorry.'

'Your position?' Rose cried. She was incensed by the steady reasonableness of his tone. 'Do you ever think of anything except your position? What about my position?'

'You knew what you were letting yourself in for when you started all this. I don't mind that if it's what you want to do - I never did. I don't even mind the publicity . . .'

'It's all news, I suppose!'

'Quite.' He seemed unaware of her sarcasm. 'But I can't publish my wife's letters on so controversial a subject. It would smack of favouritism.'

'So I'm to go undefended? Is that it? The Royal Family and the wives of newspaper editors must never answer back?'

'Someone else might write in your defence,' Alex said. 'If they do I'll publish it.'

'Pigs might fly!' Rose said scornfully. 'The people who would defend me hardly know how to write. If they could they'd tell you I don't threaten family life. I try to improve it. I don't persuade women not to have babies. I teach them how to have them at reasonable intervals, not to have more than they can cope with – for the sake of the baby as well as the mother. And I don't work for wives against husbands. I try to make things better for both of them. I thank God every time – rare though it is – that a man comes with his wife to my surgery . . .'

'All right,' Alex said. 'Calm down!'

'I will not calm down,' Rose cried. 'These people know what I'm trying to do! How is it the so-called better classes can't understand? Everyone knows that the middle classes practise birth control, one way or another, so why do they want to deny it to the poor, who have far more need of it?'

She was suddenly weak and shaking, all her strength gone. Why did she always have to fight for things? Nothing came easily. It was not fair. It was not fair! She burst into noisy tears, which immediately brought Nurse Dobson from where she lurked on the other side of the bedroom door.

'Dear me, dear me, we can't have this!' she cried. 'We'll turn our milk sour, and then where will poor baby be? I knew all this activity would end in tears! Mr Bairstow, call me interfering if you will, but I really must ask you not to upset my patient like this!'

Rose lifted her head, accepted the handkerchief Alex offered her to dry her eyes. 'Don't blame my husband, Nurse,' she said wearily. 'It's my own fault. I shouldn't have got so worked up.'

'Indeed you should not!' Nurse Dobson straightened the counterpane, shook up Rose's pillow, and shooed Alex from the room.

At the end of a fortnight Rose parted thankfully from Nurse Dobson. She felt guilty that she was so pleased to see her go. The woman was a good nurse and had done her duty as she saw it. Because of her guilt, Rose gave her a large box of expensive chocolates and two pairs of fine silk stockings on top of her fee.

Tomorrow she would open her surgery here, and in a week or two's time, perhaps sooner, she would be back in Babcock Street.

Chapter Eleven

Rose glanced around the sitting-room, checking that everything was in order; chairs more or less in a circle, ashtrays to hand. It was the afternoon of the Mothers' Holiday Fund Committee meeting and it had been agreed, in view of Rose's present circumstances, to hold it here. She turned to speak to Annie, who came into the room carrying a vase of bronze chrysanthemums.

'Put them on the small table there, I think.'

'Right-ho, Doctor,' Annie said.

'Jenny went straight to sleep after her two-o-clock feed. With luck there won't be a sound from her for two or three hours. But if she should cry you'll go to her, won't you?'

'She'll be all right with me, the little pet,' Annie promised. 'Don't you worry!'

Rose viewed herself in the mirror over the mantelpiece and wondered if the members of the Committee would see any difference in her. Physically she looked well now. She had benefited from the enforced rest and her hair, which had not been at its best when she was pregnant, had regained its bounce and bright colour. She was as slender as ever, except that her breasts were rounder and fuller, which was an improvement.

It was the way she felt which was so different. Since Jenny's birth everything in life seemed bigger, brighter, more significant. Far from being discouraged about her work in Babcock Street, as she had momentarily been on the evening of that silly outburst, she felt more than ever fitted for it and knew that nothing, least of all stupid letters in the *Record*, would stand in her way.

She wished that her marriage ran as well as her job. She and Alex, though now amiable enough on the surface, seemed to have less and less to say to each other. His interest in the baby seemed already to have abated, though in any case Jenny was usually asleep long before he arrived home. If he was around when she was having her late evening feed he would glance at her, perhaps touch her on the cheek. That was the sum of his physical contact with her. He never picked her up, never held her.

'I'll ring for tea at about a quarter-to-four,' she said to Annie. 'There'll be seven of us.'

'I know,' Annie said. 'You told me.'

So she had. Everything was catered for. There was no reason at all for the nervousness she was feeling. So she told herself, but it was not true. She was apprehensive about meeting John Worthing, whom she had not seen for so long, he having missed the last meeting. Would he find her different? It should not matter, but it did, and she faced the fact that it always would. Though nothing could ever come of it, she wanted always to be desirable in his sight.

Rose answered the ring at the door herself. Miss Nesfield, matron of a home for unmarried mothers and, with Rose, one of the two women on the Committee, stood on the doorstep with the Reverend Thomas Francis, a Wesleyan minister and Chairman of the Committee. Behind them, inches taller, stood John Worthing. His eyes, serious, lacking their usual glint of humour, met and held Rose's until her attention was claimed by the Reverend Francis.

'Councillor Worthing kindly gave us a lift,' he said. 'Such a help!'

Before they were in the house the other members arrived, with the punctuality of busy people. The Reverend Francis settled himself in the most comfortable chair and made a start.

'The main business this afternoon, as we all know, is to decide where we shall have our second holiday home. We have two proposals. One is that we should use the money we've accumulated, plus the substantial sum we inherited under the will of the late Mrs Sebastian Preston, to enlarge our existing home in Ilkley; the other is that we should acquire a house at the seaside – Blackpool has been mentioned. If, as we said at the previous meeting, we want to open the house next Spring, then we must make our decision today.'

'I've brought details of one or two properties in Blackpool,' one of the members said. 'Good, sound places; not too expensive.'

'We're fortunate in having an estate agent on our

committee,' the Reverend Francis said. 'Thank you, Mr Mortimer. But perhaps we should decide in principle where we're to go - Ilkley or Blackpool - before we begin to look at properties.'

That, as Rose and everyone present knew, was the bone of contention.

'I vote for Blackpool every time,' she said decisively. 'Nothing against our house in Ilkley, but Blackpool would be such fun for the mothers. It's lively - always something happening.'

'Too lively by half!' one of the men said. 'And is fun the object of our exercise? Remember that these ladies would be in Blackpool without their husbands.'

'These are grown women you're talking about, Mr Barber,' Miss Nesfield interrupted. 'I'm sure they're capable of conducting themselves properly.'

'Capable, ay - but will they?' Mr Barber questioned. 'If I may be so bold, I'd remind you that yon place you're running is for women who've failed to do just that. We don't want to go looking for trouble, do we?'

Miss Nesfield turned on him sharply. 'And may I remind you, Mr Barber, that none of my girls would be where she is now but for the connivance of some man! Immaculate conception does not take place in Akersfield!'

'Ladies! Gentlemen!' the Reverend Francis pleaded.

John Worthing had so far taken no part in the proceedings. He seemed preoccupied, distant. But when he looked up and spoke now the others stopped to listen. It was always the same. He was a man who compelled attention.

'I agree with Matron. Our purpose is to give these women a much needed holiday, not to be public guardians of their morals. Freedom to enjoy oneself is surely part of a good holiday. So the point is, where would they do that most? Come to think of it, anyone who has a mind to do so could go astray in either Blackpool *or* Ilkley!'

'Ilkley is a very healthy place,' one member ventured.

'So is Blackpool,' Miss Nesfield countered. 'I feel better the minute I get off the train there.'

Rose looked across at Miss Nesfield with interest. She had not thought of her as a devotee of Blackpool. A quiet holiday in Filey, even two weeks in Torquay, but not Blackpool. What did she do there? Did she go on the Big Wheel, or dance the night away in the Tower ballroom? But then she remembered that Miss Nesfield had nursed abroad through four years of war, serving in the thick of danger. Blackpool would hold no terrors for her.

'Well, we must put it to the vote,' the Reverend Francis said eventually.

Three were for Blackpool, three for Ilkley. 'So I must use my casting vote,' he said.

To Rose's amazement he said, 'I choose Blackpool. And now we must appoint a sub-committee who will undertake to visit some properties there.'

John Worthing, Miss Nesfield and Mr Barber, the latter presumably to hold the other two in check, were appointed. 'Perhaps Doctor Rose?' someone said. Rose looked at John Worthing, read the invitation in his eyes.

'I can't,' she said quickly. 'I'm feeding my baby. I can't be away from home for so long.'

She longed to go, to be with him for an entire day, even though in the presence of other people. But she knew it was just as well that she could not.

When the meeting was over and they were ready to leave, Rose said to John, 'Could I see you for a few minutes? There's something I want to ask you about.'

He waited behind when she showed the others to the door. When she came back into the sitting room he was standing with his back to her, looking into the fire. She doubted that he had heard her come into the room. Seeing him so, she had this deep longing to go to him, to touch and stroke the back of his neck where his dark hair, always worn a little longer than was the fashion, curled over the edge of his stiff white collar. If she could do only that, she told herself, it would be enough. She would be content. Only let her touch him.

Suddenly aware of her, he turned, and caught the longing in her face before she could hide it from him. He moved quickly towards her and took her in his arms, his lips seeking hers. There was no resistance in her and the lips she offered him were as eager as his own. How had she borne to be without him all these months? How could she ever bear it again? She stretched up her hand to touch and caress the back of his neck and his hands began to move over her body, caressing, demanding. Hunger for him rose strongly in her and she found herself responding fervently to his touch. She felt lost, as if she was moving through a dream and had no power to direct herself. And then, as he made a movement to manoeuvre her on to the sofa, she all at once came to, with a sharp, painful awakening from the dream.

She wanted immediately to return to that dream world. She resented whatever strong power had called her from it. She told herself she had heard her baby cry, but it was not true. What had brought her back was that censor in her mind which would not allow her to assuage her body's needs. With Alex she could not do so because she could think only of John Worthing. With John her sense of duty – to her husband, her child, her profession – rose up like a great barrier between them. It was impossible to give herself to either man, though the longing was there, deep and strong.

With all the resolve she could muster she tried to push John away from her, to escape from his arms.

'John, we mustn't.' It sounded childish.

He held her fast. 'Why mustn't we?'

'You know why not.'

'If you don't want me to touch you,' he said, 'you must not look at me in the way you did. How do you expect me to resist you?'

'I do want you to,' she said softly. 'To touch me. You know that, John. I don't deny it.'

He held her at arm's length now, but not letting her go; looking into her face as if he had found magic in it.

'I wouldn't believe you if you did, my love. Your body tells a different story. But do you know that it's the first time you've admitted it?'

'I do know,' Rose said. 'I'm never going to deny it again. Even so it has to stop.'

'You can't stop it,' he said. 'Any more than you can stop the sun rising each morning.'

'I can't stop the feelings,' she admitted. 'I can only refuse to act on them.'

'Such a controlled lady!' There was an edge of sarcasm in

his voice which was more than Rose could bear.

'I'm not!' she blazed. 'I'm not! I don't want to be controlled, cool, contained! My blood runs as fast and as warm as yours. I want everything you want, and as desperately. Can't you see that? Can't you understand? I just have to accept that it's impossible. It's not only because I'm married - though that counts a great deal. There's more to it than that. If I weren't . . .'

'If you weren't a doctor,' he interrupted. 'I know.'

'It's difficult to explain. It's something I chose, it's part of me. Aside from those laid down for me, I set my own standards. However priggish it sounds, they don't include adultery; especially deliberately entered into, and repeated; made a way of life as ours would grow to be; a life hedged about with petty deceptions. But my feelings are real enough, John. I'm not some efficient machine. Please try to understand.'

He looked at her bleakly, let her go, almost pushing her away from him. She was trembling so that she could hardly stand. She sat down on the sofa, knowing that now he would not sit beside her.

'I try,' he said. 'Perhaps I can understand, but I can't accept. I can't live up to your standards, Rose. It's not in me.'

But you have standards, she thought. You can't leave a wife whom you think needs you. But now, even if he would, it was too late for her. She had Alex and Jenny. She wondered if, in the last few minutes, she had finally lost John Worthing.

In the silence between them he lit a cigar, making a small ceremony out of lighting it, as if to mark a change of mood. His hands, holding the flame to the tobacco, were steady, while her own hands still trembled. He puffed the aromatic smoke into the air and spoke to her as if the last few minutes had not happened.

'What did you want to see me about?'

Rose caught her breath. How could he be so cool, so calm on the instant, while her own feelings were in a ferment? She wanted to strike him, to knock the cigar from his fingers. For a moment she almost hated him for his swift change of mood, and then hated herself because she could not be so quickly dispassionate.

'The Denbys,' she said, trying to pull herself together. 'Eva Denby says that the Council is building new houses at Marton Green. She feels - and I must say I agree with her - that if only they could get out of Paradine Street, live somewhere decent, it might change their lives. You're on the Housing Committee aren't you? I wondered if you could help?'

'Has the husband applied for a house?'

'No. He thinks it's hopeless unless you know someone with influence.'

He looked stern, concentrated on the problem. The man who had taken her in his arms only minutes ago had vanished. But it was part of the fascination this man had for her, that there were so many facets to his character. He was unpredictable, volatile; it was his intrinsic challenge which made her feel that she - she alone - could be the one to tame him.

'Tell Mrs Denby that she must get her husband to go down to the town hall and make an application,' he said. 'After that I'll do what I can. It might help if you, as a doctor, backed up Mrs Denby's case.'

'I can do that with the utmost conviction. Whether Jim Denby will like it is another matter. I'm not especially keen to tangle with him again. By the way,' she said, remembering, 'I saw a patient recommended by you a couple of weeks ago.'

'Gwen Mayfield? Yes, she told me she'd seen you.'

So did they see each other often? Rose wondered. She felt a small, sharp prick of jealousy.

'She mentioned some idea of helping you with your Mothers' Club,' John said.

'We did discuss it briefly,' Rose agreed. 'Would she be any good, do you think? Nothing against Mrs Mayfield, of course, but my mothers are important. I want the best for them.'

'Gwen would be quite good, I reckon. She's intelligent, warm-hearted, understanding under that brittle surface.'

'You sound enthusiastic,' Rose said.

John Worthing gave her a quizzical look.

'I am. All that's wrong with Gwen is that over the last

year or two she's had too little to do and too much time to think. You'd be doing her – and your mothers – a favour if you took her on.'

Do I want to do her a favour? Rose asked herself. Out loud she said, 'Well I'll think about it.'

She saw him to the door, watched him as he walked swiftly down the path and got into his car. She stood there watching until he was out of sight.

The Babcock Street surgery was in full swing again. Rose pressed the buzzer for the next patient to enter.

'Hello, Mrs Palmer,' she said to the woman who came in. 'How are you?'

Mrs Palmer was a regular. She came with her shilling – sometimes it was only sixpence – hoping that the hard-won coin would somehow buy from the doctor a solution to her troubles. She was one of several who came with the same idea. Rose knew well enough that she had no answer to the ordeal of lasting unemployment, to the burden of bringing up large families on a meagre dole, in squalid surroundings. It seemed beyond the reach even of politicians and governments to do anything about it. They had laid upon the local councils the responsibility of building houses to rent, but little had been done so far. As for jobs, there seemed no prospect of any improvement, ever.

'Is your husband still out of work?' Rose asked. She was examining Mrs Palmer carefully, sounding her heart, listening to her lungs. She needed to do none of this to know that what her patient needed was some good food, a decent place to live, a lightening of her worries; but she knew that by the act of examining Mrs Palmer she was assuring her that someone was taking notice.

'Three years since he had a job,' Mrs Palmer said. 'I reckon them politicians down in London have forgotten we exist up here! They have it easy down there. But they didn't forget when they wanted them for the war, did they?'

'You're a bit congested,' Rose said. 'I'll give you a bottle of medicine, and see you take it!' She was convinced that many of her patients came for a talk, rather than for the medicine, and who was to say which did most good? 'You can get dressed now,' she said.

175

'You remember that Lord Kitchener pointing his finger from the posters?' Mrs Palmer said. '"Your Country Needs You!" Young kids like my brother rushing to join the Bradford Pals, pretending they was eighteen!'

Rose knew that Mrs Palmer's brother had been killed on the Somme on the warm July day which was his seventeenth birthday.

Mrs Palmer fastened her blouse, put on her jacket.

'It was as well a lot of 'em didn't come back,' she said bitterly. 'There'd have been nowt for 'em. Thirty men after every job as it is.'

She opened her purse, scanned the contents with anxious blue eyes. 'Will sixpence do this time, Doctor? I'm a bit short this week. I'll pay you when things are better.'

'Sixpence will be fine,' Rose said.

At least, she thought, as Mrs Palmer left, she hasn't got pregnant again. At least that was something she'd been able to do for her. A sixth child would have made life impossible.

Most of that morning's patients were regulars, from the surrounding streets, their problems pitifully similar to Mrs Palmer's, but there were a couple of women from further afield who had heard that Doctor Rose Bairstow would give them birth control advice which their own doctors denied them. It was with grim satisfaction that Rose heard one of them say, 'I read about you in the *Record*, when your baby was born. I didn't agree with the letter.'

When Rose thought she had seen the last of her patients there was a knock at the door and Gwen Mayfield entered.

'Why, Mrs Mayfield, I didn't expect to see you here!' Rose said. 'How is it you didn't go to my home surgery? Not that you're not welcome here, but . . .'

'But I'm out of place,' Mrs Mayfield finished the sentence for her. 'I came out of curiosity. I wanted to see what your mothers were like.'

Rose lifted her chin, looked hard at Gwen Mayfield. She would not have her patients patronized by this young woman.

'They're women, like you and me,' she said coldly. 'Down on their luck, most of them, but like you and me inside.'

'Sisters under the skin?'

'Something like that,' Rose agreed. 'I'm not sure that I

could cope as well as they do in the same circumstances. I don't know about you.'

'I'm sure I couldn't,' Mrs Mayfield said. 'I really didn't mean to be uppity, you know. I came because I've been thinking over what you said about your Mothers' Club. In short, I'd like to help if you'll have me, if you think I'd be any good. I was nervous about the women, about whether I'd be acceptable – to them as well as to you. But I've listened to them in the waiting room this morning, even talked to one or two. I think perhaps I could be, given a chance.'

In spite of herself, Rose liked Gwen Mayfield. And why in spite of myself? she thought. All she really had against the woman was that she came *via* John Worthing, that she presumably enjoyed his friendship. I'm jealous, Rose admitted to herself.

'I'm sure you could be,' she said. 'I think you could be a great help. Could you possibly come around to my home – would next Monday evening suit you? We could talk about it in detail then. We're going to my home village for our baby's christening at the weekend and I'm going to be a bit busy until then.'

As if on cue Jenny, in her basket in the corner of the room, began to cry.

'Goodness!' Mrs Mayfield exclaimed. 'I hadn't even noticed she was there! Is she always so quiet?'

Rose, picking up the baby, holding her close, laughed. 'Not always. She's pretty good, though. She doesn't always sleep; sometimes she just gurgles – don't you my precious?' She looked down with love on the downy top of Jenny's head, where the dark hair was already showing red glints.

'What do your patients think, seeing a baby in the surgery?' Gwen Mayfield asked.

'I think they rather like it. But my husband doesn't,' Rose said.

Alex had protested about it from the first. 'I don't want my daughter spending her time in Babcock Street,' he'd said. He didn't usually say 'my daughter', Rose thought. He must feel quite strongly about the situation.

'It's not suitable,' he objected. 'She could pick up anything.'

'Not in my surgery she couldn't!' Rose said. 'And you'd better not let Mrs Foster hear you say that! She keeps the place as clean as an operating theatre. Anyway, do you suppose I'd take Jenny there if I thought she'd come to any harm?'

'In spite of all you said beforehand, I'd hoped you'd ease off work a bit when you had the baby,' Alex said.

'But Alex, you must have known I wouldn't,' Rose said. 'I never gave you to think otherwise.'

'We could stretch to having a nursemaid,' Alex persisted. 'A girl to look after her here, at least on the days you were in Babcock Street.'

'But I don't want that,' Rose said. 'Don't you understand, I want to look after her myself. I'm just lucky that my job allows me to do that.'

'I met your husband in Akersfield,' Gwen Mayfield was saying. 'We literally bumped into each other in Market Street. I wasn't looking where I was going. He took me for a cup of tea. But I expect he told you.'

He hadn't. But no matter, Rose thought. He had no doubt forgotten all about it.

'I must get home now,' Rose said. 'Can I drop you anywhere?'

'No, thanks. I thought I might walk around here a bit. Get the lie of the land.'

'You won't like it,' Rose warned her. 'Still, it's a good idea. I'll see you next Monday evening then. Shall we say about eight o-clock?'

Within the hour, spent mostly in attending to Jenny's needs, Rose was ready for the first patient in her home surgery. In spite of her fears, most of her private patients had come back to her. In addition Dr Lewthwaite, because of her knowledge of birth control, had sent her a few new ones from his own practice. 'You know as well as I do that we were taught nothing of it in Medical School,' he'd said. 'And I think I'm too old now to enter the fray. But I approve of what you're doing, young lady, and I sympathize with your struggle. More power to your elbow!'

She had been heartened by Doctor Lewthwaite's words as she had not been by anything else in ages. It would be a long time before women could go to their physician, or to a clinic, and receive expert advice, but in the old doctor's attitude she read the signs that one day it would happen. It would be part of everyday life. She did not consider herself an expert, far from it, but she studied whatever was available and she had not hesitated to turn for advice to Doctor Marie Stopes, that much villified and maligned expert on birth control. Though Rose had never met her, Doctor Stopes had always been helpful and encouraging in correspondence.

Jenny was now six weeks old and Rose was looking forward to the weekend in Faverwell and the baby's baptism in the church there. Mrs Stanton had paid one of her rare visits to Akersfield, and Christopher had brought Emily and the girls over for the day, but it would be the first time her father had seen the baby. He could not leave the Ewe Lamb.

'I'm longing to see Dad,' she said to Alex. 'What with one thing and another, I haven't seen him since Easter. It's too long.'

When Rose saw her father, when they arrived at the Ewe Lamb on Saturday afternoon, she was shocked by his appearance. It was difficult for her not to cry out at the sight of him as he greeted her with his usual loving warmth. His wasted frame, the hollows in his cheeks which could have concealed a pigeon's egg, the overall grey of his complexion, told a story which she, as a doctor, could not help but read and understand.

Emily was there, with the children. When they had left her father in the bar, Rose took Emily's arm and led her upstairs to their former bedroom, closing the door behind them.

'Why didn't you let me know?' she demanded angrily. 'Why didn't you write, or telephone?'

'We decided not to, because of the baby. With your record so far, we didn't want to take the risk.'

'But you were over in Akersfield after the baby was born. Why didn't you tell me then?'

'You were so happy with Jenny. We didn't want to spoil it. And Mother was there. We're still not sure how much she realizes. You know what Mother's like. She won't let on.'

'All the same you should have told me,' Rose said. 'Supposing he'd . . .'

'Died? Doctor Harper said there was time. He said we could wait for the christening. Oh Rose, I did want to tell you. Even with Christopher and the children here, I felt so lonely!'

The two sisters sat side by side on the bed in the room where they had spent their childhood together. Tears streamed down Emily's face. Rose put her arms around Emily and they held each other close.

'Oh Rose, it's so awful,' Emily sobbed. 'You don't know how glad I am to see you here at last!'

It was a pity, Rose thought, that it took great unhappiness to unite people, even when they were members of the same family. She had not felt as close to her sister for a long, long time.

George Stanton was present on Sunday afternoon, with the rest of the family and many of the villagers, for the christening of his granddaughter. Rose looked across at him, standing by the font. She saw him watch closely as the Vicar performed the ceremony of baptism. The baby, quiet until now, yelled lustily as the water trickled over her forehead. It was a good sign, they said hereabouts; a sign that the devil had been driven out. Rose saw the look on her father's face as he heard the cry. It was if he, too, had been liberated. She knew as she watched him, her heart filled with sadness, for what reason she would next be in this church.

In the evening her father agreed to let Christopher and Alex take over in the bar. It was an extraordinary concession on his part, but the afternoon had tired him.

'I've a mind to listen to Evensong on the wireless,' he said. 'When I were a lad in the choir, I liked Evensong.'

He joined in the *Nunc Dimittis*, his sweet tenor voice suddenly and surprisingly strong. 'Lord, now lettest Thou thy servant depart in peace . . . for mine eyes hath seen Thy salvation . . .'

'The chap who said that had been waiting to see the baby brought to the temple,' he said to Rose. 'Didst know that, lass?'

Chapter Twelve

'If we could rehearse in your house it would be really helpful,' Gwen Mayfield said. 'My place is too far from the centre of Akersfield for the mothers to get there. And we simply can't afford to rent a room.'

'I can only offer you the attic,' Rose said doubtfully. 'It's big enough, but it might be rather cold up there. I suppose we could put in an oil stove?'

She was ashamed that her offer was half-hearted, hoped that her reluctance didn't show. Gwen Mayfield had worked miracles in the Mothers' Club in the last six months and she was truly grateful to her. 'How do you do it?' Rose had asked.

'Well for one thing,' Gwen admitted, 'I see to it that we have a bit of fun, that we don't spend *too* much time improving our minds, or learning ten ways to cook a penny herring!'

She had organized a series of evening meetings and activities which had been surprisingly well attended, right through the winter. Now she had this idea of producing the women in a play.

'But Gwen, do you think they'll turn out for rehearsals two evenings a week?' Rose queried.

'Oh I know they will - if they can get their husbands to look after the children. And it will do them good to get away from home.'

'Well I agree with that,' Rose said.

'At first they weren't too sure about being in a play - none of them had done anything like it before - but now they're terribly keen. And with properties, stage managing, etcetera etcetera I've managed to involve just about everyone.'

'Well if the attic is any good to you, it's yours. Mondays and Wednesdays, isn't it?'

Pleased though she was about the success of the Mothers' Club - and Gwen Mayfield, with time to spend and with a decided flair had achieved more than Rose could ever have hoped to – she did not look forward to this invasion of her home. She faced the discomfiting fact that it was not the mothers she minded; it was Gwen. Gwen seemed, these days, to be too large a part of life in Beechcroft Road, popping in or telephoning frequently, though always with some good reason. But she was amiable, friendly, a favourite with both Jenny and Alex. Rose chided herself for her ungenerous feelings towards Gwen. But at least my prescription worked, she thought. Immersing herself in a job of work had made a new woman of Gwen Mayfield.

'That's marvellous,' Gwen said. 'I'm really grateful. And if you would let a couple of mothers come down to the kitchen to make a cup of tea, that would be a bonus. Endless cups of tea, I've discovered, is the real secret of my success with them.'

And what is the secret of your success with Alex? The thought came swift and disturbing into Rose's mind. Well not tea, that was for sure. Alex was more and more a whisky man. The demands of his job gave frequent opportunities for drinking, and he did not let them pass. She wondered how he could afford it all, even on an editor's salary. But though he drank a lot, he did not get drunk and she was thankful for that.

Whatever the secret, if there was one, Gwen Mayfield and Alex got on together famously. In Gwen's presence Alex came alive, as he had not been since the early days of Rose's pregnancy. When she was there he seemed to throw off the constraints of his job – or whatever it was which was changing him into a quiet, often morose, man.

'Expect us Mondays and Wednesdays, then,' Gwen said. 'We won't disturb you. We'll creep upstairs like little mice!' She began to pull on her gloves, fastened up her coat collar against the early April wind which was blowing outside.

'Alex should be home any minute,' Rose said. 'Stay and have a drink.'

Now why had she said that? Why, when with one part of her she resented Gwen Mayfield, with another part of her did she want the woman to stay? Perhaps because with Gwen around that first half hour of the evening was made easier. Alex would be more relaxed, not so silent. There would be less of the acrimony which since Jenny's birth had crept into Rose's own relationship with him. Almost every day of her life now, Rose decided that she and Alex must talk, must sort things out. Alex did not attempt to initiate such a discussion, and on her side Rose was too well aware of her own guilty part in the change in him, too afraid to bring the subject into the open.

'Oh he won't want me here when he gets home, tired out,' Gwen protested.

Rose looked directly at her.

'You know that's nonsense, Gwen. He's always pleased to see *you*.' The asperity which Rose failed to keep out of her voice, the emphasis in the sentence, was plain to both women. Now whatever made me do that? Rose asked herself. Gwen, who had been ready to leave, quietly sat down again.

'What do you mean by that?'

'Nothing. Nothing at all!'

'Why . . . why do you dislike me, Rose?'

'But I don't . . .'

'Don't deny it, Rose,' Gwen cut in. 'I'm not stupid. You tolerate me because of the Mothers' Club. If it weren't for that . . .'

Rose floundered. 'I don't! That's not true. It's nonsense!' She felt the flush which stained her cheeks.

'It's not nonsense, and you know it. But why? What have I done to you?'

'Nothing at all. I don't understand what this conversation is about!'

'Yes you do.' Gwen's voice was steady; not unfriendly. She was in command of herself. 'But I've taken nothing from you, Rose. Perhaps I could have. You seem to want to throw it away. But I haven't, I assure you.'

Had Alex offered her the chance? It was Alex they were talking about, they both knew that. And if he had, how much would I care, Rose asked herself, apart from the hurt to my pride? Was it only upset pride which was causing her stomach to churn as she faced the other woman, or was there more to it than that?

A more insistent voice asked her how much of this was her own fault. Was it true, what Gwen Mayfield said, that she was throwing away Alex's love? But Gwen did not know everything. How could she? Who was she to interfere?

'I think we should stop this conversation,' Rose said. 'I'm sorry if I sounded rude.'

Gwen managed a cool little smile.

'Oh, you're never rude. You're civilized and well-mannered, and on the whole, so am I. If we'd been two of the mothers in the club we'd have been scratching each other's eyes out by now. And maybe that's better – healthier than pushing things away, pretending they don't exist. I'd have thought as a doctor you'd have known that.'

'There are lots of things I know as a doctor,' Rose said. 'Carrying them out as a woman is another matter. I still have to contend with my own temperament.'

All at once a wave of weariness swept over her. She had an almost overwhelming desire to talk to this calm-faced woman, whom she suddenly no longer saw as an enemy. She wanted to lay before her all the problems of a marriage which in her heart she knew was deteriorating, wearing away a little every day. In her daily life, in her practice, she was always at the receiving end of other people's troubles; always the strong one, seeking solutions, offering comfort. At this moment she yearned desperately, with a depth of longing which only the strongest could experience, to be weak, helpless, to shift the burden to someone else. To lean, in fact, on Gwen Mayfield of all people.

It was naturally out of the question. Repentance she had in plenty, but confession was not for her. And there being no confession, there could be no absolution. She must sort it out for herself.

'They say the onlooker sees most of the game,' Gwen was saying. 'It's true. What I'd like you to understand is that I'm fond of you both and I wish I could help. Forgive me for speaking so frankly, Rose. But I owe a lot to you. Sometimes I think you saved my life!'

'Rubbish!' Rose said. 'You'd have done it yourself in the end.'

'I'm not so sure. Anyway, under this cool exterior there beats a heart full of gratitude.' Her tone was lighter. The mood, for both of them, was passing.

'Then you can show your gratitude by staying for a drink,' Rose said. 'I mean it when I say you cheer Alex up. In any case, I have a patient due before supper, so he'll be even more glad of your company.'

Ten minutes later Alex arrived home. Without asking, he poured a dry sherry and handed it to Gwen.

'Your tipple, I believe?'

He queried Rose with a look. She shook her head. 'Not for me, thank you. I have a patient due.'

He replaced the sherry decanter and poured himself a large whisky, almost half a tumbler, Rose noted. And he had already had some. She had smelled it on his breath when he came in. She said nothing, but could not help raising her eyebrows.

'Ah! I sense disapproval!' Alex said. 'Give me one good reason why I shouldn't drink it.' He sounded reasonably pleasant, but Rose recognized the edge in his voice. She knew that but for Gwen's presence he would quickly become argumentative. Either that, or he would lapse into complete silence. Either way, it would be another unpleasant evening. She shrugged her shoulders, watched him take a long drink.

'Because it's no good to you,' Gwen answered him. Her words dropped cool and clear into the silence. Alex looked at her in surprise.

'Oh I know it's none of my business,' Gwen said. 'I just claim the privilege of friendship to say what I think.'

'Does it matter?' Alex did not sound as annoyed as Rose expected him to be, as he would have been if she had said it.

'Of course it matters,' Gwen said. 'To anyone who cares two hoots about you, which includes your family and your friends.'

'I'm gratified,' he said mockingly.

'In any case, does it do what you want it to?' Gwen asked. 'Does it solve whatever makes you drink it in the first place? Pressure of work or whatever?'

'Temporarily it does,' Alex said. 'Pressure of work and . . . whatever.'

'I tried it,' Gwen said. 'I found everything came back next morning.'

She's treading on dangerous ground, Rose thought. Alex wouldn't stand for being lectured. So far and no further. Besides, the reasons were nothing to do with Gwen. Or could they be? Even in so controversial a discussion there was a rapport between she and Alex.

The doorbell rang.

'That will be my patient,' Rose said.

'You see what it's like being married to a doctor?' Alex said to Gwen. 'Always on the job!' His tone was bantering, falling just short of complaint.

'I'm sorry,' Rose said. 'It is rather a special appointment.'

'Don't apologize,' he said. 'We all know the job comes first, the husband last in this house.'

'You're talking nonsense,' Rose said, trying to keep her tone light. 'You know I never see a patient as late as this unless it's for something special. Anyway, supper won't be too long. Will you stay and eat with us, Gwen?'

'Thank you, no,' Gwen said. 'I must go as soon as I've finished my sherry.'

'Then I'll say good-bye,' Rose said. 'I might be a little while in the surgery.'

She was glad to escape from the atmosphere of the sitting room. In her surgery she knew where she was, what was what. It was her domain. She was particularly happy to see this evening's patient – a young woman who was coming on Doctor Lewthwaite's recommendation, with her husband, seeking advice on planning the family they both wanted. A year ago, without breaking her patient's confidence, she would have wanted to share that small triumph with Alex. Now she would not bother to mention it.

When she returned to the sitting room, Gwen had gone.

'I'm sorry to keep you waiting for supper, Alex,' Rose said. 'It really was quite important.'

'Oh I'm sure it was,' Alex said. 'Everything to do with your job is important!' He reached for the whisky decanter and started to pour himself another drink.

'Please don't,' Rose begged. 'You've had enough for one evening.' She put out a hand to restrain him.

He shook off her hand, poured the whisky into his glass and drank deeply.

'Don't tell me what to do!' he said furiously. 'I'll drink what I like and when I like!'

'But why, Alex? Why?' Rose pleaded. 'What's gone wrong between us?'

186

He stared at her in disbelief. 'You ask me that? You hypocritical bitch!'

She recoiled before the anger in his eyes, the savage look on his face. This was an Alex she did not know. She had seen him lately in many dark moods, but never one like this.

'I don't understand,' she said.

'Oh yes you do, Madam!'

He had risen to his feet and was standing over her, his whole body trembling, the glass in his hand shaking. She put out a hand to take the glass from him but before she could do so he flung the whisky in her face. Then with a violent throw he sent the glass to smash into a hundred pieces against a table. Gasping, with the whisky stinging her eyes, Rose moved quickly to evade him, trying not to step on the slivers of broken glass which covered the carpet but hearing one crunch under the heel of her shoe. She did not move quickly enough. He caught her, and held her by the wrists, thrusting his face close to hers. She struggled to break free but his grip was too strong.

'Let me go, Alex!' She tried to speak calmly, to show that she was not afraid. How could she possibly be afraid of Alex? But now she was.

'Please let me go,' she begged. 'You're hurting me!'

As suddenly as he had attacked her, and as if he could no longer bear to touch her, he flung her away from him. She caught her foot in the rug and fell to the floor, miraculously missing the scattered glass. She lay there for a moment, her head buried in her arms. This couldn't be true! It couldn't be happening! Slowly, dizzy and shaking, she started to get to her feet. Alex moved swiftly to help her up. He sat her on the sofa and folded his arms around her.

'I didn't mean it, Rose!' he cried. 'I never meant to hurt you!' Feeling his arms around her, she burst into tears.

'What is it, Alex?' she sobbed. 'What has gone so wrong? It wasn't like this when we married.'

He moved away from her, sat at the other end of the sofa.

'When we married you were decent to me,' he said. 'Oh, I knew you didn't love me. That was the risk I took. But you acted as though you did and I fooled myself that that would do.'

'But I do love you, Alex,' she said.

'Don't lie to me, Rose. Don't insult me by pretending.'
She heard the pain in his voice, and wanted to assuage it,
but could not.

'I never pretended. I told you from the first that I didn't
love you as you loved me. But in my own way I love you a
great deal.'

'What sort of way is that? I didn't marry you because I
wanted a sister or a friend.' His voice was bitter and angry.
'I wanted a wife. What sort of wife denies her husband her
body for months on end, as you've done me? Do you know
just how long it is since I had you? We made love twice since
before Jenny was born!'

Guilt flushed her face crimson.

'I've tried to explain,' she said. 'A woman has odd
feelings after she's given birth. It takes time. It's no
reflection on you. I'm truly sorry, Alex.'

'Medical clap-trap!' He was on his feet again, pacing up
and down, shouting. 'It's more than six months since Jenny
was born. Is this how you teach your precious patients to
limit their families?'

'You know it isn't,' she protested. 'And I'm not proud of
myself for feeling like this. I'm truly sorry. But I repeat, I
need time.'

'Time? What do you call time? Six months, six years?
The trouble with you is, you're besotted!'

She stared at him. He could not know, he could not
possibly know. What she felt was in her own heart. Only
she was aware that, mixed up with her aversion to sex with
Alex, which had started early in her pregnancy and showed
no sign of diminishing – though she had tried, God knew
she had tried – was a longing for John Worthing which
never grew less. She had done everything to stifle it but it
would not be stifled. The most she could do was to bury it
deep inside her. It was true that she was besotted, but she
had determined that it should never touch Alex.

'You're besotted by your work,' he cried. 'You think of
nothing else. It takes all your strength. Even the baby comes
second.'

Relief surged through her. She could cope with his
accusations about her work. It was a frequent cause of

minor arguments between them, but she felt no guilt about her work.

'No more than you are with yours,' she said. 'I'm in our home more than you are. But I allow for the fact that you have to work long hours, work hard.'

Alex sat down again, leaned back in the chair, his eyes closed. The fight was over, leaving them both dejected, nothing solved.

'I'll get supper,' Rose said after a while.

Supper was eaten in silence. Rose cast around for some safe topic to break it.

'Gwen is going to rehearse the mothers here in a play, Monday and Wednesday evenings,' she said. 'Shall you mind?'

'Not in the least.'

'You like Gwen, don't you?' Rose ventured.

He lifted his head and looked at her. His face was bleak, his blue eyes tired.

'Gwen Mayfield has more warmth in her little finger than you have in your whole body!'

She flinched at the bitterness in his voice. And what he said was not true. Somewhere inside her, waiting to be released, was all the warmth and passion in the world. She knew it, she felt it. But she recalled John Worthing's taunt after the Committee meeting. 'It's women like you who drive men into other women's arms.' They had been talking *then* of Gwen Mayfield.

'I'm sorry, Alex,' she said. 'I *will* try. I really will!'

That night she turned to him in bed, pulling him towards her. In the darkness, silently, they made love. But it was no good and they both knew it. They had gone too far away. They could never get back. When it was over they lay back to back, bodies not touching. Rose lay awake until morning and she knew, from his breathing and from his unnatural stillness, that Alex was awake too.

'Prepare yourself for a surprise,' Mrs Foster said when Rose arrived at Babcock Street with Jenny the next morning. She took the child from Rose and placed her in the playpen to which, since she had long been sitting up and could now

189

wriggle herself around, she had been promoted.

'There you go, chicken!' Mrs Foster said fondly. There was great rapport between Jenny and Mrs Foster though they saw each other for a few minutes only before the morning surgeries.

'A pity your Dad didn't live to see her grow up a bit,' Mrs Foster said. 'He'd have been that proud!'

George Stanton had lived just a week after the christening. A wild, November storm, sweeping down the dale and bringing with it the first flurry of winter snow, had inappropriately attended the funeral of this quietest of men. He had been buried in the churchyard with his ancestors and Rose had returned to Akersfield heavy hearted. She had known her father's love ever since she could remember anything and nothing had ever spoilt the bond between them.

'I know,' Rose said. 'I know he would have loved her. By the way, my mother's coming for a short visit next Monday, so I shan't be bringing Jenny. She'll stay with Ma. Now what did you mean by a surprise?'

Mrs Foster nodded mysteriously. 'You'll never guess. And if I was to tell you it wouldn't be one, would it? So I'll be off then. Ta-ta!'

Rose did not have long to wait. She heard the doorbell and called out to whoever it was to come in, and was amazed, not so much to see Eva Denby as to see that she was accompanied by her husband. Rose felt a moment's apprehension. She had sent a letter of recommendation, on Eva's behalf, to the Housing Committee, but she had heard nothing more since then. It was possible that Jim Denby did not even know she had done it.

Eva and her husband advanced into the room and stood before Rose's desk. It was almost three years since Rose had seen Jim Denby. Then he had been shouting drunk; now he stood quietly, cap in hand. They both looked thinner and shabbier than ever, though nothing could quite dim Jim Denby's attraction.

'He has something to say to you, Doctor,' Eva announced. She nudged her husband. 'Go on then! You promised!'

Jim Denby took a deep breath, and reluctantly spoke.

'We've come to tell you we've got a Council house.'

'I had to go in front of the Committee and a bloke there told me I should thank you. So that's what I've come to do.'

'Why, that's wonderful news!' Rose cried. 'I'm delighted. Is it at Marton Green?'

'Yes,' Eva said. 'Number eight, Firth Avenue. Three bedrooms, hot water out of the taps, a bathroom, and a lavatory to every house. Just in the doorway. You don't have to go down the yard. There's a garden back and front with railings round, and your own front gate!' The words bubbled out of her. Rose had never seen Eva so lively. 'And a school quite near for the children,' she continued.

But Jim Denby had not finished his own speech. He silenced Eva with a look and continued in a low voice, filled with embarrassment.

'I've come as well to apologize for what I done to you in the past. You didn't deserve it and I'm sorry. I was in the drink, you see. I hope I didn't muck anything up proper.'

'It's all in the past,' Rose could think of nothing else to say.

Had he 'mucked up anything proper'? she asked herself. Well, but for him she might still be at the Clinic. But for him she would not have thrown up her job, almost left Akersfield, married Alex. But that last was not true. She had married Alex because she had realized she could never have John Worthing. Perhaps, one thing leading to another, if Jim Denby had not behaved as he had she would not be here in Babcock Street. Perhaps she would be still looking after other women's babies, never have had Jenny. If things were not going too well with Alex – well, everything had a price and perhaps that was the price she had to pay. But she wished with all her heart that Alex did not have to pay it too.

'It's all in the past,' she repeated.

'Well it looks as if things might work out for me', Jim Denby said. 'This is the first bit of luck I've had in a long time.'

'Any sign of a job?' Rose asked.

'No Doctor. So if you hear . . .'

'If I hear of anything at all, you can be sure I'll let you know,' Rose promised.

'There's just one thing,' Eva said shyly. 'We wondered if . . . that is, I thought . . .'

'Yes?'

'I wondered if, when we get in, you'd come and see us? It won't be smart, of course.. We've nothing new to put in the house - except Mam has promised me some lace curtains. But you'll be very welcome. It'll be after Easter.'

'I'd be glad to,' Rose said. 'Let me know just as soon as it's convenient.'

Mrs Foster was right, Rose thought when they had left. She never would have believed it, not of Jim Denby. Even now it did not quite ring true. But if things had always gone right for him, if it had not been for the war, and for all the years without a job, would he have been a completely different man? Who could tell? But she could not quite believe it.

On Monday afternoon Rose met her mother at Akersfield station. When George Stanton had died it was at first thought that his widow might take over the licence of the Ewe Lamb and continue to run it. But in her husband's lifetime she had never identified herself with the running of the inn, and she doubted that she was cut out to do it on her own, even if help could have been afforded for the heavy work. When it seemed that the Ewe Lamb must finally pass out of the hands of the Stanton family, Emily and Christopher had suddenly decided to sell the farm and take over the inn.

'How's everything going?' Rose asked her mother when they were settled in at Beechcroft Road, drinking tea, eating the curd tarts her mother had carefully carried from Faverwell.

'All right,' Mrs Stanton said. 'The alterations are finished, and with the extra built on there's a nice dining room and even bedrooms. Christopher reckons that with more people travelling about since the war - cars, and people walking and cycling everywhere - bed and breakfast will be the thing. Considering he's invested all the money he got from the sale of the farm, let's hope he's right!'

On Tuesday evening Miss Nesfield telephoned. 'I'm due to go to Blackpool again tomorrow,' she said. 'Now something's cropped up here and I can't possibly get away. Can you take my place? I think it's important for a woman to go.'

The negotiations for the house which had first been chosen in Blackpool had fallen through at the last minute and now another had to be found.

'You don't have surgery on a Wednesday and you've finished weaning Jenny, haven't you?' Miss Nesfield said.

'All except the early morning and late night feeds.'

'Well you could bring her here. Plenty of people to look after her.'

'That's all right. My mother's here for a day or two,' Rose said. 'It's just that . . .'

It was impossible to say that she did not want to spend the day with John Worthing. It would also be untrue. She longed to do so. But perhaps he was not included in this trip, in which case she could go with a clear conscience. She turned to Alex.

'Do you mind if I go to Blackpool tomorrow? Miss Nesfield suddenly can't go.'

He did not lift his head from the book he was reading. 'Makes no difference to me,' he said.

'I'll willingly look after little Jenny,' Mrs Stanton volunteered.

Rose turned back to the telephone. 'Yes, I'll go,' she said. 'Who's going and where do we meet?'

'Councillor Worthing and Mr Mortimer. Mr Barber's dropped out – he really can't stand the place. Anyway it makes more sense to have an estate agent in the party. They'll pick you up at your home at ten o-clock if that's all right.'

'I'll be ready,' Rose said. 'I'm sorry you can't go.' But she was not. She was wildly glad. And she need feel no guilt since she had engineered none of it, though she wondered if John Worthing had suggested her to Miss Nesfield.

She dressed with care next morning, pleased that in the last sales she had treated herself to a new coat. It was of dark green facecloth, with deep cuffs and a high collar of moleskin. She would be glad of that in 'breezy Blackpool'. Even in mid-April the weather could be chilly there. Her round velour hat in the same shade as the coat sat well down on her forehead and covered her ears.

'Those hats might be fashionable,' Mrs Stanton said, observing her daughter standing in the hall, nervously waiting to be called for, 'But to my way of thinking they're like overturned plant pots – or worse! Now in my days hats *were* hats. Plenty of width and lots of trimming. Still, I must say, you do look quite nice, Our Rose.'

Promptly at ten o-clock the doorbell rang and John Worthing stood on the step. He looked at Rose with appreciation but said nothing until Mrs Stanton had closed the door on them.

'You look delicious,' he said. 'I've explained to Willy Mortimer that you have to ride in the front of the car because you get travel sick.'

'But I don't . . .' Rose began.

'Yes you do. Don't argue!'

There was some traffic between Akersfield and Skipton but after that the roads were almost empty until they reached Preston. John Worthing drove fast and they were in Blackpool by lunchtime.

'We'll eat at the Imperial,' he said. 'They give you a good meal there. Does that suit you, Willy?'

'Capital,' Mr Mortimer said. 'I hope you're feeling all right after the drive, Doctor Rose?'

'Fine,' Rose said.

John Worthing ordered cocktails, and a bottle of Muscadet to drink with the fish which they all chose as the main course.

'We shall see all the houses through a pleasant haze,' Rose said happily. 'Let's hope it doesn't cloud our judgement.'

She was determined to enjoy this day. Even the presence of Mr Mortimer could not be allowed to spoil it. In any case, he was a nice man.

'They're three desirable properties we're going to see,' Mr Mortimer said. 'All three different. The difficulty will be making a decision.'

After a final cup of coffee they set off to inspect. The first property was to the south of Blackpool, where it joined with St Anne's. It was a fair-sized house in a quiet avenue, ten minutes' walk from the soft sandhills which comprised St Anne's beach.

'It is pleasant,' Rose said. 'But I think it's too far out of Blackpool. It would mean a tram ride, and our mothers don't have much money for that.'

'It's a lovely house and a select neighbourhood,' Mr Mortimer pointed out. 'But let's reserve judgement until we've seen the others.'

'I don't know that we're looking for a select area,' John Worthing said. 'It won't be what these ladies come to Blackpool for.'

The second house was in the centre of the town, two streets back from the promenade and near to the station; a tall, narrow house which had been run for some years as a private hotel.

'It's handy all right,' Rose said. 'Even a bit noisy. But perhaps that doesn't matter.'

John Worthing tapped wood, examined pipes, stared up at ceilings. 'It'll need a lot of repair,' he said. 'It's been neglected.'

But when they saw the third house there was no doubt in any of their minds that this was the one. It was brick built and solid, in an area not too quiet and not too noisy, and a short distance from the bracing North Shore. It had six spacious bedrooms which could be split up to give more privacy, and a large garden with lawns and flowerbeds, sheltered behind high walls.

'Moreover, at fifteen hundred pounds the price is right,' Rose said.

It took them no more than ten minutes to decide upon it.

'Right!' Mr Mortimer said. 'I know the agent quite well. I'll pop along and ask him to hold it, pending a decision from the Committee. But it'll have to be a quick decision. This house is a snip!'

'I'll see that it's quick,' John Worthing promised.

'And now if you'll excuse me, I'm going to leave you good people,' Mr Mortimer said. He looked a little embarrassed. 'I have this friend in Blackpool. She'd never forgive me if I didn't look her up. And I'll not travel back with you, I'll make my own way back by train. So if you'll drop me anywhere near the Winter Gardens that'll be fine.'

'Did you know he was going to do that?' Rose asked when Mr Mortimer had left them, scurrying away into the labyrinth of streets behind the Winter Gardens.

'I didn't,' John said. 'I shall be forever grateful to him and his lady friend. What would you like to do now?'

'Go home, surely?' Rose said. 'It's four o-clock.'

'Must we, Rose?'

I can't stay, she thought. I can't. I could tell him I have to see a patient, or that my mother, or Alex, expects me back. It would be untrue. Alex would be out and her mother's last words had been, 'I'll expect you when I see you.' Also, it being Wednesday, Gwen Mayfield would be holding a rehearsal, which would be company for her mother if she needed it. Above all, and with all her heart, she wanted to stay.

'Two or three hours,' John said. 'When shall we ever have two or three hours alone together? And that's all it will be, Rose. Just being together, no-one else to consider. You want it as much as I do. Be honest, Rose.'

She wanted to stay here forever; wanted time to stand still.

'I'll stay,' she said quietly. It could harm no-one, three short hours out of life.

'How shall we spend the time? What would you like to do?'

Rose was silent for a moment. She knew what she wanted, knew that John wanted it too.

'We could go to an hotel, Rose,' he said softly.

'At four o-clock in the afternoon?' With no luggage?'

'I could fix it.' His voice was husky with longing.

Her own longing was no less than his, but she could not do as he asked. If this time together was not to cast its guilt over everything that came after, they must avoid all that was too serious. They must do nothing which subsequent regret would spoil. She knew that in the future she would want to take out these few hours, like a precious jewel from a case, and look at them. She had to be able to do that without remorse.

'No John,' she said. 'I'm sorry! But maybe I'd like to do all the little things, the silly things, I've never had a chance to do. I'd like to do them just with you. Go on the Big Wheel;

drive to the Pleasure Beach and try the Water Chute; play the slot machines on the pier, have my fortune told!'

She saw the disappointment on his face. Was she being a fool, throwing away what might never come again?

'It's fatuous, isn't it?' she said. 'Perhaps we should, after all, go home. We've had a happy day so far. Perhaps we should leave it at that?'

She watched him hide his disappointment under a smile.

'No,' he said. 'We'll do everything you say. And since we're right beside it, we'll start with the Big Wheel!'

It was not as frightening as she had expected. They were totally encased in the glass carriage, which moved up and around in a slow, stately manner, the whole of Blackpool spread out below them.

'Quite staid, really,' Rose said when they were back on the ground.

The Water Chute on the Pleasure Beach was another matter. Rose screamed with the rest as the small boat shot down the steep ramp and launched itself with a tremendous splash into the pool below. She clung for dear life to John and he held her in his arms. By the time they staggered off the boat their former mood had changed – for both of them. They were happy in the simple fact of being together; free, uninhibited. Arm in arm, they sampled everything the Pleasure Beach had to offer – swings, roundabouts, coconut shies, various games at which Rose showed no skill at all, and at which John won a box of chocolates, a large stuffed rabbit, and a cheap brooch set with green stones which he insisted on pinning on her coat.

'I want to give you diamonds and pearls,' he said.

'This means more to me,' Rose told him, fingering the green glass. 'I'll keep it always.'

When they had exhausted the Pleasure Beach they found the car again and drove to the North Pier. The incoming tide brought a strong, damp wind from the Irish Sea, so strong that, getting out of the car, Rose found difficulty in standing against it. She buried her chin in the warmth of her fur collar and was glad of John's arm around her for support.

They passed through the turnstile and walked forward to the very end of the pier. It was deserted. Easter had come and gone. It was low season from now until Whitsuntide. Most of the resort's visitors would, in any case, be in the warmth of the Tower, or in one of the cinemas or music halls; or if they wanted a free show, in one of the booths along the Golden Mile where a pianist, foot on the loud pedal, thumped out the latest popular song while his partner, with the words on a huge song sheet, encouraged the audience to sing and afterwards sold them the sheet music.

John and Rose stood alone, facing the sea, their backs to the lights of the town. They watched the great waves hurl themselves against the massive iron structure beneath the deck of the pier, pitting their strength against the strength that was man made.

'The sea will win in the end,' John said. 'One day the pier will no longer exist. It will rust, and fall into the sea.'

Rose shivered at the thought. It threatened the moment they were standing in, and she wanted to be assured that this moment would last forever.

'You're cold,' John said, feeling her shiver against him.

'Not really. For a moment the sea frightened me. But only for a moment. I like the sea, really.'

'I'd like to sail away with you,' John said. 'Just the two of us. No-one else in the world.'

'Where would we get to?' Rose asked. 'If we sailed away from here, from the end of this pier?'

'Ireland. But we wouldn't land there. We'd turn south, and then west. We'd cross the Atlantic in our ship. Then we'd turn south again and we'd find an island . . .'

'A desert island?'

'What would we want with other people?'

He turned and drew her close to him, kissing her fiercely. His lips, hard against hers, were salty with sea spray. Held in his embrace she felt that life, new life, his life and vitality, flooded through her, filled her to the brim. She loved this man as she had never thought it possible to love anyone. If she could not have him, what else was there to live for, what else mattered?

'I love you, Rose,' he said. 'It's real and it's forever. There is no other woman in the world for me. Tell me you love me, Rose. I know you do. Tell me! I want to hear it.'

'I love you,' she said. 'Oh John, how I love you!'

He kissed her again. Her lips felt bruised from the strength of his kiss. She never wanted anyone else to kiss her again, ever. Like an adolescent girl who has been kissed for the first time, she felt she would carry the feeling on her lips forever.

'What are we going to do, Rose? We can't leave it like this. You know we can't!'

The tide was racing in now. The noise of the sea and of the wind enveloped them, but they were oblivious to them as they stood there in each other's arms. Looking only at each other, they did not see the giant wave which broke against the end of the pier, knew nothing of it until they were drenched in heavy spray and broken apart by its force. Afterwards, remembering, it seemed to Rose that the elements themselves, jealous observers of their love, had conspired to separate them.

John found her hand and they ran for shelter in the lee of one of the pier buildings.

'Are you very wet?'

'Not as much as I thought,' Rose said. But she was shivering with cold now; and with more than cold – with the knowledge that the moment had passed and that it would not come again. For a short space of time she had been prepared to throw everything aside. Now her mind and her spirit, as well as her body, had received a cold douche.

John took her into the shelter of his arms again.

'Rose, my darling . . .'

But the madness was over. The madness was over, but not her love or her desire. Her body ached for him.

'John, we must go,' she said.

'Where shall we go, Rose?'

There is nowhere for us to go, she thought. No warm, desert island. In all the world there is no place for the two of us. Tears, which she could no longer check, ran down her face, and while John held her close, deep sobs shook her body.

Eventually she said, 'Take me home, John. Please take me home!'

He kissed her gently.

'I shall always love you. Never forget it, Rose.'

'And I you,' she said, the words almost inaudible against the sound of the wind and the sea.

They turned their backs on the sea and began to walk towards the bright lights of the town.

When Rose arrived home her mother was waiting up for her. There was no sign of Alex.

'He took Mrs Mayfield home after the rehearsal,' Mrs Stanton said. 'It was raining and she'd missed the tram. Did you have a nice day, then?'

'Yes thank you, Mother.' Already it belonged to another world, though it was never to be forgotten. She was glad Alex was out.

'I'm rather tired,' she said. 'If you don't mind, I think I'll see to Jenny and then go to bed.'

She fell asleep thinking of John Worthing. Later, she wakened from a dream in which she was drowning in the sea just off the North Pier. She called for help but, though everyone she knew was there on the pier, no-one heard her, no-one answered.

She looked at her watch. It was two-thirty. Alex was not in bed and when she went downstairs to warm herself some milk, he was not in the house.

Chapter Thirteen

Rose had lain awake most of the night. It was not only Alex's absence, and the likely reason for it, which had kept her from sleeping, but the turmoil of her thoughts after the day in Blackpool. Round and round in her head the people spun: Diana Worthing, Alex, Gwen Mayfield, herself and, above all others and every minute of the dragging hours, John Worthing. They twisted and wove in an impossible dance of which no-one knew the steps, trying to weave a coherent pattern. It was no use. Everything was chaos; everything was impossible.

Her ears attuned to the slightest sound, just before dawn she heard Alex's car, and then the sound of his key in the front door. She waited apprehensively for him to come up to the bedroom, ready to feign sleep. There was no way they could talk to each other at this moment. But he did not come.

She heard him go into the kitchen, turn on a tap; but he moved around quietly, from which she deduced that he was sober. When he had drunk too much he tended to crash around. In fact, he had not taken a drink at home since the evening he had thrown the whisky in her face and she doubted that he had, since then, had much during the day. 'Whatever happens between us,' he had said next morning at breakfast, 'you will never have to endure such a scene again.'

It had been fully daylight when she had fallen asleep and now, next morning, she was exhausted, reluctant to obey the summons of the alarm clock. Thought came flooding back as she stretched out a hand to turn it off. She longed to sink back into a deep sleep. But it was not possible; she had early surgery at Babcock Street and she must get herself and Jenny ready to leave.

She found Alex asleep on the sitting-room sofa. Standing over him, she thought how young and carefree he looked in his sleep, as if something in his dreams released him. With all her heart she wished she had not failed him.

'Alex, it's half-past eight!'

When she was sure he was awake, she left him. There was no time for explanations, for the confrontations which she knew the day must bring; nor could she bear them now.

In the kitchen Annie was preparing breakfast.

'I'll take my mother a tray,' Rose said. She did not want her to come down before Alex had removed himself.

Mrs Stanton was sitting up in bed, looking perky.

'You're spoiling me,' she said. 'I'm not used to this. I'm used to being up and doing!'

'It won't do you any harm,' Rose said. From her mother's demeanour it seemed likely that she had heard nothing.

'You don't look all that bright,' Mrs Stanton observed. 'I'd have thought a day at the seaside would have put new life into you.'

'I'm fine,' Rose said. 'Will you be able to look after Jenny this afternoon? I've promised to visit Eva Denby.'

'Of course I will, and glad to,' Mrs Stanton said.

When Rose went downstairs again Alex was in the dining room, drinking tea, eating toast.

'I'm sorry if I worried you last night, coming in late, he said. Rose was surprised at the steady calm of his voice.

'I would have called it early rather than late!'

She realized with surprise that worry about what might have happened to him, about the possibility of accident or illness, had not been one of her emotions. She had been too occupied with other thoughts.

'We have to talk,' Alex said.

'Not now, Alex. I'm already late for surgery.' She didn't want to talk. Everything was too muddled.

'This evening then. No matter what you say, Rose, we *have* to talk.'

Firth Avenue was not an avenue, but a collection of houses built around a large circle of grass which had been split into four quarters by narrow concrete paths. Two or three children played on the grass but the rest were on the road, most of them with a skipping rope stretched across its width, a few playing hopscotch. Would they never get used to playing on grass? Rose wondered.

When she stopped the car outside number eight, half-a-dozen children left their games to stand and stare. No-one in Firth Avenue, and practically no-one who visited there, owned a car. 'Don't touch it!' Rose warned, getting out.

Number eight was the end house of a block of four. The whole of the estate had been built in harsh red brick, though every other building in Akersfield had, for centuries, been built in the local stone. But since all the stone buildings in Akersfield were coal black from the smoke, perhaps red brick was more cheerful. The doors were painted a dark, serviceable green and there were lace curtains at most of the windows. As Rose walked down the path, Eva opened the front door.

'Doctor Rose! Please come in!'

She smiled a welcome. How happy she looked, how different from the girl in Paradine Street, though she had been here only a few weeks. Rose followed her into the living-room – and gasped in astonishment. Everything was clean, everything was bright, everything was new. The oven range, let into one wall, shone black in its iron parts from the application of blacklead, silver in its steel trim from hard work with emery paper. The newly-plastered walls were distempered a fashionable shade of pale mauve and the floor was covered with glossy new linoleum patterned with red and yellow roses on a brown background.

'It's all quite splendid!' Rose said.

'Isn't it just?' Eva agreed. 'Look at the suite!' The three-piece suite was equally new, equally brightly flowered.

'A chesterfield with a drop end,' Eva explained. 'The tallest man can lie stretched out on it. Ten pounds the sofa and two chairs at Butterfields. It's very good value, the man said.'

There was a small, square dining table with bulbous legs, and two smaller chairs.

'It's wonderful!' Rose said. 'Jim must be doing very well at his job.'

She knew that Jim Denby was working now. Mrs Foster had told her that he'd been given a job as a chauffeur-handyman – he had learned to drive in the army – to a business man who had a large house in Marton Green. 'It'll be a miracle if he keeps it,' Mrs Foster said. 'He never has yet!' Rose, surveying the new possessions, hoped that Mrs

Foster would be proved wrong.

'He's doing ever so well,' Eva said. 'Three pounds a week regular, and he likes the work. We got all this lot on easy payments - hire purchase - the first week. Thirty poundsworth of goods you can get for twelve shillings a month! When we've paid for these we might go in for a bedroom suite.'

'Marvellous!

'But you haven't seen everything,' Eva continued. 'Come and look at this!'

On a rickety stand - one of the few pieces Rose remembered from Paradine Street - stood a square, dark oak box.

'Columbia Hornless Gramophone!' Eva said proudly. 'Five guineas, on easy payments too. And we've got two records. I could play you one if you liked. Though perhaps that's a bit silly. I expect you've got a gramophone of your own.' She was suddenly unsure of herself.

'As a matter of fact we haven't,' Rose said. 'But we have the wireless.'

Astonished delight lit Eva's face.

'Fancy me having something you haven't got!' She picked up the two records in turn, handling them with reverence.

'You can have the Black Dyke Mills Band playing "*Il Travatore*",' she said 'Or Layton and Johnstone singing "Tea For Two".'

'Let's have Layton and Johnstone,' Rose said. Alex had taken her to see them once. It had been a happy occasion.

Eva wound up the gramophone, fixed a new needle and gingerly lowered the head. The music filled the small room and the two women sat side by side, listening; Rose deep in her own sad thoughts, Eva, a pleased smile on her face, beating time and then joining in with the chorus until, three-quarters of the way through, she jumped quickly to her feet and began to wind the gramophone handle.

'It's beginning to run down,' she explained. 'You mustn't let it run down. It sounds awful! Shall I turn it over to the other side? It's "I Want to be Happy".'

'Please!' Rose said.

The words were so slick, she thought as she listened. As if happiness was easy to come by. And yet, watching Eva with

204

her head swaying to the music, it seemed to be so for some people. Such little things - a three-piece suite, a square of bright linoleum, two gramophone records - made Eva supremely happy. Rose's own parents had never had to seek far for happiness. So why did it run away from her, and why did she seem unable to give it?

'I'll make a cup of tea,' Eva said. 'We'll play "*Il Travatore*", afterwards. It's a bit sad but I love it.'

'Where are the children?' Rose asked.

'Out playing. They've already made friends. There are some nice people around here, you know. A cut above Paradine Street.'

Or is it that better surroundings make better people? Rose wondered.

'Is Dorothy doing well at school?' she asked.

'Ever so well,' Eva said proudly. 'She's in the top class of the infants and she can read. She goes up into Standard One next year when she's seven. They learn to knit in Standard One.'

'And Meg?'

'She goes to school later this year.' Eva suddenly looked serious. 'If it hadn't been for you, Doctor Rose, I doubt I'd ever have reared our Meg. I owe a lot to you, one way and another. Who would have thought, five years ago, that I'd have been sitting where I am right now?'

She looked around at her home, at her beautiful new possessions. When her gaze came back to Rose her eyes were filled with happy tears; tears of gratitude for the turn that her life had taken.

Rose leaned forward and took Eva's hand. 'I'm truly glad that things are going better for you,' she said. 'It was about time you had a bit of luck. Now, are you going to show me the rest of the house before I go?'

It was quickly obvious that every resource had been put into the living room. The three bedrooms, one of them the size of a cupboard, had no floor covering and the rickety double bed from Paradine Street, plus a narrow single one in which the children slept together, comprised almost the whole of the furniture. There were no curtains at the windows except for the lace ones which looked so respectable from the outside.

'We have to get undressed in the dark,' Eva giggled. 'Lest anyone might see us! Of course we *shall* get curtains, *and* all the rest. Now that Jim's bringing money home regular there's nothing to stop us. But you can't get curtains and suchlike on hire purchase.'

'Why not?' Rose asked.

A shadow crossed Eva's face.

'Well you see, if you weren't able to keep up the payments they couldn't take curtains back, could they? Not like . . . other things.'

'I'm sure that won't happen to you,' Rose said.

Eva's face brightened again. "Course it won't! Not a chance!'

I wish I could believe that, Rose thought. But where Jim Denby was concerned it all seemed too good to be true. There must be a catch in it somewhere.

Every Thursday Rose held an evening surgery, specifically for the very few mothers who worked during the day, and for married couples who might wish to attend together. There were very few of the latter. Mrs Foster had popped in this evening, ostensibly to do a few odd jobs but really, Rose knew, to hear about that afternoon's visit to Eva.

'I could hardly believe it!' Rose said. 'Such a change.'

'I told you you wouldn't,' Mrs Foster said. 'What's more, I don't! It's too good to be true – knowing that Jim Denby as I do. There's a catch in it somewhere. I just wish I knew what it was.'

'I'm inclined to agree with you,' Rose said. 'Let's hope we're both wrong.'

Mrs Foster's answering snort expressed disbelief, derision and incredulity.

'It doesn't look as though anyone else is coming this evening,' Rose said, changing the subject. 'I'm not sure that this Thursday evening clinic is worthwhile. I doubt I'm ever going to get the husbands.'

'More's the pity,' Mrs Foster said. "Course, it's not always that they don't agree with you, but they're not going to show it in public, not going to walk into the surgery. Most of them reckon it's the woman's job, anyway.'

She took a step closer to Rose and lowered her voice.

'Would you believe, Doctor,' she said, speaking confidentially, 'that during the war, in France, they issued Our Boys with . . . well, you know what! French letters! So they could have it off with them mademoiselles and not leave a cart load of little half-breed bastards behind, I suppose! They say the Government gave 'em out like rations! Pity they don't do that now, when the men can't afford 'em. It'd be cheaper than paying the dole for all the kids!'

Mrs Foster went off home. Rose knew that it was time she did likewise. There would be no more patients this evening. But she was loath to go, knowing that she must face Alex. From time to time, during a day in which John Worthing had scarcely been out of her thoughts, she had reminded herself that Alex knew nothing of the day in Blackpool beyond the fact that she had been, and had returned. The events of *her* yesterday were not for display. They were buried in her own heart and must remain there. Alex had other problems which Rose, though knowing herself to be deeply involved, did not want to face with him.

But face them she must. She began to gather her things together, getting ready to leave, when the surgery bell rang. When she called out to the patient to come through, Gwen Mayfield walked in. She was pale, with blue shadows under her eyes, as if she too had not slept.

Gwen seated herself in the chair in front of Rose's desk.

'You know why I'm here,' she said without preamble. 'I told Alex last night that I was coming to see you. He didn't like the idea, but I wanted us to talk. Two rational women!'

Am I rational? Rose wondered. I don't feel it. I don't know what I feel. Her heart and mind were still full of those moments on the pier. She resented anything which might usurp those thoughts.

'I haven't spoken to Alex,' she said. 'I had to leave in a hurry this morning.'

'But you can guess why I'm here?'

'I think so.'

'You know Alex spent the night with me?'

Rose flinched at Gwen's hard directness.

'I took it he had,' she said.

'You might not believe it, but we talked most of the night.'

207

'But not all of it?'

'Not all. No.'

All those hours, Rose thought. What did they find to talk about? How far was all this serious and how far was Alex simply turning to Gwen for comfort? For the comfort his wife failed to give him.

'We didn't talk all the time about you,' Gwen said. 'Alex is nothing if not loyal. I'm not sure what we did talk about. Alex's work, our differing childhoods, my marriage, the war. Alex hadn't taken me home with the intention of staying the night, you know. It just happened.'

'Even the fact that the whole night wasn't spent in talking?'

For the first time, Gwen looked uncomfortable.

'Even that,' she said. 'And it was the first time. I'd like you to believe that.'

'I do,' Rose said.

Would I have acted any differently, she asked herself, if John and I had been in similar circumstances? If we'd been together in a warm room instead of standing on the end of the pier with the wind and the rain in our faces? Should they have gone to an hotel, as John had wanted? But that was futile thinking. It could never happen to them now.

'I have to tell you that I love Alex,' Gwen said. 'I really and truly love him. I didn't want to, I didn't seek it; but it's there. It won't go away.'

'And Alex?'

'I must leave Alex to speak for himself,' Gwen said.

'You sound confident. You must know how he feels.'

Gwen hesitated only for a second.

'I do know. He loves me. Not as much as I love him, but he loves me.'

Do two people ever love each other equally? Rose wondered. She wanted to believe that between herself and John Worthing it was so, but would it be true if they could put it to the test?

'Why are you telling me this?' she asked. 'Is it because the affair between you and Alex is to continue?'

'It hasn't been an affair so far,' Gwen said. 'There's been nothing clandestine; no secret meetings, no stolen kisses when your back was turned – though it would have been easy. You were often busy with your work. But you're my friend. I wouldn't do that to you. I won't now. What I want to say is, that if you and Alex are going to make a go of your marriage, I'm prepared to fade out of the picture. I'd leave Akersfield if I thought that would happen.'

'You must love him quite a lot.'

'I do.'

'But you don't think it will happen?' Rose said.

'Frankly, no! I don't believe your marriage with Alex has the seeds of happiness in it. You're two nice people who simply bring each other unhappiness.'

'He's stopped drinking.'

'I know,' Gwen said. 'We talked about that. It's genuine.'

Why couldn't he talk to me? Rose asked herself. Why can't we communicate? Her life was one of constant communication with people, so why not with her own husband?

'Listen, Rose,' Gwen was saying. 'Don't hang on to Alex from pride, or duty. If you can't love him as I love him – if you can't make him happy as I know I could – then let him go! Rose, I beg of you to let him go.'

'There's more to it than that,' Rose said. She felt confused, unutterably tired, deeply lonely. 'I must talk to Alex.'

Gwen nodded. 'Yes, you must. I'll leave you now, Rose.'

Rose watched her go, then gathered her things together and went home to Alex.

'Before we go any further,' Alex said, 'I have to tell you that I spent the night with Gwen. We made love. More important than that, I love her.'

'I've seen Gwen,' Rose interrupted. 'She came to see me this evening in Babcock Street.'

A shadow of annoyance crossed Alex's face. 'I didn't want her to do that. I wanted to tell you myself. I'm sorry.'

'It doesn't matter,' Rose said.

They had picked at their evening meal in near silence because Annie was in and out of the dining room, serving and clearing away. After supper Alex had rushed them both into the sitting room. The fire was lit, for the late Spring evenings were cold.

'I've always known that you were attracted to her.' She didn't really know what to say to him. It was all so unreal.

'I've made no secret of it,' Alex said. 'She's warm, she's lively. I've learnt that she's loving.'

'I'm sure she is,' Rose said wearily. 'Please spare me a recital of her virtues. I realize that I possess none of them - at least in your eyes.'

'What do you mean by that?'

'Nothing. Nothing at all.'

'You used to be warm and lively,' Alex said. 'I hoped that you might grow loving.'

'I tried,' Rose said quietly.

'The effort was only too clear,' Alex said.

Annie came in.

'Can I clear the coffee?' she asked.

'Please do,' Rose said. 'And we shan't need anything more this evening. I'll get my mother's bedtime drink when she comes in.' Mrs Stanton was spending this evening at the Mothers' Club, talking to the members about life in the Dales.

'So where do we go from here?' Rose asked when Annie had left the room. 'I don't see that the decisions are mine. Either you give up Gwen and we try to make a fresh start - really try, I mean - or we agree to drift along as we've been doing.'

'I can't give her up,' Alex said stubbornly. 'I won't. I've told you, I love her.'

'You loved me,' Rose said. 'It doesn't seem so long ago.'

'You threw it back at me.' Alex's voice was bitter. 'You didn't want it. You wanted marriage, a child, a career. I was able to provide them. You didn't want *me!*'

He glanced around, she thought for the drink he would normally have had to hand. But he did not get up and pour one. He was stone cold sober. She felt sick at his words. Was it true, what he said? Possibly she had always known it, though even to herself she had never put it into words. In the beginning she was sure she had genuinely tried her best, and she was willing to do so again.

'Shall we make a fresh start, Alex?' she said.

'No,' he said. 'I don't think we can.' He was quietly implacable, no give in him. 'Not to beat about the bush,' he said. 'I want a divorce. I'm sorry, Rose, but it's the only way.'

'Divorce!' All the horror she felt was in her voice. 'We can't divorce. It would ruin both of us!'

'It wouldn't ruin you,' Alex said. 'You would be the innocent party, the wronged woman. It might even gain you a few patients!'

'Don't joke, Alex. I can't bear it. And what about *your* career?'

'I'll take the risk,' he said. 'Divorce isn't exactly common, but I won't be the first. It's easier for a man than for a woman.'

'Naturally,' Rose said. But she knew that he did not approve of divorce. He must love Gwen Mayfield very much to contemplate it. 'I suppose you've considered that every nasty little bit will be printed in the newspaper?' she said. 'Especially in the *Record*. Is Gwen prepared to face that? Or in this case will you use your God-like position as editor to suppress it?'

'I shall suppress nothing,' Alex said. 'It's not my way, as you know. But Gwen won't come into it. There are other ways, as you know.'

'A night in an hotel with a hired woman? A chambermaid surprising you both in bed?'

'If I have to. I didn't make the divorce laws.'

Rose jumped to her feet, moved to the window, drew back the heavy plush curtains and looked out. She wanted to escape. It was a soft, dark night with no moon. Lighted windows shone in the darkness over Akersfield to the distant edge of the town where the dark moors merged into the black sky. What was taking place behind all those windows? Love, hate, birth, death - and a thousand more trivial things? It seemed to her in this moment that she was to be lonely for the rest of her life. She turned back to Alex.

'What about Jenny? Where does she fit into all this? Have you given a thought to Jenny?'

She flinched at the swift anger in his face.

'Of course I have! A thousand. But Jenny will never be mine as she's yours. You've seen to that. You always will.'

'It's not true . . . !'

'You know it is. From the day she was born you've tried

to keep her to yourself. But I shall see Jenny often. It never occurred to me that you wouldn't agree to that.'

'Thank you for those kind words,' Rose said. 'And what if I won't divorce you?'

'Then I shall leave you just the same. You won't keep me by refusing to divorce me. But I don't expect you to take that line, Rose. It would be unlike you.'

The sick feeling had passed but she felt weak, all her strength spent, as if at any second she might collapse.

'I'm very tired. I must go to bed,' she said. 'I'll give you your answer in a day or two. In the meantime, where are you going to sleep? You can't expect . . .'

'I shall sleep on the sofa in here tonight. You take your mother back to Faverwell tomorrow. From then on I'll have the spare room until things are settled.'

Not only did he not expect to sleep in her bed, he had no desire to do so. Though she did not want him, the thought was bitter.

'I'm very sorry about all this, Rose,' he said. 'Truly sorry.'

'I should not have married you,' Rose said. 'It was wrong of me to do so.'

She wanted to go to bed and sleep and sleep and sleep. She went into the kitchen and left a note for her mother on the top of the Ovaltine tin, then went upstairs. On her way up to the bedroom she looked in on Jenny. The child was lying face down, her chubby legs bent up, her clenched hands above her head, in a frog-like position as if ready to leap away. She was deeply asleep and did not stir as Rose pulled the blanket over her shoulders.

It was a silent journey back to Faverwell. Rose wondered how much her mother knew, or suspected; but Mrs Stanton was not a woman to pry. They arrived at the Ewe Lamb in time for the midday meal and Emily insisted on Rose drinking a glass of sherry before they sat down to eat. 'You look as though you could do with a bottle of whatever you give your patients when they're under the weather,' she said. 'In the meantime, a glass of this won't do you any harm.'

It was better sherry than her father had kept, Rose judged. There were other signs, too, that the Ewe Lamb was changing: flowered curtains at the windows, new display shelves behind the bar, holding a selection of drinks with which her father would have had no truck. In the built-on wing the dining room boasted an Axminster carpet on the floor and eight tables with immaculate damask cloths and small vases of flowers.

'How are things going?' Rose asked.

'Very well. We were busy at Easter – one or two room bookings as well as plenty of passing trade. We reckon we'll have a good summer.'

There was no doubt that Emily had found her *niche*. Gone was the look of discontent which had been in her eyes for so long, though to those who knew her there would always be a sadness for her son. Christopher, too, though he had little time to stop and talk, looked happy and healthy.

'It was a wrench, selling the farm,' he admitted. 'I've lived there all my life. But it turned out for the best.'

'I visited Eva Denby the other day,' Rose told Emily. 'She's in seventh heaven.' She felt that everyone's life, except her own, was prospering.

After the meal she left Jenny with her mother and went for a walk, climbing down the narrow path by the bridge to walk along the river bank. The river was in full spate from the Spring rains, and for the same reason the grass on its banks was a brilliant emerald green. A kingfisher, a blinding flash of iridescent blue, flew low over the water and was lost again under the darkness of the bridge. She had watched the kingfishers every year of her childhood. They were part, as she was, of Faverwell. This was where she belonged and, right now, she wanted to stay here forever; to make no more decisions, face no problems. It was impossible, of course. This evening she must return to Akersfield, must make decisions.

She understood, or thought she did, that Alex might love someone else. How could she not when she thought of John Worthing? But she had always determined not to let John intrude into their marriage. So was Alex being self-indulgent or was he simply more honest than she? It was beside the point. He was going. Whether she would consent to free him legally or not, he was going. She must build a new life which did not include him, a life from which it seemed marriage and love, and the prospect of more children, must be excluded.

She turned and began to walk back. By the time she reached the Ewe Lamb she had decided that she would divorce Alex. She owed him that much. But she would not tell her family just yet. They would be horrified and deeply hurt. Divorce was unknown in the family, almost unknown among all the people they knew. They would see it as disgrace. But the disgrace was not in the divorce, Rose thought; the real disgrace was in her failure to make a proper marriage.

She drove back to Akersfield on an evening so clear, so golden, that it mocked the misery of her thoughts. When she walked into the house, carrying Jenny, the first thing she saw was Alex's suitcase in the hall. She began to tremble. Dear God, not so soon? Surely not so soon? It was less than twenty-four hours. She put Jenny down on the floor and sat herself on the hall chair, her whole body shaking.

Alex came down the stairs, another suitcase in hand. At the sight of him her misery turned to anger.

'Did it have to be like this?' she cried. 'You might well have gone without me seeing you! Is that what you intended? Am I so unbearable that you can't stand me another day? Or is it that you can't wait for her?'

'I'm not going to Gwen,' Alex said quietly. 'I'm going to stay with Mrs Crabtree for a while. If you consent to a divorce I shall stay there until it's over. If not . . .'

'I'll divorce you,' Rose said. All the anger, it seemed all the life, had suddenly gone out of her.

They faced each other awkwardly. 'There's no rehearsal for this situation,' Rose said. 'I don't know the lines. Except to say that I'm sorry for whatever part of it was my fault.'

'I'm sorry, too, Rose. I'll give you the evidence quickly. And from then you understand that I mustn't see you until it's all over. The courts are hot on collusion.'

'Collusion?'

'Once you've started proceedings against me you must have no more to do with me until after the decree absolute. If it was thought that we'd agreed to this divorce, it wouldn't be allowed to go through. I'll see you don't want for money, for yourself or Jenny.'

He lifted Jenny from the floor and kissed her.

'Now please go,' Rose said.

He put Jenny down, gathered up his suitcase, and left.

Looking back, Rose realized that she measured the months after Alex's departure by the ailments among her patients at both her surgeries. There was an epidemic of diarrhoea – which among her poorer patients, with the lack of sanitation in their homes, went on all summer – followed by measles in the autumn, with its legacy of chest complaints made worse by Akersfield's cold, damp winter. Before they cleared, an early spring flu epidemic set in. Rose supposed she was thankful to be busy, though from fatigue, and from the other things which were happening to her, she felt stripped of even that emotion.

On her first birthday Jenny took her first, faltering footsteps across the sitting room and soon after that Rose engaged a young nursemaid to look after her. It was not easy to find the ten shillings a week to pay for Moira, but somehow she managed.

She was presented with evidence that Alex had committed adultery with a woman in an hotel in Blackpool – the choice of place gave her a nasty stab. Later she was granted a *decree nisi* and, six months later still, a decree absolute. She was no longer married. She was a free woman, with no idea what to do with her freedom.

On the day after the announcement of the decree absolute appeared in the *Record*, John Worthing telephoned her.

'I can't pretend I'm sorry,' he said. 'It's a step nearer. At least nothing now stands in *your* way.'

She was shocked by the directness of his approach. 'You're quite wrong,' she said. 'Your wife stands as much in my way as in yours. You can't persuade me otherwise.'

She wished that he could. Over the months she had seen him whenever the Committee met, but there had been nothing more. She longed for him: on some sleepless nights she had, in her loneliness, physically cried out for him. But though she longed for him, she was not ready to take him

215

for her lover. It would, in any case, be only part of the answer. To have him as her lover, with meetings snatched in secret, when and where they could, would only accentuate his absence from the rest of her life. She wanted him not only sexually, but in every other way. She wanted the daily companionship, the shared domesticity, the evenings spent together, the births of children who would belong to them both.

As she put down the telephone on John Worthing, Annie came into the room.

'There's a Mrs Denby to see you. Says it's urgent. I told her you was busy.'

'Show her in at once, please,' Rose said. It must be important. Eva had hardly ever been to Beechcroft Road, and never without an invitation.

Eva burst into the room. She was hatless, her hair not combed; she still wore a pinafore under her unbuttoned coat. Her eyes were red from weeping.

'I had to come,' she cried. 'I didn't know where to turn! Mam's gone to see Auntie Dora in Halifax!'

'Whatever is it, Eva?' Rose had never seen her in such a state.

'Jim's been arrested! They say it's been going on for months! Something to do with his employer and some money. The police came and took him away! They took him in full view of the neighbours – handcuffed! Oh, Doctor Rose, what am I going to do? What am I going to do?'

The words poured out in a torrent, then gave way to noisy sobs as Eva collapsed on to a chair. She lowered her head to her knees, her shaking back and shoulders a long curve of hopelessness.

Chapter Fourteen

When Rose arrived at the Babcock Street surgery next morning a child, standing on the doorstep, thrust a note into her hand.

'Mrs Foster said I was to gi'e it to yer.'

'Wait until I read it, in case there's an answer needed,' Rose said.

He knew there was no answer. Mrs Foster had said so. But if he waited the Doctor was always good for a penny which, together with the one Mrs Foster had given him, would be a bit of all right.

Rose unfolded the note.

'Dear Doctor (she read)
    I can't come this a.m. on account of the bastard is up in court and I got the children here while Eva goes.
            Yours truly and oblige
            J. Foster (Mrs)'

Rose took a penny from her purse and handed it to the messenger. 'No answer,' she said.

In the act of unlocking the surgery door she paused. If she hurried, there was time to pop in on Mrs Foster before surgery. She felt anxious about Eva. The girl's white face, stained with tears and sick with worry, had occupied her mind since yesterday's visit. She felt she had done little to help her.

In Mrs Foster's living room Dorothy and Meg sat at the table which was spread with a clean newspaper as a tablecloth. In her darker moments Rose had sometimes thought that to have tea and treacle and soup spilled over it was just about what the *Record* deserved. Mrs Foster handed thick slices of bread and margarine to the children, then spooned skimmed, condensed milk into the cups of strong tea which she placed before them. In the area around Babcock Street most people had forgotten what fresh milk tasted like, and now they had come to prefer the

217

sticky, sweet substance which they called 'Swiss milk'.

'This is a bad business,' Mrs Foster said. 'I can't say much, though.' She gave a warning jerk of her head in the direction of the children. 'Little pigs have big ears!'

'Where is Eva?' Rose asked.

'Already down there. He has to appear this morning, though the Lord knows what time. She could be there for hours, all on her own. I wish I could have gone with her, only I can't be in two places at once.'

She was untypically harassed and, divested of her usual hat, her sparse white hair drifting away from its hairpins and straggling around her face, she looked an old woman.

'I'll finish surgery as quickly as I can,' Rose said. 'Then I'll pop down there myself. How was she?'

Mrs Foster shook her head. 'Upset! Can you wonder? If I could speak my mind . . .' She checked herself, seeing the wary curiosity on the faces of her grandchildren. 'But it's very kind of you to offer to go down there. God bless you, Doctor!'

Fortunately the surgery was a light one. Rose reached the courtroom, and was allowed in by the constable on duty who recognized her, just as Jim Denby's case was called. There was no time to speak to Eva as she slid into the seat beside her but she took the girl's ice-cold hand and held it for a moment in her own.

In the dock Jim Denby looked diminished, all the bravado gone from him. He gazed fixedly ahead, his face expressionless. If he knew Eva was in court he gave no sign of it.

The case started, and was over, with surprising speed.

'You are charged with stealing, by a trick, the sum of five pounds, the property of the Akersfield Building Society, which trick you perpetrated by means of a bogus telephone call.'

The magistrate's tone of voice said that no tricks surprised him. He had heard them all.

'However,' he continued, 'I am informed by the police that other and far graver charges will be alleged against you. I do not therefore propose to try you in this court, but to remand you in custody for one week.'

Eva clutched at Rose's arm, gripping her until it hurt, as

Jim Denby was led away.

'Let's go,' Rose whispered.

Outside in the street Rose said, 'I'm going to take you for a cup of tea. I'd like to give you something stronger but the pubs aren't open.'

The café to which they went was the one to which Alex had taken Rose on her first day in Akersfield. So much had changed since that day that it seemed - if indeed it had ever existed - half a lifetime away.

'Would you like something to eat?' she asked Eva.

Eva shook her head. 'It wouldn't stay on my stomach. It was good of you to come, Doctor.'

'If you like I'll come with you next week,' Rose said. 'I'll make arrangements about the surgery.' Next week's ordeal, she was sure, would be far worse than today's.

'What will they do to him?' Eva said.

'I don't know. I don't know what he's done, do you?'

'No. I swear to God I don't know anything. I thought he was doing so well with his job. When he gave me a bit extra he said it was overtime, or he'd come up on a horse. I suppose I should have known it couldn't last. Nothing good ever does, least of all with me and Jim.'

'It might not be as bad as we think.' Rose tried to sound more reassuring than she felt. 'Grave charges' the magistrate had said. And Jim Denby had a record. 'I believe he's been in trouble before?' she said.

'Before we were married,' Eva said. 'Right from being a kid. He was in Borstal. Then he was in the glasshouse in the army. His own mother warned me. But you don't take any notice, do you? Will it be in the *Record*?' she asked anxiously.

'Only a line or two, I daresay.' Rose had seen one of Alex's reporters in the court, scribbling away.

'But next week?'

The two women looked at each other. They could not pretend that if the case was substantial the *Record* would not make a meal of it.

'That's what I dread most,' Eva said desperately. 'I can't stand for the neighbours to read it. I can't stand for the children's friends to point them out. They will, you know.'

'Surely not?'

'*You* don't know, Doctor. Oh, I mean no disrespect. But the people on the Marton Green estate are a cut above some. They won't like anything of this nature.'

'But they won't take it out on you and the children,' Rose said. It was strange that Eva made no mention of what it would be like for Jim, or how she would face the separation, how she would manage for money. Her entire concern seemed to be with the effect of the likely newspaper report.

'Oh yes they will,' Eva said. 'People can be very cruel. I can stand it for myself, though I was just beginning to get to know people, starting to make friends, and I suppose that'll all finish. But it's the children, you see. Other mothers won't let their children play with mine when all this comes out.'

'I think you're wrong,' Rose said. She refilled Eva's cup and for a minute they sat in silence.

'Doctor Rose,' Eva said.

'Yes?'

'I wouldn't ask you if it wasn't for the children . . .'

'You know I'll help if I can, whatever it is.'

'You're so good to me, Doctor. I hardly know how to ask. But do you think you could ask your husband . . .' She flushed with embarrassment. 'Oh dear! I mean Mr Bairstow. I know he's not your husband now and perhaps you're not on speaking terms with him any longer . . .'

'We are on speaking terms,' Eva said gently. 'And I think I know what you want me to ask him. You want him to keep the case out of the *Record*.'

Eva nodded vigorously, her face showing its first sign of hope.

'I'm sorry,' Rose said. 'He wouldn't do that, Eva. He wouldn't do it for me, nor for anyone. He would call it suppressing the news, and it's against his principles.'

Eva looked at her in disbelief.

'But he's the editor! He can print what he likes, can't he? He could keep it out if he wanted to.'

'I daresay he could,' Rose said. 'I'm never quite sure. But I know he wouldn't. He says the readers have a right to know.' She thought of their own divorce, which had been reported in full, every sordid detail of it, no matter how it told against him.

'But the readers wouldn't be any better off for knowing Jim had been sent to prison!' Eva protested. 'No-one would be better off, only me and the children would be a lot worse off.'

Rose saw the tears well up in Eva's eyes, and made up her mind.

'All the same I'll ask him,' she said. 'But don't build up your hopes, Eva.'

'Oh I won't, Doctor!' Eva said, immediately brightening. 'I won't, I promise!' But Rose knew she would.

'We'd better get back,' she said. 'My car's close by. I'll give you a lift to your mother's. In fact, we would pick up the children there and I could take you all back to Marton Green to save you bothering with the tram.'

They collected Dorothy and Meg and Rose drove back to Firth Avenue.

'Will you come in?' Eva said.

'Well, just for a minute.'

Wanting to get home, she would have refused but for the nervous look on Eva's face as, when they saw the car approaching, a group of children gathered outside the gate of number eight. They stood there silently, curious and unsmiling; but not hostile, Rose thought. There was really no need for Eva's nervousness. The children were simply nosey-parkers. She often encountered the same behaviour when she was visiting patients.

She helped Eva and the children out of the car and crossed the pavement with them. As they walked through the group of children a girl, younger than the rest, called out to Dorothy.

'Your Dad's a Bad Man, Dorothy Denby!'

Eva took her daughters' hands and ran with them into the house. Rose turned to the little girl.

'Who told you that?' There was no way anything could have appeared in the paper yet.

The little girl looked scared at the sharpness in Rose's voice and an older girl spoke up for her.

'We saw him being taken away by the police. He was handcuffed. We saw!'

'There you are, you see!' Eva cried when Rose went into the house. 'It's started already! What will it be like next week when it all comes out?'

'My husband used to tell me that people soon forget. He said all these things were a nine days' wonder.'

'The people it happens to don't forget,' Eva said bitterly. 'It lasts a lot longer than nine days for them. Dorothy and Meg might remember for the rest of their lives!'

She sat on the bright new sofa in the bright new home, her daughters on either side of her, all three of them looking at Rose, who felt powerless to help them.

Rose had seen little of Alex since the day he had left her, almost a year ago now. They had made arrangements whereby he would collect Jenny and have her with him for a few hours at a time, but it had proved unsatisfactory. She was not yet two years old and she did not take kindly to being whisked away by this man who had already become a stranger to her. Most of the time she was with him she fretted for her mother and for the familiar surroundings of her own home. It seemed kinder, in the end, to discontinue the arrangement.

'But then she'll forget me,' Alex protested.

Rose nodded.

'Perhaps she will. I'll try to see that she doesn't. I've no wish to deprive you of your daughter, or Jenny of her father, but I suppose it's one of the consequences of divorce when a child is so young. Perhaps you can come back into her life again when she's a little older.'

She doubted that he would. By that time he would probably have a new family who would replace Jenny. He had not yet married Gwen Mayfield, but Rose was sure it was in the offing.

On the day after Jim Denby had been remanded in custody Rose went to see Alex. Yesterday's court case had been reported in the *Record*. She had known she would not be in time to stop that, but it had been a brief report, not in a prominent position in the paper. She had little hope of the same treatment in a week's time.

'You're looking well,' Alex said when she was shown into his office.

'You too,' Rose replied. He was an attractive man, no

222

doubt of it. Since he had left her he had put on some weight, and it suited him; but his face was not so puffy, nor his colour so high. She thought that he was probably not drinking. She was interested to find that she could view him so dispassionately. Sitting opposite to him, she harboured no hard feelings, had no animosity towards him.

'How is Jenny?' Alex enquired.

Rose thought he sounded uneasy. Was he worried about her visit? Was he perhaps expecting her to ask for money?

'She's well. She's talking a lot now. New words every day. But I'm not here on my own behalf or Jenny's. We're doing fine. I'm here about Jim Denby. You know he's been remanded in custody? But of course you know! It was reported in the *Record*.'

She watched his eyes grow wary as she was speaking.

'So I'm sure you can guess why I'm here,' she continued. 'I'm asking you to keep it out of the paper . . .'

'Impossible!' He did not wait for her to finish. 'You know I can't do that!'

'Won't, not can't! Then will you promise to give it the least possible publicity, Alex? For the sake of Eva and her children?'

'I can't possibly promise that,' he said. 'It will get the amount of publicity it merits; no more, no less. But I have to warn you, it looks like being an interesting case.'

It was suddenly not true that she had no strong feelings about this man. A tide of dislike rose in her. She wanted to wipe the cool, implacable expression from his face. But even so, she realized that it was the editor in him she disliked. The man she had first known, or thought she had known, had disappeared behind the job. He was the God Almighty Editor.

'You don't care at all about people, do you?' she flared. 'As long as you can titillate your readers, feed their vulgar curiosity, that's all that counts, isn't it?'

She was shouting her accusations. She knew she could be heard all over the outer office but she did not care. She would like to shout it all from the Town Hall steps.

'Do you ever give a thought to what you do to people?' she demanded. 'Does it never worry you that you might ruin their lives? Don't you *care?*

Alex, on his side of the desk, remained calm and imperturbable.

'I'm not the one who ruins their lives,' he said. 'I haven't ruined Eva Denby's life. Her husband did that. I shall do no more than report what the court says *he* has done.'

'My God, you make it sound like you're doing the world a favour!' Rose cried. 'Did *you* never go wrong? Did *you* never go astray?'

'When I did,' he said quickly '– if we're to call it wrong – when you divorced me it was all reported in the *Record*. I didn't lift a finger to stop it. You must know that. You must have read it.'

'I did,' Rose said sharply. 'Every sordid detail! Thank God Jenny was too young to understand. But Eva's children aren't too young. They can read – and even if they couldn't, people would soon tell them. I wouldn't have your job, Alex. I wouldn't have it for a king's ransom!'

'It's a job,' Alex said. 'I'm a professional – every bit as much as you are, though I know you like to think you're way above a mere newspaper man. But I don't tell you how to run your professional life. I leave it to you because I expect you to know best, to know where your duty lies. Why should you expect to run mine? Come to that, how many people strongly disagree with what *you* are doing – but you never let it stop you. Nor shall I let you interfere in mine.'

'So that's your final word?' Rose said. It was no use. She was defeated.

'I shan't give the Denby case any special publicity, any particularly prominent position,' he said. 'Nor shall I play it down. It will get exactly the space and position it deserves; no more, no less. Until the case is heard we don't know what that will be. And now can I give you a cup of tea, Rose?'

'No thank you.' She stood up, ready to leave.

'Before you go,' Alex said, 'I want to tell you that Gwen and I are getting married in two weeks' time.'

Rose began to tremble, and clenched her hands so as not to show it. She felt weak, and near to tears. How could she have thought, not many minutes ago, that she was devoid of feeling for Alex? The love, of a kind, the affection and friendship, the shared lives over five years, could not be wiped clean away by a form of words in a divorce court. It was not as easy as that.

'I hope you will both be very happy,' she said quietly.

'Thank you. And while you're here, Rose, let me say how much I appreciate your attitude to Gwen over the Mothers' Club. She'd have hated to give it up.'

'That was never on the cards,' Rose said. 'She's far better at the job than I am. I'm not really needed now. In any case, it's the club members who are important, not Gwen or myself. I have my professional standards too, you see!'

'You don't have to tell me,' Alex said.

Rose noted with some misgiving that the courtroom was almost full. She supposed the magistrate's words, duly reported, had brought people in. 'Graver charges to follow', he had said, but what did it mean? Eva had been allowed to see her husband during the past week but he had revealed nothing.

'He said he'd been advised not to,' she told Rose.

So the general public, to whom a morning in court was a way of passing the time agreeably, would hear at the same time as Eva what would so deeply affect her life. And if the case didn't take too long it would make this evening's edition of the *Record*, and the world of Akersfield, Eva's world, would know all.

Eva, pale and silent, sat beside Rose, her hands clenching and unclenching as she waited. When Jim Denby was led into the dock she closed her eyes as if she could not bear to see him. He looked even more defeated than he had a week ago, not even raising his head as the charges were read out.

'You appear on three charges,' the Stipendiary Magistrate said. 'You are charged firstly with obtaining, by false pretences from your employer, sums amounting to ninety pounds. Secondly you are charged with obtaining a cheque book from the Akersfield and District Bank; thirdly you are charged with obtaining by false pretences parts for a car amounting to twenty-three pounds fifteen shillings.

In a voice no more than a whisper, Jim Denby pleaded guilty to all three charges.

'I don't believe it!' Eva gasped. 'All that money.'

There was plenty to interest the crowd in the court-room, Rose thought as the tale unfolded. Doing odd jobs in the home of Mr Freeman, his employer, Jim Denby had come across the man's passbook for the building society. Noting the account number he had written a letter, purporting to come from his employer, saying that the pass book was lost and asking the Society to pay the bearer of the letter the sum of twenty pounds. It had worked like a dream. Denby signed for the money in a fictitious name, pocketed it, and repeated the process on four more occasions, never asking for too much. It was only when he took the short cut of impersonating his employer on the telephone, instead of writing a letter, asking the Society to pay a small sum of money to a messenger he would send to collect it, and the clerk called Mr Freeman back on some small point, that the fraud came to light.

The details of the other charges revealed equally devious plots, each of which he had got away with in the beginning, all of which were bound to trap him in the end. How could he be at once so clever and so utterly stupid? Rose wondered. Her heart ached for Eva, listening to these revelations which her husband did not deny. At one point she lifted her hands and covered her ears as if she could bear to hear no more.

The Stipendiary appeared to enjoy the summing up as much as he had enjoyed the recital.

'This case is very serious,' he said. 'The prisoner has pleaded guilty to acts which might have led him to be charged with forgery, for which I would have had no alternative but to send him to penal servitude.'

A quiet moan escaped Eva. 'It's all right,' Rose whispered. 'He's not going to.'

'You have been committing these wicked acts notwithstanding the fact that you were in regular employment. You have given no thought to the consequences for your wife and children . . .' On and on he went. Jim Denby sat as though not hearing a word. Only when the Stipendiary pronounced sentence – 'You will go to prison for twelve months in all' – did he raise his head and look across the court to where Eva sat. But Eva did not see him. Her face was buried in her hands as she wept, and she did not even see him led away. Her voice came muffled through her sobs. 'You don't understand! You don't know the worst! I'm going to have a baby! My baby will be born when its father is in prison!'

Rose gasped. 'Eva, why didn't you tell me? Does Jim know?'

'Nobody knows. I didn't tell anybody. I couldn't believe it – it's been so long. But it's true all right. What am I going to do, Doctor Rose? What am I going to do?'

It was all there in the next edition of the *Record*.

AKERSFIELD MAN'S FRAUDS
Forged Letters
Twelve Month Sentence

As well as everything about the crimes, every word of the Stipendiary's summing up, homily, dire warnings to Youth, they printed Jim Denby's home address and the names and ages of his wife and children. Nothing was left out. As she read those last details, Rose felt a tremendous anger against all newspapers and against Alex Bairstow in particular.

A week after Jim Denby had been sent to prison the quarterly meeting of the Mothers' Holiday Fund took place in Rose's house, which had become the recognized venue for them.

'The house at Blackpool has turned out very well,' Miss Nesfield said. She turned to Rose. 'You made a very wise decision that day in Blackpool, Rose!'

Rose's eyes sought and met John Worthing's. She read in his the question which had so often been in her own heart since that day. 'Did we make the right decision?' She was lonely; she admitted it. At the end of each day, when work was over and Jenny was in bed, there was nothing left for her. Often, physically tired though she was, she welcomed the urgent night calls which took her out again, pitched her into life. Work was all that was left to her, and it was not enough; even though it was going so well, it was not enough. She needed to share the success she was having, as well as the setbacks. But there could never be anyone. She would never again make the mistake of thinking that someone else could take John Worthing's place. The question burned in his eyes now as he looked at her. She turned away quickly, brought her mind back to the business in hand. There was no future in such questions.

When the meeting was over and the members were leaving, Rose standing in the hall seeing them out, John Worthing said, 'I wanted a word with you about the Denbys. Can you spare me a few minutes?'

'Of course,' Rose said.

She closed the door on the others and went back into the sitting room, John Worthing followed her.

'It's a bad situation about the Denbys,' Rose said. 'Eva is pregnant, but what obsesses her is that the baby will be born while Jim is in prison. She doesn't seem to care for his sake – though why should she. I'd say she'd lost all feeling for him. But she's bitterly upset that this is going to be the baby's start in life – as if it was a curse on the child. And she's already sure that one day it will find out . . .'

She broke off. He wasn't listening. He was standing there, looking at her. A *frisson* of fear, pleasure, wonder, went through her at the intensity of his look.

'Where's Jenny?' he asked quietly.

'Out with Moira.'

'And Annie?'

'Gone to see her mother. Why?'

'Then we're alone?'

'John, why do you . . .' Rose began.

But she was in his arms and he had stopped her words with his kiss. His mouth was hard on hers and she knew that he would bruise her lips. But she wanted him to do so. She wanted him to hold her so hard that he would crush her bones, crush the life out of her. She raised her arms and locked them around his neck, running her fingers through his hair, caressing his head, stroking his neck. And then they were on the sofa, and then on the floor. She pulled his head down to her breast and his fingers trembled as he unfastened the buttons of her blouse. A shudder went through her body as his fingers sought, and found, her nipples.

It was over violently and quickly. As the climax came they cried out together, and then she shuddered, and began to weep. He was infinitely tender with her then.

'I'm sorry,' he said. 'I didn't mean to hurt you, Rose. I never meant that.'

'You didn't,' she said. 'I wanted you to. It had to be like that. We waited so long.'

'And now the waiting is over,' he said.

'What do you mean?'

'I mean we can't go back, my darling Rose. Not ever again.'

But she knew, it was instantly clear to her, that they could not go on.

'I love you,' he said. 'You know that. I love you as I've never loved any other woman.'

'And I love you,' she replied. 'I do truly love you, my dear one. But it's impossible.'

'What's impossible, Rose? Nothing is impossible between you and me, except marriage. I want that as much as you do. You know that's true. But what we have is better than you'll find in a thousand other marriages.'

'I know that, too,' Rose said. 'Don't think I'm not tempted, John. I am. And never more so than at this minute. I want you every bit as much as you want me. But I can't do it. I've explained to you before that for me it has to be marriage or nothing.'

He let go her hand, moved away from her. She watched the tight, hostile look come into his face.

'Don't play about, Rose. I'll not stand for that. If you're trying to blackmail me into marriage, it won't work. Diana is sick. She needs me. It's you I love, but as long as she's ill – and she *is* ill – I won't leave her. I've always made that clear.'

'But I need you too!' Rose cried. 'I need you every day of my life! What about my needs? As for blackmail – how can you *say* that?'

'I'm sorry!' John said.

'But I have my boundaries, too. You can't leave your wife while she's sick. I can't have an affair with you while you're married to Diana.'

'We always get back to the same place,' he said.

'We always will,' Rose answered.

She stood up. She felt drained, hopeless. 'I think you should go now, John. Moira will be back with Jenny soon.' He would never know the effort it took her to send him away. It was as if she was amputating a limb, cutting out her heart.

He gave her a long look, searching into her. Then he took her hand and, with that foreign way he had, lightly kissed the backs of her fingers.

'Good-bye Rose,' he said.

Chapter Fifteen

On the twenty-third of December Rose decided to go to Marton Green to visit Eva. She was ashamed that, though from time to time she had sent things by way of Mrs Foster, she had visited only once in the months since Jim had gone to prison, and that in the early days. Her excuse – she knew it was a poor one – was that with the steady increase in both her practices she had been too busy.

Before leaving home she went upstairs to the attic, which had now been furnished as a nursery for Jenny, with the adjoining smaller attic as a bedroom for Moira. The warmth and comfort of the nursery, a bright fire burning in the grate behind the heavy metal fireguard, the floor carpeted, met her as she opened the door. Jenny sat on the floor, surrounded by toys; building bricks, dolls, a teddy bear, a wooden cart. She held out her arms to Rose as she entered.

'Mummy play with bricks?' she invited.

'Well only for a minute, darling. I have to go out,' Rose said. She picked her way through the scattered playthings and knelt down beside her daughter. Jenny had far too many toys. Some *must* be given away. But many of them were presents from patients and it would be wrong to part with them just yet.

'You're going out yourself,' she said to Jenny. 'Moira will take you just as soon as she's finished ironing your clothes.'

She turned to Moira. 'See that she's well wrapped up. She must wear her thick leggings and her fur cap. It's bitter out. In fact I'm wondering if you should go at all. It's so snug in here.'

'She enjoys her outing, Doctor,' Moira said. She appealed to Jenny. 'Don't you, my pet?' What was more, she herself wanted to go out. She planned to change her library book again. There was a new young man in the library she rather liked the look of; moreover, he had promised to save her the new Ethel M. Dell. The doctor was a good employer, but she was so set on Jenny that she sometimes forgot that other people had their own lives to live. Much as she loved Jenny, Moira did not intend to look after other people's children forever.

'Very well then,' Rose said. 'But don't keep her out too long.' She turned back to Jenny. 'I have to go now, love. We'll have a game later, I promise.'

She kissed the top of her daughter's head. Such pretty red hair she had. 'She's the spitten image of you when you were little,' Rose's own mother had said on her last visit. 'I only wish your Dad could be here to see her.'

When Rose drove into Firth Avenue it seemed that all the children in the neighbourhood were engaged in making slides: thankfully not on the road, but on the asphalt paths which bisected the green, where the surface was like glass from black ice. They queued behind each other to take turns on the slide. The less brave went upright, one foot in front of the other, down the slope; the bolder ones shot down crouching, and the bravest of all crouched on one foot, the other held out stiffly in front of them. All over Akersfield, Rose reckoned, children were sliding on the ice. It was amazing that she did not have to deal with more broken limbs.

Eva was so long in answering her knock that Rose wondered if she was out, though she had spotted Dorothy and Meg in the crowd of children. In the end she came, opening the door no more than an inch or two until she was sure who stood there.

'Why, Doctor Rose, I didn't expect to see *you*!' The absence of any reproach in Eva's greeting made Rose feel more guilty than ever.

'Come in, Doctor!'

Rose, following Eva into the living room, was appalled by what she saw. She should not have been so shocked. Mrs Foster had told her more than once that things were not going well for Eva, but Rose had never pictured it like this.

Gone was the three-piece suite, with the much-prized chesterfield; gone was the bulbous-legged table and the two upright chairs. In their place were a small, deal table with a scrubbed white top, plus three old stools. The range no longer shone black and silver but, worst of all on this bitter winter's day, there was no fire in the grate.

'Why, Eva!' Rose exclaimed.

'They took the furniture back,' Eva said. 'I couldn't keep up the payments, you see.' She was ashamed to admit it, as if it was a fault in herself.

'Even the oilcloth from the floor?' Rose asked.

'Yes. Though I don't know what good it was to them. It was cheap stuff. The pattern was already wearing off.' The floor was bare now, except for a shabby, tabbed rug in front of the fireplace.

'The only things they didn't take were the two gramophone records,' Eva said. 'I reckon they forgot those. But they're not much good without a gramophone, are they?'

She picked up the records in their cardboard cases, fingering them, stroking them, as if by some magic she could bring out the music, hear the mellifluous harmonies of Layton and Johnstone once again.

'I Want to be Happy,' Rose thought. What an ill-chosen one that had turned out to be!

'Why have you no fire?' she asked – and could have bitten out her tongue at the stupidity of the question. There was only one reason for not having a fire on a day like this.

'Actually we have a little bit of coal in the coalhouse,' Eva said. 'I'm saving it for Christmas Day. The curate from Saint Thomas's said the church would be sending me a bag of coal but I'm afraid of it not coming in time. The children are out playing, so they can keep warm.'

'So they do still play with the other children?' Rose asked gently.

Eva's face shadowed. 'If it's a crowd, like playing on the ice today. But it's not liked if they're playing with just one or two others. Nothing much is said, but I watch the other bairns being called home by their mothers. And of course they're never invited into anyone's house.'

'But that's monstrous!' Rose cried.

Eva shrugged. 'It's the way things are. It's as if they were infectious. I try to make it up to them in other ways, but it's not the same.'

It was freezing cold in the house. Rose resisted the temptation to draw the fur collar of her coat closer around her neck. She wanted to weep at the sight of Eva in the bare little room, where only the lace curtains remained of its former glory, hiding its poverty from the world outside.

'The worst bit was when the van came to take the furniture away,' Eva said. 'All the neighbours seeing it. They put the chesterfield down in the road while they were loading up and some of the children came and sat on it. It was worse, in a way, than when they came and took Jim.' She sat there, remembering.

'And how have you been?' Rose asked, breaking the silence. 'In yourself, I mean?'

It was hardly necessary to ask. Eva was as thin as a stick, her face chalky and hollow-cheeked, her hair lank. In contrast to the thinness of the rest of her body her belly, filled with the coming child, swelled out in front of her like a balloon. As always, Nature had taken priority over the mother's food to nourish the baby, leaving almost nothing for Eva's own needs.

'I'm all right,' Eva said. 'The baby's due in January, a month before Jim comes out - if he gets full remission for good conduct, that is.'

'And will he?'

'Oh yes! He's a very good prisoner, it seems. Did Mam tell you I'd been to see him? The church paid my fare, though I never go there. When the baby is born I'm going to have it christened there. They've been very good to me.'

While I did almost nothing, Rose thought.

'Thank you for the things you sent with Mam,' Eva said. 'It was kind of you.'

'How do you manage for money?' Rose asked.

'I get relief. They give me a bit of cash, and a voucher for food that I can spend at the Coop.'

She did not add that she walked two miles each way to the Relieving Officer's premises, and then queued for an hour for the handout; nor that she was allowed to use the food voucher only for certain basic items. Not for her the gratification of a pregnant woman's fancy for a tin of salmon or a bit of real butter on her bread.

'I'm very lucky, though,' Eva said. 'The lady next door

sends me in a bit of their dinner two or three times a week, when they have a cooked meal themselves. Just while I'm pregnant, she says. I have to promise not to share it with Dorothy and Meg, though, and that's hard. It's all right when they're at school because they get tickets to go somewhere for dinners, but it's school holidays now and they get real hungry.'

'I've brought a few things,' Rose said. 'Nothing much really.' She unpacked the bag on the table; sugar, tea, some tins of food, a packet of biscuits, cheese, a jar of her mother's home-made jam.

'Oh, Doctor, how good of you!' Eva cried. 'Strawberry jam of all things!'

'It's nothing,' Rose said quickly. Seeing Eva's poverty she felt it keenly that she had been able to pick these things from her well-filled larder almost in passing.

'It's a great deal,' Eva said. Her face shone with gratitude.

'And there are three small Christmas presents here, one for each of you. Not to be unwrapped until Christmas Day.'

At the sight of the three parcels, neatly wrapped in coloured tissue paper and tied with ribbon, Eva broke down. Tears ran down her cheeks. She collapsed on to a stool, laid her head on her arms on the table, and wept. She wept as though the misery of months was pouring out of her. She wept, not in anger or despair, but in relief that something good had happened, Rose went to her and stood with her arms around Eva's shoulders. There were tears in her own eyes that something which had cost her so little could mean so much to Eva. Hers were tears of shame at herself, and of anger against life which did this to people like Eva.

Presently Eva lifted her head, dried her eyes. 'I'm sorry, Doctor,' she said. 'But you don't know what these presents mean to me. You see I'd racked my brains as to what I could give the children. There wasn't anything. It would have had to be a Jaffa orange in each of their stockings, and some nuts. The trouble is, they believe in Father Christmas. It's one thing to be poor the rest of the time - children can cope with that somehow - but if you

235

think that Father Christmas has left you out - well, it's too much to bear isn't it? You can't understand why. You wonder what you've done wrong.'

Rose felt anguished. She must do something more. The little she had done was not enough. There must be some fund - surely the *Record* had such a fund? She would go to Alex.

'Don't tell the children the presents are from me,' she said to Eva. 'Let them be from Father Christmas.'

There was a knock at the door. 'That'll be Norman,' Eva said.

'Norman?'

'The lady's son from next door. He brings my dinner in if he's working nights. Can he tell I've been crying?' she asked anxiously.

Not waiting for an answer to his knock, Norman came into the house carrying two plates put together.

'Your favourite today, Eva! Liver and onions with fried potatoes! Oh, I didn't know you had a visitor! I'm sorry!'

'That's all right,' Rose said. 'I'm just about to leave. Eat it while it's hot, Eva. It smells delicious.'

The door opened again and Dorothy and Meg came in. They were small and pinched-looking, red noses in faces white from the cold. Not speaking, they looked longingly at Eva's plate. Eve glanced unhappily at Norman.

'It's no use,' she said. 'How can I eat it?'

He shook his head, non-plussed.

'Ma says you've got to, for the sake of the baby. She's only sorry she can't do the same for Dorothy and Meg. She would if she could.'

'I know,' Eva said. 'She's a kind woman.'

'I'll tell you what,' Norman said. 'I'll take the kiddies around with me and see if I can't rake up something. Come on you two!'

'Wait a minute,' Rose interrupted. 'Isn't there a fish-and-chip shop near?'

'Five minutes away,' Norman said.

Rose opened her purse. 'Here's a shilling,' she said to Dorothy. 'Can you get fish and chips for you and Meg and me? A fish-and-a-pennyworth each? You could take Meg with you while your mother finishes her dinner.'

'A fish?' Dorothy was incredulous. 'Not just chips?'

'That's right,' Rose said. 'I'll stay and eat with you. We three will have dinner together.'

Eva beamed, was transformed. 'Oh Doctor Rose, are you sure?'

'Quite sure!'

Eva turned to the children. 'There'll be three-ha'pence change, Our Dorothy,' she said. 'Mind you don't lose it. Get off with you then.'

'I'll leave you to it as well,' Norman said.

'Now I must set some plates,' Eva fussed when they had gone. 'I'm right sorry I don't have a tablecloth.'

'Get on with your dinner before it goes cold,' Rose ordered. 'We don't need a tablecloth, nor plates either for that matter. It won't be the first time I've eaten fish and chips from a newspaper.'

Eva tucked into her liver and onions with a clear conscience and a sharp appetite. 'Some say they taste better that way,' she said through a mouthful. 'Especially if they're wrapped in the *News of the World!*'

They came – hot and delicious, the white fish covered in crisp, golden batter – wrapped in the Akersfield *Record*. 'I put salt and vinegar on them in the shop,' Dorothy said.

When they had eaten the last delectable mouthful, and drunk a cup of tea which Eva insisted on making, Rose left. Her home surgery was not until six o-clock but she was determined to see Alex this afternoon.

'Close the door after me,' she said to Eva. 'Don't come outside. It's a bitter day.'

When she was getting into her car Norman came out of his house to speak to her.

'I just wanted to ask you, is Eva going to be all right? Having the baby, I mean?'

'I'm not her doctor now,' Rose said. 'But I think she should be. Thanks in no small part to your mother.'

'We do what we can for her,' he said. 'We think a lot of Eva. She doesn't get out enough. I wanted to take her out this coming New Year's Eve, but she won't come. Says it wouldn't be the right thing. My Ma agrees with her.'

'I daresay your mother's right,' Rose said. 'More's the pity. Eva doesn't get much fun.'

'I'll let you into a secret,' Norman said eagerly. 'She's going to get a wireless set for a Christmas present! I'm building it myself from a blueprint. Two valves, with a loud-speaker!'

What a pity Eva didn't meet you first, Rose thought as she drove away.

She had seen nothing of Alex since their stormy meeting in the week before Jim Denby went to prison. She had not communicated her disgust at the spread given to the case in the *Record*. It would have done no good and he already knew how she felt. She had read the account in the paper of his marriage to Gwen and a rumour had filtered through, by way of a member of the Mothers' Club who knew Mrs Foster, who told Rose, that Gwen was already pregnant.

So could I have been, Rose thought, driving into the town. I could have been carrying John Worthing's child. One sexual act, as she often told her disbelieving patients, was all it took. Nature had been at it too long to require several months of practice. On the one and only occasion John had made love to her they had taken no precautions. There had been none of the forethought she preached to others, no considerations except of the body's demands at that moment. Nothing else had mattered. She was fortunate that the episode's only legacy was a deeper understanding of her patients' actions in similar circumstances.

Was she fortunate? Above everything else she could think of she would like to have John Worthing's child in her. But no matter. It had not happened, and now it never would.

Alex was surprised to see her. He greeted her politely, though there was a shade of anxiety in his voice.

'Is something wrong with Jenny?' he asked.

'Nothing at all. She's as fit as a fiddle. You could come to the house to visit her, you know, if you wished to do so.'

His face closed up. 'It wouldn't do just now. Gwen is pregnant. It would upset her.'

'Surely not?' Rose said. 'I've always considered Gwen a

sensible, down-to-earth woman.'

'That's true,' Alex said. 'But women are different when they're pregnant. You must know that. You see them often enough. By the way, I'm glad to hear your work's going so well. I suppose you saw the letter of appreciation in the *Record* a few weeks ago?'

'I saw it,' Rose said. 'I was encouraged. I'm sure public opinion *is* changing – but so very slowly. It will be a long time before more than a handful of people describe doctors in my line of work as "public benefactors". To most of the population we're quite the reverse.'

'Well, what can I do for you?' Alex asked.

'The Denbys again. Or rather, Eva. I went to see her this morning. I was appalled at the conditions she's living under. Two days before Christmas and she has no coal, hardly any food, no money in her purse. She's being fed a few dinners by the kindness of a neighbour, but until school starts again the children are going hungry. In addition to all that she's eight months pregnant. Isn't there a fund which can help her?'

'There's the Christmas Relief Fund,' Alex said. 'Run by the *Record*. Why hasn't she applied?'

'Presumably because she doesn't know about it and nobody thought to tell her,' Rose said. 'There isn't time for her to go through all the red tape of applying before Christmas. Can you cut any corners for her? To be really useful she needs the money in time to buy things for Christmas – and tomorrow is Christmas Eve.'

'I'll have a word with the Powers-that-Be. I expect they'll award her five pounds as she's in such straits.' Alex took out his wallet, extracted a note. 'I'll jump the gun and give it to you myself – and redeem it from them.'

'Thank you very much,' Rose said. 'I can't tell you what a difference it will make. I'll get Moira to go to Marton Green on the tram later this afternoon, to take it to Eva.'

There seemed nothing more for them to say to each other. She wanted to ask him if he was happy. He looked contented enough. She wanted to assure him that she felt nothing but friendship for him now. But the words would not come. Perhaps he understood all that, anyway.

'I'll be off then,' she said. 'I hope you have a good

Christmas. Congratulations about the baby. I'm truly glad for both of you, Alex.'

'Thank you. We're pleased about it. What are you doing at Christmas?'

'I'm taking Jenny to Faverwell on Christmas Day. Just for a few days. Doctor Lewthwaite is covering for me.'

The two of them stayed in Faverwell until the twenty-seventh of December. Rose had closed up the house in Beechcroft Road so that Annie and Moira could go home to their families for the holiday. When she returned there was a note on the mat from Mrs Foster.

'Dear Doctor,

This is to let you know that Eva had her baby on Boxing Day (yesterday). A fine little boy and both well though he was before his time. The coal came Christmas Eve so they was kept warm and a big hamper from someone ~~amon~~ . . . ~~anyom~~ . . . from persons unknown.

Yours truly and oblige,
Mrs Foster

Who had sent the hamper? Rose wondered. She had not done so.

On New Year's Eve Rose attended a party given by Doctor Lewthwaite. It came as no surprise to her when, towards the end of the evening, John Worthing came in. He was alone. She had long ago realized that in Akersfield everyone ran across everyone else all the time. It was one of the reasons why she could not keep John Worthing out of her life. Even so, she had not met him or spoken with him since the day he had made love to her. Now she felt his hand under her elbow and knew without turning around that it was he. No-one else in the world could send this wave of feeling through her. A moment ago she had been with a group of people; now, as if by magic, she was just with him.

'It's almost midnight,' John said. 'A few more minutes and it will be nineteen-twenty-seven. What does this remind you of?'

'I know,' Rose said. 'I remember the first time. It's strange how we think the year just about to begin is going to be the best ever.'

At that other party, looking towards nineteen-twenty-one from the last days of nineteen-twenty, it had seemed that everything good was before her. She had been ready to start her job at the Infant Welfare Centre; Alex was her good friend; John Worthing . . . with John it had seemed no more than perhaps the lightest of flirtations ahead.

'Everything seems set to go in one direction,' she said. 'Then before you know where you are it all changes.'

'I haven't,' John said. 'I knew what I felt about you then. I haven't changed.'

'Please John, let's not talk like this!' Rose begged.

'Why not? If we can't be emotional at the end of the old year, looking into the new, when can we?'

'I can't cope with it,' Rose said. 'I don't want to make a fool of myself in front of all these people. Unless we can change the subject I shall walk away from you.'

'Then we'll talk about anything you like,' he promised. 'Only stay with me until it's midnight. I want you to be the first person I see and touch in nineteen-twenty-seven.'

'I shall be,' she said.

'So what do you want to talk about?'

She cast around for a topic of conversation. All she wanted was to be with him, not to have to talk at all. But people would notice if they stood in silence.

'Is there anything to be done about Jim Denby?' she asked. 'He's due out in February, with not much prospect of a job. If he stays out of work long, then I think that whole family will just go under. But who will give him a job now?'

'I will,' John Worthing said.

Rose stared at him in disbelief. She had asked the question with no hope of a reply.

'*You* will? But how? What?'

'I'm getting a second car. I shall need a chauffeur, mostly to take Diana around. Her health doesn't improve. Sometimes me also, if I have to go to dinners or functions in the evening. He's a good driver, I believe?'

'There's nothing wrong with his driving that I know of,'

Rose said. 'But what about the risk of . . .'

'I'll take the other risks,' he interrupted. 'There won't be a lot of opportunity for him to go wrong. I don't propose to employ him in the house. He'll be strictly for the car.'

'I understand he's vowed to go straight,' Rose said. 'I went to see Eva and the new baby yesterday. She'd had a Christmas letter.'

'I daresay he has,' John said. 'For what it's worth. Let's hope he sticks to it.'

A sudden thought struck Rose. Why had she not thought of it before?'

'Did you by any chance send a hamper to Eva Denby at Christmas?' she asked.

'Quiet!' he said. 'It's striking midnight.'

When the last stroke from Doctor Lewthwaite's silver-toned clock had died away John Worthing turned to Rose, gently pulling her around so that she faced him.

'A Happy New Year to you, my dearest Rose,' he said quietly. 'A happy nineteen-twenty-seven.'

She raised her glass.

'And to you, John. Happy New Year!'

Jim Denby, driving the new, maroon-coloured Daimler, felt good. It was a superb car, a pleasure to handle. Sometimes, sitting up here in front, he could almost imagine it was his own. And he himself matched the car in smartness, in his well-fitting maroon uniform with silver buttons and the peaked cap which Mrs Worthing had chosen for him. She was a woman of taste, and not mean like so many of them who had money. She had sent him to a good tailor to have the uniform made, no expense spared. It flattered his figure. Though he had lost some weight in prison, he still had a good pair of shoulders on him.

He turned into the forecourt of the Queen's Hotel in Harrogate and drew to a smooth halt in front of the main entrance. Jumping quickly from his seat, he went around the back of the car to open the rear door. No good chauffeur ever went around the front of a car: he had learnt that as he was learning many things now. It was a good job he'd landed, and he was determined to make the most of it. There would be picking, opportunities of course – of that he was sure. Now if Madam would let him handle the buying of the petrol for instance . . . Everyone knew it was a thirsty car. And in time she'd trust him to do little errands for her. He'd be happy to serve. He held open the door deferentially while Mr and Mrs Worthing stepped out.

'It's seven-thirty,' John Worthing said. 'Be back here at ten-thirty sharp, Denby.'

'I will, Sir,' Jim said. 'Do you want me to stay with the car, Sir?'

'Not necessarily. You can garage it. Do what you like as long as you're back here on time.'

Jim watched his employers walk into the hotel where they were attending a dinner. They were a smart couple; good-looking, well-dressed. She always remained the lady and she treated him all right. Come to that, so did the boss, though he didn't have much to say. Rumour was that he was sweet on Doctor Rose, but in Akersfield, that one-horse town, rumour said anything. She was an attractive bit of stuff though. He'd always thought so, even when he'd hated her – which he didn't any longer as long as she kept her nose out of his business.

He parked the car safely in the hotel garage, locked it up, and deposited the keys with the man in charge. Nearly three hours to kill – say two-and-a-half to be on the safe side. He knew Harrogate well enough now. He sometimes brought Mrs Worthing here. While she was shopping in Parliament Street or browsing around the antique shops down by the Spa, where they said you could often see Queen Mary, he was free to explore the rest of the town. He had discovered a nice little pub near to the station and that was where he meant to go now.

'A pint of Tetley's,' he said to the barmaid, who was a new one. 'And something for yourself?'

'Ta very much. I'll have a glass of port if it's all the same to you!' She favoured him with an intimate smile, which he put down to the smartness of his uniform. It usually had that effect on the ladies. She was the type he liked: good figure, well-rounded. Eva was too skinny these days.

All the same, she'd stood by him when he was inside. And then there was the boy.

At the thought of his baby son a smile played around his lips. The barmaid turned away to serve another customer and Jim went to sit with some of the regulars. He'd be back with her later if he had time. He was quite friendly with one or two of the regulars now.

'How's the bairn?' one of them asked.

'Spit of his Dad!' Jim said. 'And he'd better be!'

He called for a round of drinks, and when they came he said 'I'll ask you to drink to my lad. Wilfred – after Wilfred Rhodes. The greatest cricketer of them all – and a Yorkshireman!'

After that they drank to various people; other men's sons, mothers, wives, sweethearts. They drank to King George, Queen Mary and the Prince of Wales. The people of Harrogate were very loyal. When Jim looked at his watch he was horrified to see the time. The evening had gone by in a flash. It was twenty past ten when he reached the garage and only by the cooperation of the man in charge was he able to get the car out quickly, and be round at the front door of the hotel on the dot of half past.

He waited no more than a couple of minutes before his employer came out. Mrs Worthing was leaning heavily on her husband's arm. She didn't look at all well and the Guv'nor seemed concerned about her – which in a way was lucky because it meant that he wouldn't notice that his chauffeur had had one or two. Not more than he could carry, of course.

'Straight home, Denby,' John Worthing said. 'If the roads are clear you can step on it.'

Jim did just that, and the car responded with alacrity. He was driving well this evening. He quite looked forward to getting home, wondered if Eva would be waiting up for him and if young Wilfred might wake up.

The long, steep hill was clear of traffic. It was a still night; dark sky, touch of frost in the air and on the ground. He gathered speed down the hill, letting the car have her head, like a horse at the gallops. That fellow in the pub had given him a cast-iron tip for the two-thirty at

York tomorrow. What was it called?

At the bottom of the hill, where the river ran, the road turned sharply over the bridge. The road turned, but the big car, careering down the hill, did not. It went at an angle into the wall at the beginning of the bridge. It went through the wall, which was weak at this point. As it plunged nose first towards the river it turned completely over, so that the top of the car was under water first. But it would not have mattered either way. The water was deep at this point, and swollen even more from the heavy Spring rains. In no time at all the whole car was submerged. The bubbles which rose to the surface were lost in the torrent of water. A peaked cap, maroon, with a shiny black neb, floated to the surface and was quickly carried downstream by the current.

Chapter Sixteen

Rose knocked hard on Eva's door, a second time, but to no avail. No wonder, though, that she couldn't be heard. Loud music filled the house, escaping through the open window, floating in the air around number eight, Firth Avenue. Rose turned the knob and went in. Neither Eva nor Norman, who sat on either side of the table, heard her. They were visibly enraptured by a spirited brass band rendering of the 'William Tell' overture from the gramophone. In the split second before the baby, playing on the rug by Eva's feet, looked up and gave the alarm, Rose thought how totally happy they looked. She was glad that, for Eva at any rate, things seemed to have worked out.

'Oh, Doctor Rose! I'm sorry! I didn't hear a thing!' Eva sprang to her feet, shouting over the music. Norman lifted the gramophone head from the record and stopped the sound.

'I didn't know you had a gramophone,' Rose said. Just in time she stopped herself saying 'again'. Now was not the time to remind Eva of that earlier instrument which had been so cruelly snatched from her.

'Norman bought it me for a wedding present,' Eva said. 'And three more records!'

How different the house was since that sad visit she had paid last Christmas, Rose thought. It had not been restored to the shining glory of that first easy payment splurge, but there were some comfortable chairs, and a decent table with a crocheted runner and a glass vase filled with marigolds. Eva, following Rose's glance, said:

'Norman grew them. He's done wonders in the garden in such a short time. We've got lettuces and radishes and other things too!'

Norman Ackroyd had come to Eva's aid from the first awful moments of her widowhood and had looked after her ever since; and always would. Perhaps they would have children of their own? At twenty-seven Eva was young enough, and the way this kind man looked after her, she would soon regain her strength.

'I had to make a visit out this way,' Rose said. 'I thought I'd call and see how you were getting on.'

Eva's smile as she looked at Norman was full of pride. 'We're getting on very well, aren't we, love?' she said. 'We've been married six weeks now, you know!'

'I know,' Rose said. She had been a guest at the quiet wedding in the church which had been so good to Eva when she was in need.

'Wilfred looks well,' she said.

Eva looked fondly at the baby. 'He's into everything now that he's crawling around,' she said with pride. 'He was in the coal scuttle yesterday. You should have seen him. Black as the fireback he was! Ma's looking after him tomorrow. Me and Norman and the girls are going to Morecambe on a *charabanc* excursion, it being Akersfield Tide Saturday.'

'So Mrs Foster told me,' Rose said.

'I've promised Eva that one of these days we shall go for a whole week's holiday,' Norman said. 'I've made up my mind on it. Perhaps in two or three years. I'm one of the lucky ones, you see – a steady job in the dyeworks. I manage to put by a shilling or two each week.'

He was such a good man, Rose thought, looking at his round, pink face, his earnest brown eyes. He had taken Eva's three children as if it was a privilege for him to do so, showing them as much love as if he had fathered them. He must love Eva a great deal.

'How is that nice Mr Worthing?' Eva asked. 'Is he keeping well? I shall never forget how good he was to us when Jim came out of prison. And then to me when Jim . . .'

She faltered. Norman stretched out and took her small hand into his huge one.

'It's all over, love!'

'I know,' Eva said. 'All the same, I don't forget a kindness. I often think what a miracle it was that he wasn't drowned when his wife and poor Jim were. The *Record* said if he'd been trapped like them he couldn't have saved himself. He came to see me, you know. After he came out of hospital.'

At first, when Rose had visited John in hospital, he had not wanted to talk about the accident, but gradually over the weeks, from the little he had said and from the report which had appeared in the *Record*, she had pieced together the story.

In the seconds after the car had plunged into the river John Worthing, finding himself free, had tried at once to save his wife and his chauffeur, but it had been impossible. In any case he had recognized that they were already dead – most likely from shock. He had swum to the river bank, heaved himself out of the icy water, and gone to look for help. The rest of the story had been told to the *Record* by the couple whose cottage John had reached.

'It were a bitter night, with a keen frost,' the man said. 'Me and the wife had gone to bed when the knocking came on the door. I shall never forget the sight of him standing there, like something from the grave; shaking and shivering, the water running out of him and making a pool at his feet; his face bleeding. The wife looked after him – got his wet clothes off, wrapped him in blankets – while I ran to the vicarage to get them to phone for the ambulance.'

As a result of that night, John had taken pneumonia. On the day of his wife's funeral he had a raging temperature and could not leave his bed in the private ward of Akersfield General Hospital. For several days, when it seemed that he might die, life to Rose had seemed cold, black, hopeless. She could not envisage a world without him. Now, though she had seen little of him since he had left hospital, she was grateful every day of her life for his recovery.

'I think he's quite fit again,' she said, answering Eva's question.

When she had drunk the cup of tea which Eva insisted on giving her, she said, 'I must go. I have several calls to make. I'm glad to see everything is going so well.'

Eva went out to the car with her.

'Doctor Rose . . .' she said hesitantly.

'Yes?'

'I hope you don't think it's disrespectful of me, marrying Norman so soon after Jim died. I did try with Jim, you know. And there was nothing went on between Norman and me, no funny business, even when Jim was in prison. I wouldn't have had that, nor would Norman.'

'You did the right thing,' Rose assured her. 'It's clear to

me that Norman worships the ground you walk on.'

'And I love him the same,' Eva said. 'I shall try to be a good wife to him. I hope one day you'll be as happy as me, Doctor Rose.'

Rose drove to Babcock Street. She had an afternoon surgery there today. It was, in many ways, a replica of most of her surgeries. And yet they were all different and she never tired of them. People were not carbon copies of each other even when, as in Babcock Street, their problems were so similar.

There were problems among her patients she was powerless to solve. Unemployment was fractionally better than when she had started in Akersfield, but there were still hundreds of men who had not worked for years and perhaps never would, their families existing on the small dole for which the men queued. Rose saw those long queues day after day, in all weathers, as her route to Babcock Street took her past the Labour Exchange. And until the problems of bad housing and overcrowding were dealt with, no doctor would ever eradicate the diseases and infections which arose from them. Eva had shaken it off, but Paradine Street still stood, its bug-ridden houses still inhabited, the rats still playing on the middens. Such places should be razed to the ground.

The last patient at that afternoon's surgery turned back as she was on the point of leaving.

'There's one thing you've done for us, Doctor, those of us who take advantage. You've shown us how not to have children we can't afford to feed, having to watch them starve, sharing out too little food amongst too many mouths. It isn't that women don't want children, Doctor. Most of us do, and life wouldn't be the same without them. It's that we want to be able to look after them properly. I reckon children are best born to folks who love 'em and want 'em *afore* they're born.'

Rose smiled. 'I know that, Mrs Laycock. It's what I've been trying to get across for years.'

'But things *have* changed a bit,' Mrs Laycock said. 'It's not all that long ago that working-class wives like me had to insert a bit of sponge, soaked in olive oil – or cooking oil if you couldn't afford better – if we didn't want to have a 'bairn. Sometimes it worked, sometimes it didn't, but it was a right messy business, I can tell you. And then all that douching afterwards!'

It was the attitudes which needed to change, Rose thought as Mrs Laycock left. She was convinced that as attitudes changed, research would produce what was needed. It seemed to her – it always had – that attitudes lagged a long way behind science.

She packed her bag and left for home. When she arrived, Jenny was in the hall to greet her.

'You promised to take me to the Tide,' she said.

'I know, and I will,' Rose assured her. 'Straight after evening surgery. Did you do as I suggested and have a good sleep this afternoon? You're going to be staying up rather late for a little girl.'

'She slept well,' Moira said, coming into the hall.

'Good! Then we'll have tea, and then it'll be time for surgery.'

It would be a short surgery this evening. Apart from the fact that there were fewer illnesses in the summer months, the first week in August was Akersfield Tide. 'Tide' was the West Riding word for 'fair'. It was the week when all the mills closed down and those who could afford to go on holiday flocked to the seaside. But there were far more for whom a holiday was impossible and in the tide they had a substitute. It could, at a pinch, be enjoyed for nothing. It cost nothing to walk around and look. But it was far better if one had even a little money.

Rose saw a few patients – stomach upsets, insect bites, sunburn; a stye on the eye of a pretty girl who was mortified by her appearance on the eve of her holiday.

'Bathe it with boracic lotion. Also I'll give you some ointment,' Rose said. 'Cheer up! It doesn't look half as bad as you think. It'll clear up in a day or two.,' Rose had long ago concluded that there were a great many ailments which would clear up as quickly of their own accord as from any remedy she might hand out, but it was another matter getting patients to believe this.

The girl was the last of her patients, but as she started to clear her desk there was a knock at the door.

'Come in,' she called.

When she looked up, John Worthing stood before her. Her heart gave its customary lurch at the sight of him. However calm her outward demeanour she could never, in his presence, control what went on inside her.

He looked well. Leaner, perhaps, since his illness – but more handsome than ever. He was better looking, even, than he had been seven years ago, the few grey hairs amongst the dark ones merely adding to his distinction.

'I thought you were a patient,' Rose said.

'I decided I would be. It seems the easiest way, these days, of seeing you. Do you ever do anything but work, Rose?'

'I've been really quite busy,' Rose said defensively.

'Nonsense! I know perfectly well that this is the slackest time of the year for you. You paid me more attention when I was in hospital than I ever get from you now.'

'Well that's a doctor for you! The sicker the patient, the more attention they get.'

'I wasn't your patient.'

'Well, no. But I always have one or two people to visit in hospital.'

'So you fitted me in? Thank you!'

'You know that's not true,' Rose protested. They both knew that she had visited him night and day, had hardly been able to keep away. But as a doctor she had been able to do that inconspicuously. Now that he was home again . . .

'Have you come for something special?' she asked.

'Very special. I've come to ask you to marry me.'

'Oh John, what am I to say?' They were the words she had waited so long to hear, but now that he had said them she was suddenly unsure of herself, afraid. She wanted, at one and the same time, to shout with happiness and to burst into tears. Why was she being such a fool?

'You are to say "Yes", my darling Rose!'

'But I don't know . . .' She fended him off. 'It's too soon . . . Your wife . . .'

'Nonsense!' he said. 'Look at Eva Denby. She's been married nearly a couple of months already.'

But to Eva life seemed so much less complicated. In spite of her disastrous experience of marriage, she had had no hesitation in accepting Norman. She had that simple faith in the future which Rose longed to possess.

'I want an answer, Rose.' He was stern, demanding.

'You'll have to wait, John.'

He looked at her for a long time before speaking again. When he did so his voice was quiet, yet firm.

'It's nearly seven years since I fell in love with you, Rose. You sat buried in that big chair in the Committee room. Your hair was escaping from under your severe little hat and I thought that your spirit was as fiery and irrepressible as your hair. I fell in love with you then and I wanted you for my wife. Whatever stood between us then, Rose, is past.'

She was trembling from head to foot. What was she to say to him? Her mind was in a turmoil.

'Do you remember the bit in the Bible?' he said.

'What bit?'

'"And Jacob served seven years for Rachel and they seemed unto him but a few days for the love he had to her." That's what it says. Well, I've served it, Rose, but it hasn't seemed a few days to me. It's seemed a long, long time. An eternity.'

It had been a long time. So much had happened. She had gone through all the things they had told her would make her a better doctor; marriage, motherhood, the death of her father – even the break-up of her marriage. Had it made her a better doctor? She didn't know. What she did know was that she wanted to be a doctor for the rest of her life, that nothing would ever take its place. But could she at the same time be the kind of wife John Worthing wanted – and deserved? She didn't know.

'Yes,' she said. 'It's been a long time. Don't think I don't feel that, John. But it's myself I don't trust. I've failed so badly at marriage once, caused a lot of unhappiness. And the reason is – as far as I can tell – that I want more out of life than marriage. Even marriage to someone I love as much as I love you. I'm greedy, John. I want the best of all worlds.'

'Are you trying to tell me that you can't give up your career?' John said. 'Well I don't expect you to, any more than I expect to give up mine.'

'I don't even think of it as a career any longer. I'm not looking for personal advancement. But I couldn't give it up, and I know that sometimes I would put it before you.'

'I'd not stand in your way,' he said. 'I'd not prevent you

doing anything you wanted to.'

'There's more to it than that,' Rose said. 'Alex felt sometimes that I belonged to my patients, not to him. He was right.'

'But this is different, Rose. You and me . . .'

'I know. I love you so much. But it could happen.' Seeing him standing there on the other side of the desk, she wanted to rush into his arms, to be held by him forever.

'I do understand, Rose,' John said. 'I don't think you have anything to fear. I can cope with it if you can – and I know you can. We can face anything if we're together.'

Rose looked at him – and her eyes pricked with tears at the love in his face. What had she done to deserve it? She could never do anything which would let this man down.

'John, I can't give you an answer yet. I want to, but I can't. But I promise not to keep you waiting long.'

'How long, Rose?'

'I don't know. Not long. And whatever I say, that will be final. John, I have to go now. I promised to take Jenny and Moira to Akersfield Tide. They're waiting for me.'

He looked at her without speaking, and then in the end he smiled. She felt an enormous relief that he was not angry with her.

'Then I'll come with you if I may,' he said. 'You can't refuse that. I haven't been to Akersfield Tide for a long time. I don't suppose you've ever been?'

'No. Moira put the idea into Jenny's head but I didn't want Moira to take her alone. If you're coming with us you'll have to go on the tram. That's part of the bargain with Jenny.'

They took the tram, also at Jenny's request riding outside on top. For the past two days Rose, out and about in the town, had seen the tide engines arrive; giant steam engines whose big iron wheels clanged over Akersfield's cobbled streets, whose size held up the trams and all other traffic. 'Mighty in Strength and Endurance', one of them had in letters of brass on its side. It was a good motto since they pulled behind them caravans and trucks, or platforms holding the big roundabouts, and once on the fairground they would generate power.

'We must keep close together,' Rose warned Jenny as

they alighted from the tram and walked up the lane to the tide field. 'It's going to be very crowded.' It was wage night in Akersfield. Anyone lucky enough to have a little money would be here.

With Jenny between Rose and Moira, holding hands, and John Worthing at Rose's elbow, they walked around.

'You may have some brandy snaps,' Rose said. 'It's a very clean stall.' There was fresh sawdust on the ground around the stall and the woman who weighed out the crisp, golden curls of brandy snap wore a clean white coat.

Rose took Jenny on the big cockerels, both of them clinging for dear life to the twisted brass rails. Then John took them all on the luxuriously appointed motor cars. From the centre of each big roundabout the music – each with a different tune – blared out, mingling with all the other noises of the fairground. Moira alone tried the 'Waltzer', each seat of which whizzed around independently as the roundabout also circled. When she came from that, looking as pale as winter, they watched while John tried the 'Test Your Strength' machine.

'I was a dab hand at this when I was twenty,' he said. 'I don't know about now!' He raised the big hammer above his head, swung it violently, hit the pin, and was cheered by the crowd as the indicator shot up the steel slide and rang the bell at the top. He acknowledged the cheers with a satisfied grin.

They patronized the coconut shies and moved on to the 'pot' stall, where John bought 'fairings' for the three of them; china kittens for Moira and Jenny and a pair of china lovers, entwined in each other's arms, for Rose. Next to the pot stall they admired the rippling muscles of 'Samson' in his leopardskin leotard.

'And now we really must go home,' Rose said. 'It's way past your bedtime, Jenny.'

'I want to go on the children's roundabout,' Jenny pleaded. 'I want to go on by myself.'

'It's safe enough,' John said to Rose. 'It can only go as fast as the lady in the middle can turn the handle. Let Moira watch Jenny while she goes on this. I want to take you on the "Shamrock".'

Rose gasped. 'I wouldn't dare to go on that thing! I'd be terrified!

'Not with me you wouldn't,' John said. 'Remember how I looked after you on the Big Wheel, and the Water Chute in Blackpool?'

'I remember.'

She had been recalling that all evening as they had walked around the fairground. Did he hold in his mind every moment of that day, as she did? Did he think back to the moments on the pier when they had seemed to be alone, only the sea and themselves in the whole world? Such a brief time, but she would never forget it.

'Shamrock' was the name of the huge steam yacht. It was fitted with brass rails to which the passengers clung as the Shamrock gathered speed and swung ever more violently. The underside of the Shamrock was painted with the Union Jack, and when it reached the greatest height of its swing the whole of the flag was visible to the people on the ground. There was always a crowd around to watch the Shamrock and their screams were drowned only by the louder ones of the Shamrock's passengers. John took Rose's arm and led her towards it.

'I can't!' Rose cried, though with part of her she knew she wanted to. She enjoyed the physical thrill of such things.

'Yes you can,' John said.

When the Shamrock came to a standstill and disgorged its passengers, John led Rose up the steep steps and they climbed aboard.

The huge boat swung gently at first, lulling its passengers into a false security. Then it started to go faster - and faster, higher and higher. It was horrific! Terrifying, breathtaking, wonderful, and deliciously frightening. As the violent movement flung them first in one direction and then in the other, Rose clung desperately to John. He folded his arms around her and held her close. Only then did she feel safe. He spoke to her, but the screaming and shouting of the other passengers drowned his words.

'WHAT DID YOU SAY?' Rose shouted back.

'I SAID WILL YOU MARRY ME? I'VE WAITED TWO HOURS SINCE I ASKED YOU. WILL YOU MARRY ME?'

Hurtling through the air, swinging to and fro, though now the Shamrock was slowing down again and she was being rocked gently in John's arms, Rose knew, suddenly, in

255

this most incongruous of places, as she had never known before, what her answer must be. There could be no other.

'I shan't let you go,' John said. 'I shall keep you in this contraption until you say "Yes".'

'Yes,' Rose said. 'Yes, I will marry you. Oh John, my love, I will, I will!'

The Shamrock slowed down, and finally stopped. Arm in arm they descended to where Jenny and Moira were waiting.

THE END